Praise for
Joseph A. West

"Old-fashioned storytelling raised to the level of homegrown art told in an American language that is almost gone."

—Loren D. Estleman, four-time
Spur Award–winning
author of *White Desert*

"Original, imaginative."

—Max Evans, Spur Award–winning
author of *The Rounders*

"Wildly comic and darkly compelling."

—Robert Olen Butler, Pulitzer Prize–winning
author of *A Good Scent from a Strange Mountain*

"[A] rollicking big windy." —Elmer Kelton

"Comic delight. Joseph West [has] an encyclopedic knowledge of the West. He keeps the body count sufficient to satisfy gluttons, frosts his cake with bawds, throws a few wolfers, a boxer, and a patent medicine huckster into the pot, rings in all the Western legends worth recounting, and seasons the stew with smiles. . . . Western fiction will never be the same."

—Richard S. Wheeler,
Spur Award–winning
author of *Sierra*

GUNSMOKE™

BLOOD, BULLETS, AND BUCKSKIN

Joseph A. West

Foreword by
James Arness

SIGNET
Published by New American Library, a division of
Penguin Group (USA) Inc., 375 Hudson Street,
New York, New York 10014, USA
Penguin Group (Canada), 10 Alcorn Avenue, Toronto,
Ontario M4V 3B2, Canada (a division of Pearson Penguin Canada Inc.)
Penguin Books Ltd., 80 Strand, London WC2R 0RL, England
Penguin Ireland, 25 St. Stephen's Green, Dublin 2,
Ireland (a division of Penguin Books Ltd.)
Penguin Group (Australia), 250 Camberwell Road, Camberwell, Victoria 3124,
Australia (a division of Pearson Australia Group Pty. Ltd.)
Penguin Books India Pvt. Ltd., 11 Community Centre, Panchsheel Park,
New Delhi - 110 017, India
Penguin Group (NZ), Cnr Airborne and Rosedale Roads, Albany,
Auckland 1310, New Zealand (a division of Pearson New Zealand Ltd.)
Penguin Books (South Africa) (Pty.) Ltd., 24 Sturdee Avenue,
Rosebank, Johannesburg 2196, South Africa

Penguin Books Ltd., Registered Offices:
80 Strand, London WC2R 0RL, England

First published by Signet, an imprint of New American Library,
a division of Penguin Group (USA) Inc.

First Printing, January 2005
10 9 8 7 6 5 4 3 2 1

Printed in the United States of America

Foreword

Marshall Matt Dillon here. I am honored to have been asked to write this foreword for the *Gunsmoke* books. I agreed to join the *Gunsmoke* at the advice of John Wayne (as everyone knows). It was one of the best things that ever happened to me. Being a "newcomer" on *Gunsmoke,* I wasn't involved in the decision-making processes in the beginning. In January 1955, we shot "Matt Gets It." We made another episode, "Hack Prine," so the producers would have another choice for the critical pilot program. Often that choice makes or breaks a show. They chose the more dramatic "Matt Gets It." What I never told anyone was that I always thought we should have aired "Hack Prine" first. I still feel it was a better show.

Over the years I enjoyed so many experiences with my fellow actors. We would get all wound up in a scene and then someone would start laughing and it would take us forever to settle down and start the scene over. It seemed like the most serious scenes were the ones that fell apart. I used to be the worst practical joker of the group. When someone was doing a serious part, I would stand off camera directly in the actor's line of site. Just as he started into his dialogue I would take a Popsicle from behind my back and start licking it theatrically. You should have seen the expression on the actor's face and needless to say he would crack up every time. One time we had a laughing jag so bad that a script girl, who had worked in the business many years before *Gunsmoke,* threw down the script book and started to rant and rave that she had never seen such unprofessional work in her life. It only made us laugh harder. Eventually we got her to laugh with us, and we all liked her and enjoyed working with her. There were even times when we had to take a break to get ourselves under control. Most times we ended up taking lunch to give us enough time to settle down to be able to work again. I always felt that a good laugh on the set took away the tension and allowed us to give our best performances.

We had our serious times too. During the twenty years that we worked on *Gunsmoke,* if anyone on the set had personal issues, we all rallied around him and made the situation the best it could be under the circumstances. We always remembered that we were people first and actors second. This attitude made us a true family and maintained the congenial atmosphere on the set.

One of the things that made the show a huge success was our writers. *Gunsmoke* started as a radio show, where the writers began the saga that carried over into the television show. Over the years I came to respect the writers and their ability to create show after show that would keep the audiences interested. One writer in particular, Ron Bishop, was a World War II veteran who would drive into the middle of nowhere on the twenty-thousand-acre Getty Ranch where we were filming, and write scripts. He liked to have the solitude and uninterrupted time to think. It seemed to work well for him because he wrote some of my favorite episodes. Ron Bishop passed away several years ago. He is missed by all of us.

Another great writer was Jim Burns. Jim and I are still friends to this day. His sense of humor and love of the West truly came through in his scripts. There were many terrific writers who started their careers on this show and went on to have wonderful movie and television careers. One I think of often is Sam Peckinpah, who went on to a fantastic career in the movies. One thing about all the writers is that they took it pretty well when I said things like "Matt Dillon would never say that" or "This is too long a speech for me. Cut it down." We didn't ever argue but sometimes I won and sometimes they did. In any event it always seemed to work.

I could probably spend the next twenty years telling stories about my time on *Gunsmoke*. Suffice it to say that I loved working on this show and feel like the values we portrayed carried over into my personal life. The friendships I made working on the show have continued through all these years. I was always grateful that the producers and writers maintained a high moral standard for our show. If all the letters and e-mails that I receive today from youngsters and young families telling me that they are watching *Gunsmoke* is any indication, we did it right. The show has as much impact on the audience today as it did in 1955. I continue to be amazed at the number of people who tell me that they went into law enforcement because of watching *Gunsmoke*. It makes me truly proud to have portrayed Marshal Matt Dillon.

—James Arness
"Marshal Matt Dillon"

chapter 1

Death on the Prairie

Hell lay over the next rise.

Yet the quiet, fertile and peaceful land that rolled away on all sides around Marshal Matt Dillon would seem to give lie to that statement.

The plains were green, made so by snowmelt and the coming of the spring rains, which even now hammered hard on the tall lawman's hat and the shoulders of his yellow slicker.

The downpour was relentless, steel needles slanting from a sky that looked like sheets of curling lead, spurred on by a gusting north wind. It was a day when no honest man would venture out unless driven by need—or by duty.

Ahead of Matt, the tracks of three riders scarred the wet buffalo grass to the top of the rise, then disappeared from sight.

But he knew exactly where the men were since

he'd traveled this vast, lonely country a time or two before.

On the other side of the rise—a humpbacked knoll too shallow to be called a hill—the ground sloped away gently for a hundred yards or so to a narrow stream that flowed toward the Pawnee River to the west. There were cottonwoods and willows growing on both banks, and plenty of lush grass, streaked here and there by vivid carpets of blue Johnny jump-up and yellow prairie dandelion.

A man could find shelter of a sort under the trees, and when Matt tested the breeze he smelled coffee boiling and the remembered Sunday-morning tang of frying bacon.

His hungry stomach all of a sudden growling, Matt stood beside his horse, the reins in his hand, and considered his options.

He had few and none of them amounted to much.

A man made cautious by riding many a shadowed trail in a restless and dangerous land, he had lived this long by not charging headlong into trouble.

Yet that was what he must do.

The flat Kansas prairie around the creek offered no chance of concealment. If he swung wide around the rise, then tried to ride up on the outlaw camp, he would be seen from a far distance and could be shot out of the saddle by rifle fire.

There was another way. He could walk over the crest and cover the hundred yards to the creek as quickly as his long legs would carry him—and hope to be in scattergun range before the ball opened.

Yet another was to mount up and charge hell-for-leather down the slope, trusting his rangy, long-legged bay to cover the distance in a few seconds. It would give the three outlaws little chance to recover from their surprise and start shooting.

All his options were thin, mighty thin, and did little to reassure a man.

But he knew he had to chose one of them—and soon.

Matt unbuttoned his slicker, drew his Colt and fed a sixth shell into the empty chamber under the hammer. Then he shoved the gun into the waistband of his pants where it would be handier. He hefted the Greener, thumbed it open and checked the loads. Satisfied, the big lawman snapped the shotgun shut again.

There was no doubt in Matt's mind that his attempt to arrest the outlaws would end in a gunfight and death. Violent men spoke only the language of violence and there would be no reasoning with them.

Five days before, up on the South Fork of Buckner Creek, the three had stolen a gray saddle mare and a cashbox from the two-by-twice ranch of Dutch Henry Shultz and his crippled wife, Martha.

The old couple was now dead. Matt knew this for a fact because he'd buried them both.

That Jeb and Steve Plunkett had stolen the mare and thirty-seven dollars in cash was crime enough. But the brothers had no need to kill Dutch Henry and Martha, a kindly pair who'd never let an out-of-work puncher leave their ranch unfed or allowed him to ride away without a two-dollar grubstake in his jeans.

Yet the Plunketts had shot down Henry in his barn, Martha as she lay helpless in bed. And those were two of the men Matt had been hunting for days, their tracks now leading to the top of the rain-lashed rise.

From information he had picked up along the way, Matt had learned the brothers were riding with Clem Beecham, a back-shooting killer who was crazy in the head and maybe worse than either of them.

The odds were three to one, all of the outlaws good with the Colt and Winchester, and for a brief moment, Matt allowed himself a twinge of regret, wishing that he'd brought along his deputy, Festus Haggen.

But he'd told Festus to take care of things in Dodge while he was gone, and what was done could not be undone. He was alone—and he had to do it. Matt Dillon made up his mind.

He eased the girth on the bay and dropped the reins, letting the big horse graze on the new spring grass.

He held the Greener close to his side, where it would be hidden by the slicker. Then he swallowed hard and walked toward the crest of the rise.

The rain was falling harder, hissing like an angry dragon, drawing a steel mesh curtain across the featureless land. Matt smelled the ozone tang of distant lightning and guessed that thunderstorms were rolling over and through the high peaks of the Sangre de Christo Mountains a hundred fifty miles to the west. Before this dawning day was much older, the thunder would descend upon the plains, the sizzling lightning strikes spiking spiteful and dangerous.

Would he be around to see them?

As yet, Matt Dillon had no answer to that question. But one way or another, he knew he would have his reply soon.

The big lawman's long stride took him quickly to the top of the rise; then, very aware of his own hammering heartbeat, he loped down the slope toward the stream.

Both the Plunkett brothers were squatting by the fire and Beecham was over by the horses. All this Matt saw in an instant.

He had covered half of the distance.

It was Jeb Plunkett who saw him first. The man climbed slowly to his feet, his hand close to his holstered six-gun. His brother, catching Jeb's sudden tenseness, glanced over his shoulder. Steve's eyes grew wide and he stiffened in surprise. Then he too rose. Neither man made any attempt to draw.

The Plunketts and Beecham made a sorry-looking trio, seedy, ragged and down-at-the-heel, all of them shiftless and work-shy. But as they watched Matt walk toward them, their narrowed eyes were wary and cunning, like those of deadly, coiled snakes, looking for any chance to strike.

Matt closed the remaining distance fast, and now he let them see the Greener. He swung the shotgun up and the checkered walnut forestock smacked loudly into the open palm of his left hand.

This the Plunketts noticed, their eyebrows crawling

so high up their low foreheads that they almost met their hatbands. Both had seen what a scattergun could do to a man at close range, and it seemed to Matt that this knowledge brought the brothers much unease.

Clem Beecham stepped beside Steve and Jeb and it was he who spoke first, his black eyes wild and reckless. "What the hell do you want?" he yelled. "You know better than to walk into a man's camp like that."

Matt ignored Beecham and turned slightly so he was facing the Plunketts, the shotgun aimed right at Steve's belly. Beecham stood a shade to his left, tense and ready.

"My name is Dillon"—Matt opened his slicker with his free hand, showing them the star pinned to his leather vest—"and I'm here to arrest all three of you for the murders of Dutch Henry Shultz and his wife." Matt's voice was flat and cold as he added, "And the theft of thirty-seven dollars and the gray mare over yonder."

"Dillon, I know you and you've got no jurisdiction outside of Dodge," Jeb Plunkett said. He was a tall stringbean of a man with a drooping mustache and a knife scar on his unshaven left cheek. "Now just you turn around and be on your way and there's no harm done." Jeb turned to his brother. "Ain't that right, Steve? No harm done?"

"Right as rain." Steve smiled, showing small yellow teeth in a pinched, tight mouth. "You got no authority to arrest us, Marshal. This ain't Dodge and we ain't pilgrims like them drunk cowboys you buffalo and throw in your jail. Hell, man, you're way off your bailiwick."

"The murders were first reported in Dodge," Matt said patiently, willing to talk if it would head off gunplay. "That made it my duty to investigate the crime and arrest the suspects, no matter where I found them." He hefted the Greener. "If that isn't enough, this here scattergun is all the authority I need."

Matt Dillon was well aware that the Plunketts were watching him closely and he knew what they were seeing and why the sight had given them pause.

The wind had whipped up, flapping Matt's slicker around his long legs. He stood confident and seemingly without fear, six-foot-nine in his two-inch bootheels, a high-crowned hat adding to his height so that he towered more than seven foot tall. Wide-shouldered and big in the chest, with the scattergun steady in his hands, he made a grim and terrible sight in the lashing rain.

For a moment, Matt thought the Plunketts had summed it all up in their minds and would surrender without a fight. These were hard men living hard lives in a hard land. They knew Matt Dillon had drawn the line and neither seemed much inclined to cross it.

But it was Clem Beecham, soft in the head and eager to kill, who blew whatever chance they might have had.

The man hurled a vile oath at the lawman and clawed for his gun. Matt swung the Greener and let Beecham have both barrels, low in the belly. The buckshot tore into the outlaw, blasting a bloody hole six inches wide just below his navel. Beecham screamed a wild screech of pain and stumbled backward.

Matt didn't wait to see him fall.

Both Plunketts were drawing.

The big lawman threw the Greener at Steve, who instinctively stepped to his right to avoid it, slowing his draw. Matt's own Colt was in his hand and he let Steve be, firing instead at Jeb. The outlaw took the bullet in the chest and Matt heard him gasp and drop his gun hand, quitting the fight, at least for now.

A shot split the air next to Matt's right ear. Steve had fired and missed. Now the man's legs were spread wide, as he steadied himself for another shot. Matt's Colt swung on Steve. He fired, then fired again, both shots sounding as one. Hit twice, the outlaw crumpled to the ground on his hands and knees, coughing blood. Behind him his brother threw up his hands, bright scarlet spreading across the front of his shirt.

"Dillon, I'm done!" Jeb called out, his face twisted in fear. "I'm out of it." The outlaw sank to his knees and bowed his head. "Hell, man, let me be."

No pity in him, Matt Dillon took a step toward the wounded outlaw. "Throw that Colt away," he said, a coldness icing his insides. "Throw it away or by God I'll gun you."

Plunkett did as he was told, tossing his Colt as far from him as he could. He continued to kneel, slumped over, whimpering, making no attempt to get to his feet.

Suddenly very tired, Matt Dillon looked around him at the smoke-streaked breaks between the trunks of the cottonwoods and at the rain-sputtering fire.

Clem Beecham lay on his back, rain driving into his open mouth. He was dead. Steve Plunkett was still on his hands and knees, but suddenly the man toppled over, groaned deep in his throat and was gone, his open eyes frozen, reliving forever the horror of his last moments.

Matt punched the spent shells from his gun, reloaded from the loops on his cartridge belt and shoved the Colt back into the holster.

As it always did, killing left him empty, drained, sick at heart from the mindless violence and the waste of human lives. Two men were dead and one was dying, all in less time than it took the watch in his vest pocket to tick a half dozen times.

Matt knew the right of his cause, that he'd had no choice in the matter. But such knowledge never made it any easier.

The big lawman stepped over to the fire. The bacon in the pan was cooked just right and he was hungry. He found his pocketknife and speared strip after strip of bacon, eating ravenously until it was all gone. Then he poured himself a cup of coffee.

Jeb Plunkett straightened and looked over at Matt. "I'm hit real bad," he said.

Matt nodded. "I reckon your time is short. Best you lay quiet and make peace with your Maker."

"I'm twenty-five years old," Plunkett said, his voice bitter. "It's hard for a man to die when he's twenty-five."

"Dutch Henry was seventy-five," Matt said. "But I bet he thought the same way."

"I had no hand in those killings," Plunkett said. "That was all Steve's and Clem's doing. They said they didn't want to leave no witnesses behind that could hang them."

Plunkett's eyes searched Matt's face, the blue death shadows already gathering in the hollows of his cheeks and temples. "I done my share of killing, but I never meant for those two oldsters to be harmed. They fed me and give me a handout one time, back in the winter of seventy-six. Hell, I liked 'em both."

Matt Dillon sipped his coffee, blue eyes searching Plunkett's face over the rim of his cup. "Why are you telling me this?"

"Because a man ought to die clean, at peace with himself. You ain't a preacher, Dillon, but you're the law and maybe that means something."

Matt nodded. "Well, you've told me, and for what it's worth, I believe you."

"That makes it easier," Plunkett said. He lay on his back, groaning as pain spiked at him. "Don't leave me, Dillon," he said, his voice sounding like it was coming from a long ways off. "A man shouldn't be left to die alone."

"I'll be here," Matt said.

Jeb Plunkett died an hour later, and it was still not yet noon when Matt walked up the rise and found his horse. He tightened the girth, then rode slowly back down the slope.

There could be no question of burying the three dead outlaws. At that time in the West, citizens expected justice to be done, but justice also had to be seen to be done.

Matt would take the Plunketts and Beecham back to Dodge, facedown across their saddles for everyone to see, as was the hard custom of a raw land trying desperately to emerge from lawlessness.

He rode down Front Street four days later.

Behind him, the bodies already swollen blue and smelling rank, he trailed his dead.

And before they turned away, covering their noses, the good citizens of Dodge stood on the boardwalks, as the melancholy procession plodded past, and they nodded, telling one another that indeed justice had been done.

And they had seen it to be done.

chapter 2

Evil Tidings

Matt Dillon turned up the oil lamp in his office against the gathering darkness and ruefully regarded the mountain of paperwork that had piled up on his desk during the two weeks he'd been absent from Dodge tracking the Plunkett brothers.

There were the usual wanted dodgers and notices of state ordinances, newly drafted regulations regarding vagrancy, houses of ill-repute, the carrying of firearms and other deadly weapons, the sale of intoxicating liquors, disorderly conduct and dozens of other sinful offenses, great and small.

Matt had already scratched his sputtering pen across paper to reply to a demand from the Atchison, Topeka and Santa Fe railroad that the marshal ensure the water tower in Dodge was refilled and maintained at city expense, an order from Washington that the marshal immediately investigate the proximity of privies and outhouses to the city wells and "respond without delay" and an irritable query from Mayor Kelley wanting to know what the marshal was doing to reduce the number of stray dogs within the city limits, damn it.

But the biggest problem of all was the letter Matt now held in his hands, shaking his head over it as he had been doing all afternoon.

This one, on heavy parchment with the state of Kansas seal at the top, was from Governor Anthony, requiring that the marshal do all in his power to prepare for a possible return visit to Dodge by the son of the czar of Russia. Matt now reread the letter for the tenth time and still couldn't make sense of the governor's request of him.

Sir,

I do not wish a repeat of what happened when Grand Duke Alexis visited six years ago. On that occasion, the extremely cold winter of 1872, accommodation was found for the grand duke, but none was forthcoming for his entourage. The town marshal will take immediate steps to ensure that this unfortunate and embarrassing circumstance is not repeated should the grand duke decide to revisit your fair city this fall. Reply as soon as possible and advise on the availability of accommodations for both the grand duke and his entourage.

Yours Respct. etc,
George Tobay Anthony
Governor

Matt sighed at the frivolous task assigned to him and laid the letter aside. He stepped to the door of his office and looked outside, where the day was rapidly dying and the guttering lamps were already lit along Front Street.

Dodge was full, bursting at the seams with cattle buyers and those who came to prey on the free-spending Texas cowboys. But right now the town was strangely quiet, as though holding its breath while it awaited the arrival of the fifteen hundred punchers and hundreds of hangers-on, who were even now on their way up the trails from Texas with five million head of beef.

Front Street was decked out in gorgeous array with bunting and flags, and the creaky, false-fronted stores of unpainted pine were crammed with marked-up goods of all kinds.

Doc Holliday was in town, and with him a hundred other pale, nimble-fingered gamblers who had wintered on the riverboats or cities farther east. And with these fast men came the even faster women. The girls who worked the line were back, returning from cathouses in New Orleans, Denver and Memphis for the cattle season.

Since he'd ridden into Dodge that morning, Matt had seen Big Nose Kate Elder—on Doc Holliday's arm no less—Hambone Jane, Squirrel Tooth Alice, Dirty Annie, the Galloping Cow and Sally Cottontail. There were at least fifty others he could not put a name to, for the most part young, but with hard, knowing and calculating eyes.

Over to the Long Branch, Kitty Russell had imported what she called hostesses from saloons in Denver and Cheyenne, all of them a sight prettier than the usual run of soiled doves and a whole heap more expensive.

The Alamo, the Lone Star and the town's other saloons had already stocked up with fine brandy, liqueurs and the latest mixed drinks to cater to the needs of the thirsty Texans. There was ice aplenty to keep the beer cold and even the most humble establishments advertised anchovies, crab and Russian caviar on their appetizer menus.

Matt stepped onto the boardwalk, his spurs chiming like silver bells in the quiet, and looked over to the stock pens huddled against the railroad tracks. Nothing stirred and all was in darkness. But in no time, that would change.

Day and night, the pens would be full of bawling cattle, longhorns as wild as deer but as dangerous as cougars. Clanking trains would hiss and wail like dragons and the chutes would drum with the hooves of reluctant cows being pushed and prodded aboard, a job punchers hated, especially when it was already giving rise to a derisive handle that later stuck: cowpokes.

The saloons on Front and Texas Street, now silent but for the tin-panny tinkle of a piano down at the Alamo, would be lost behind a cloud of yellow dust from the constant to and fro of cow ponies, and hundreds of human footsteps would thud and echo on the boardwalks.

Only across the tracks, in the respectable part of town, would there be quiet. The bankers, lawyers and businessmen, arm in arm with their staid wives, would go about their lawful business or attend church, later to engage in sober and profitable conversations on the weather, the price of land and crop yields.

No guns were permitted on that side of the tracks, but south of the Deadline, where Matt now stood, everything was "full up"—including the bang of the festive revolver.

And all of this was Marshal Matt Dillon's world and he loved every sight, sound, smell and moment of it.

He was a hard man, enduring and tough, bred hard for a hard land, and rawboned Dodge, for all its warts and ugliness, had become home to him.

Like the wind that whispered constantly around the roaring saloons, the bedspring-squealing line shacks, the bawling stock pens and the soft-tolling churches across the Deadline, Matt was restless and untiring. He rustled around and probed every nook and cranny of the town, seeing everything, letting nothing, no matter how small or seemingly insignificant, escape his attention. He firmly believed he would always be one with Dodge, sharing its joys, its triumphs and its tragedies.

The town had become his life, and no matter how he tried, he could imagine no other.

After one last glance up and down the quiet street, Matt reluctantly turned and was about to step back into the office when he heard the soft fall of hooves behind him.

His deputy, Festus Haggen, reined up his rangy Missouri mule at the hitching post and swung stiffly out of the saddle. Festus had a five-day growth of beard and looked tired and dirty, but then, on his best day, Festus had a five-day growth of beard and looked tired and dirty.

The deputy looped the reins around the post and stepped up on the boardwalk. He stuck out his hand. "Good to have you back safe and sound, Matthew."

Matt took Festus' hand and shook it warmly. "Good to be back."

Despite his hangdog look and perpetually shabby appearance, Festus was respected by the people of Dodge as a capable lawman. Born to the feud, he'd been raised wild in the hills of Tennessee and was sixteen when he killed his first man in a fair fight. But he'd fled the law, heading west, where he'd fought Comanche raiders and border hard cases with the Texas Rangers. He was brave, good with a gun and, to Matt's knowledge, had never taken a step back from any man.

Festus was fiercely loyal to Matt, as the marshal had come to know well. He counted Matt as one of his two best friends, the other being Ruth, his mean-spirited and cantankerous mule.

"When did you get in, Matthew?" the deputy asked.

"Early this morning," Matt replied.

Festus' right eye screwed up tight as it always did when he was thinking hard. "And them Plunkett boys?"

Matt inclined his head along Front Street. "They're laid out over to Percy Crump's funeral parlor." Matt hesitated, then said, "There was another with them, went by the name of Clem Beecham."

Festus nodded. "I've heard tell of that ranny. They say he's plumb loco and a killer to boot."

"Not anymore he isn't," Matt said, a grim smile touching the corners of his mouth. "He's over to Percy Crump's as well."

Festus absorbed all this, then feigned irritation. "Well, are you going to keep me talking on the boardwalk all night or are you going to invite me in for a cup of coffee?"

"Step right inside," Matt said. "I've got a question to ask you anyway." He stopped in the doorway, then added, "And talking about questions, where have you been all day?"

Festus walked inside and shrugged. "The widow Brady needed a new well dug, Matthew. Give me three dollars and my feed." Bringing up an old and endless complaint, Fetus poured himself coffee and said, "Deputies don't get paid much, you know."

Matt let that go, knowing how eagerly his deputy could belly up to the subject of salaries, a discussion that could go on for hours.

He walked over to his desk and picked up the letter from the governor, his thumbnail just under the word *entourage*.

"Festus, what do you reckon this fuss is all about?" he asked.

The deputy stepped close and studied the letter, his mouth working as he tried to figure out the word. Finally he scratched his hairy cheek and said: "Matthew, you know I ain't much of a one for reading writing or writing reading an' sich."

Matt nodded. "I know you're not, but climb the windmill and eyeball the pasture anyway."

Festus concentrated on the word again, biting his lip, deep in thought.

"Well?" Matt asked.

"I'm studying on it," the deputy answered. "It ain't easy." After a few more moments of deep concentration, Festus took a deep breath and said: "Matthew, you understand, I'm not setting right down on the notion, but I'd say that the key is that there ten-dollar word is en-too-raj-ee."

The big marshal smiled. "Well, however important that entourage is, it could be coming to Dodge with the Grand Duke of Russia and I have to find room for it."

Festus took the letter and studied it again. "Here, Matthew, it could be some kind of wild animal. Them furriners, especially dukes an' sich, have mighty strange ideas about critters."

"Is Doc Adams back in town yet?" Matt asked. "He knows all them big words."

Festus shook his head. "Nah, Doc is still in New Orleans. I guess his sister is still right poorly." The deputy stroked his chin. "You could ask Doc Holliday. He spouts ten-dollar words all the time. Says they're Latin, whatever that is."

Matt shook his head. "I don't plan on asking Holliday anything, except when he plans to leave Dodge." His head turned sharply to Festus. "Is he behaving himself?"

"Doc's in the chips and he's playing honest poker.

He's bought me a drink a time or three, on account of how us poor deputies can't afford to buy any of our own."

Again Matt refused to bite at Festus' worm. He poured himself a cup of coffee, carried it to the desk and flopped into his chair, tipping it back, the wood screeching in noisy protest at his two hundred fifty pounds.

He picked up the governor's letter and reread it, as though the meaning of *entourage* would suddenly become clear to him. But over the top of the paper, he noticed Festus hopping from one foot to another, a sure sign that something was troubling him.

"Festus," he said, "are you just going to stand there dancing a jig all night or will you tell me what's eating you? You don't have your salary still stuck in your craw, do you?"

The deputy shook his head. "Matthew, it's something else. I got news I've been fixing to tell since I came in here and there ain't a bit of it good."

Matt smiled, aware how prone his excitable deputy was to wild exaggeration. "Spill it, Festus," he said.

"There ain't no easy way to tell this," Festus said, "so I'll give it to you straight out."

"Then say it, man," Matt said, his patience fraying. "Get on with it."

Festus gulped a shuddering breath, his eyes troubled, and said: "Logan St. Clair is back in town. And there's worse, Matthew. Young Sean Tyree is with him."

Stiff with shock, Matt let his chair slam to an upright position.

After an absence of five years, St. Clair and Tyree were back in Dodge. This could mean trouble. Big trouble.

chapter 3

The Marshal's Tale

"Matthew, I got more bad news," Festus said. "And you ain't gonna like this any more'n you liked what I already done told you."

"Let me hear it," Matt sighed, the letter from the governor forgotten in his hand.

Festus scratched his chest, his fingers exploring under his shirt, and said: "A puncher rode into town a couple of days ago, said he was tired of eating the dust of the drag and just up and quit." The deputy's left eyebrow crawled slowly up his forehead. "Here's the cruncher, Matthew—guess who he was riding for."

"Are you going to tell me it was Clint Stucker?"

"Uh-huh, the very same."

Matt's head tilted back, his eyes steady on Festus' face, knowing what was coming. "And his son, Cage?"

"With him, ramroding the whole outfit, the puncher said. Said more too. Said the drive had hardly gotten started when young Cage killed a man south of the Red. The way the puncher told it, some two-gun ranny showed up looking for trouble and Cage gave him all he could handle an' then some. The man drawed down on Cage, but his gun hadn't even cleared the leather when Cage shot him. The puncher says both Cage's bullets clipped half moons out of the tag of the poor feller's tobacco sack."

Festus drained his coffee and wiped the back of his hand across his mouth. "Matthew, that Cage Stucker is greased lightning with a gun."

Matt nodded. "Yeah, and he's mighty handy with a bullwhip as well." He sat for a few moments, thinking things through, unease tugging at him. Finally he asked: "Where is the Stucker herd, and how many riders does Clint have with him?"

"Last I heard, Stucker was fattening six thousand head on good grass at the south bend of the Cimarron," Festus answered. "The word is that he'll split 'em up into two herds and trail 'em up to Dodge some time next week. I hear tell he's got maybe two score men with him, and I'm willing to bet they're all handy with a gun, if that tough young puncher I spoke to is anything to go by."

Festus hesitated. "Matthew, you think there could be trouble between Sean Tyree and Cage Stucker?"

Matt shrugged. "I don't know, Festus. Sean Tyree has been gone for five years and time heals a lot of wounds"—he shook his head—"unless, now that he's back in Dodge, all those years come back to curse him."

"How well do you know Clint Stucker?" the deputy asked. "An' if it comes down to it, can he rein in his son?"

"He never reined in Cage before," Matt answered. "Since Cage was a kid, Clint pretty much let him run wild and do whatever he had a mind to do. As for knowing Clint Stucker, I've been around him enough to know that he's a big rancher who dreams of being bigger. The only trouble is, his soul is too small for his dreams."

Festus found a chair and pulled it up to Matt's desk. He sat, his eyes searching the marshal's face. "How did it all happen, Matthew?" he asked. "I never did get the right of that story. Miss Kitty was going to tell me one time, but then she stopped and said she didn't know the half of it and that I should ask you. After that, it kinda plumb slipped my mind, at least until yesstidy."

Matt rose and turned up the oil lamp. Orange light spilled into the dark corners of the office. Then he found his chair again.

"Chester Goode was my deputy back then," Matt recalled, his eyes closed, remembering. "It was about this time of the year when him and me led a posse of ranchers and soldiers chasing after a band of Kiowa renegades up in the Sunflower Mountain country.

"We had a three-day running fight with the Indians among the foothills and I caught a strap iron arrow in my lower back. Chester brought me back to Dodge, and he always said I was a lot more dead than alive by the time we got here."

Festus nodded, smiling. "I've heard of Chester,"

he said. "His name was Goode and he was a good man."

"He was all of that," Matt answered. "Last I heard, he was up in the Dakota Territory, hoping to strike it rich in the gold mines."

"So," Festus prompted, "what happened when you got back to Dodge?"

Matt shrugged. "I don't remember much of it, but Doc Adams worked out the arrowhead. Then Kitty started into her fussing and fretting. She insisted on getting me a room in the Great Western across the street there because it was quiet and she could nurse me back to health, which she did."

"A mighty determined lady, Miss Kitty, when she makes her mind up to something," Festus observed.

"That she is. Well, anyhow," Matt continued, "I was still in bed, weak as a kittlin' and battling a raging fever, when Sean Tyree arrived in Dodge.

"Kitty had my bed pulled close to the window, and I saw Tyree ride in, and he was a sight to see. He was just eighteen years old then, wild and shaggy, owning nothing but the buckskins on his back, a mustang horse without a saddle and a single-shot Ballard rifle.

"But fresh out of the hills though he was, and green as mint money, Tyree put it around that he was determined to make his mark and be somebody one day."

Matt eased himself in his chair, the legs creaking, and said: "Then he ran into Cage Stucker."

"How did that come up?" Festus asked.

"Cage and his pa were in Dodge with a herd, and

Cage spotted Tyree in the street. I had the window of my room open, and I saw Cage look the kid up and down and say, plain as day: 'What the hell are you? Some kind of mountain trash?'

"Now Tyree was just a skinny, hollow-eyed kid back then, but he wasn't the kind to take a step back from any man. He didn't even bother to answer. He just swung a right to Cage's jaw. Cage was six years older, and around fifty pounds heavier, but he dropped like a felled ox.

"Then the trouble really began.

"Cage had six punchers with him, all of them mean and spoiling for a fight, and they gave Tyree a terrible beating with their fists and boots. When it was over, Tyree lying all bloody in the dust, Cage uncoiled a bullwhip and I heard him yell: 'Stand back, boys. I'm gonna cut those buckskins right off his back.'

"I tried to get out of bed to put a stop to it, but I was so weak, Kitty pushed me back into the pillow. 'Matt, if you try to go down there, they'll kill you,' she said. And thinking back on it, I guess she could have been right."

"But, Matthew, where was Chester Goode?" Festus asked. "It don't sound like he was the kind to walk away from something like that."

His face bleak, Matt answered: "After he saw that Kitty was taking good care of me, Chester rode out after the Kiowa. That fight was far from finished and those young warriors were playing hob. I didn't blame him none then, and I still don't."

"And what happened next?" Festus asked, his face eager.

"Well, like I was telling you, Sean Tyree was on the ground, pretty much dazed and helpless, and Cage cut loose with that eight-foot bullwhip.

"Every time he hit the kid, the crack sounded like a gunshot. Cage opened up Tyree's cheek"—Matt's fingers strayed to his face and he traced a line from the corner of his left eye to his chin—"here. That cut was deep. I saw it blossom open like a red flower."

His voice tense, Matt replayed the scene again in his mind, the horror of it still with him. "Time and time again, the whole of Front Street echoed to the *crack! crack! crack!* of the bullwhip until Tyree's buckskins and the skin underneath were ripped into tattered, bloody shreds.

"Cage Stucker was having a grand old time. He laughed every time the bullwhip hit and Tyree's blood sprayed into the air. Funny thing was, through it all, Sean Tyree never uttered a sound. But I saw his eyes on Cage, and they were burning with hate. In all my life I'd seen hate like that only once before, and that was in the eyes of a gut-shot broncho Apache down to the Arizona Territory."

"It's a wonder Cage didn't kill the kid," Festus said.

Matt nodded. "He would have if Logan St. Clair hadn't stepped in and saved Tyree's life."

"Gambling man, isn't he?"

"One of the best, and handy with a gun. At that time, St. Clair had killed four men, one of them Kirk

Ryan, the Cheyenne gunfighter, and from all I hear, he's added a few to his total since then."

A rider loped his horse along the street outside and Festus listened until the hoofbeats faded before he asked: "How did St. Clair stop it?"

"Well, St. Clair was standing on the boardwalk, looking down at Cage Stucker. He cleared his frockcoat away from his gun and said: 'That's enough, Stucker. I won't let you kill that boy.'

"I could see Cage think about it and he wanted to draw real bad. But you don't draw on a man like Logan St. Clair, not if you want to live to boast of it afterward.

"Cage finally threw down the whip and told St. Clair that by God he'd kill him one day. The gambler just shrugged and told Cage he'd be waiting for him anytime he cared to try.

"I watched Cage Stucker stand there, swallowing his pride like it was a dry chicken bone, and finally walk away from it. He's never forgiven St. Clair for humiliating him in front of his men like that."

Matt rose to his feet and worked a kink out of his back. "Then St. Clair picked up Tyree from the street like he weighed nothing and carried the kid to his hotel room."

Festus nodded, satisfied. "That's quite a tale, Matthew."

"It's not the end of it," Matt said, perching on the corner of his desk, looking down at his deputy. "St. Clair got Doc Adams to treat the boy's wounds, and Doc was in the room when Clint Stucker barged his way inside. The way Doc tells it, Stucker reached into his pocket and come up with a handful of double eagles.

"He spun one of the coins onto Tyree's bed and told St. Clair: 'When he's well enough to ride, give him that. He can spend it on whiskey and get drunk in some other town. Or you can use it to bury him if he dies. Either way, I don't give a damn.'

"Doc says St. Clair just looked hard at Stucker and told him: 'Clint, some day this boy will kill you for what you just said.'

"But Clint paid no mind to St. Clair. He just laughed and stomped out of the room."

Matt stepped to the gun rack and buckled on his cartridge belt and holster. "That was five years ago, Festus. Since then, Tyree and St. Clair have been wandering. I heard they'd gone from the Mississippi riverboats to Denver, Tombstone, Virginia City, Deadwood, Leadville and Creede, places where there were plenty of high-rolling gold miners with a weakness for poker.

"After that, they traveled to London, Rome, Paris and a dozen other cities in between, wherever sporting men gather to play cards."

Matt settled his hat on his head, his face thoughtful. "There's a strange thing about Logan St. Clair, though. I've been told that no matter where he wanders, he runs into plenty of old friends, all of them right gun-handy. You've seen their kind around Dodge from time to time, Festus: quiet, careful-eyed men who wear their Colts like they were born to them. They stay around for a while, watching everything, saying little, then go without as much as a so long to anybody."

"I've seen them rannies around all right," Festus agreed. "And I'd say they step kinda lightly from one side of the law to the other. They're a restless and dangerous breed, Matthew, and not to be taken lightly."

Matt nodded. "I never take any of them lightly. Some of those friends of St. Clair are prospering, others riding the grub line, but for all, he has a smile and a handshake and, for those who need it, a road stake, no questions asked and no sermons given."

Festus smiled. "Sounds like a good feller to have around."

"St. Clair is a generous man, no doubt about that. And he's taught Sean Tyree well. I hear that St. Clair showed the kid how to dress, how to behave among mannered people and how to handle the cards like a professional. If what I'm told is correct, he also taught him how to use the Colt, and there are some who say Sean Tyree is now faster than St. Clair ever was or ever could be."

Festus whistled between his teeth. "If Sean Tyree is faster than Logan St. Clair, then he could be faster than any man alive."

The deputy lapsed into silence for a few moments, thinking things through, then said: "Matthew, you made a big thing of all those good friends Logan St. Clair has. You think if there's trouble between the Stuckers and Sean Tyree, them gunfighters will come here to Dodge to back the kid up, don't you?"

Matt Dillon, too troubled to reply, merely nodded.

Festus rose to his feet, his suddenly slack-jawed face revealing his shock. "But . . . but if that happens, we'll have a war on our hands."

"Maybe," Matt said, "but I don't intend to let it happen." He turned to his deputy, his smile grim. "Let's go, Festus," he said. "We've got our rounds to make."

chapter 4

Miss Kitty's Warning

Matt Dillon sent a protesting Festus across the Deadline to patrol the respectable part of town. The deputy was right. His presence wasn't really needed, but the sight of an intrepid lawman doing his duty seemed to reassure the prosperous folks who lived in the gingerbread houses north of the tracks and, more important, immensely pleased social-climbing Mayor Kelley.

Matt stepped along the Front Street boardwalk, his spurs ringing in the quiet. The handsome, spacious saloons were all open for business, serving good bourbon and ice-cold lager twenty-four hours a day as they waited impatiently for the influx of the Texas cowboys.

The big lawman turned up Texas Street, the wind blowing off the nearby Arkansas River carrying a chill, and he leisurely walked through saloons where the gas lamps were already lit, glowing on the polished, oak-paneled bars, spreading a warm, sepia-toned light.

A full moon rose high in the sky and out on the plains the coyotes were already talking as Matt turned back onto Front Street. He walked past the darkened Comique Theater, where the famous comedian Eddie Foy would appear in a couple of weeks, then strolled past the Lady Gay Saloon, the Alamo and the Lone Star.

Now and then Matt touched his hat brim to the fashionably dressed women—some respectable, some not—he passed on the boardwalk. The looks from the soiled doves were bold and frank, bright with invitation, but the married women were less obvious, their modestly downcast eyes secretly slanting to him as he passed, long, dark lashes fluttering like fans on painted cheekbones.

To the ladies of Dodge, Marshal Matt Dillon looked like a man out for a pleasant turn around town before seeking his blankets. But the lawman's restless gaze was everywhere, probing the dark alleys with their angled black shadows. His long habit of taking measure of the men who stood at the bars of the saloons made every nerve in his body ready to react instantly at the first sign of trouble.

The doors of the Long Branch were wide-open, splashing rectangles of orange light onto the boardwalk, when Matt reached the saloon and stepped inside.

A dozen men stood at the bar, respectable townsmen mostly in broadcloth suits, gold chains slung across expansive bellies. A couple of Kitty's pretty hostesses sat at a table, earnestly engrossed in talk with two bald drummers, who had the guilty, furtive look of married men a negotiation away from adultery.

Kitty Russell, looking breathtakingly beautiful in a red satin dress that left her shapely shoulders bare, a black ribbon around her slender neck, stood at the end of the bar.

She did not notice Matt as he stepped inside, all her attention riveted on the two men who stood close to her.

Matt recognized one of the men as the handsome, elegant Logan St. Clair. The other, a livid white scar running down his left cheek, was Sean Tyree. Both men were expensively and fashionably dressed in the style of the frontier gambler. St. Clair's hair was long, spilling in shining black waves over his shoulders, a sweeping mustache adorning his top lip.

Tyree had filled out, building muscle on his shoulders and arms and, like Matt, was clean-shaven, a thing so unusual at that time in the West, when most men wore a mustache or full beard, that it was noticed and remarked upon.

Matt shaved because he was a man completely without vanity, knowing the limitations of his rugged features. He stubbornly refused to spend time on the care and cultivation of the difficult dragoon mustache, then such a beloved fashion among Western men, having decided long since that it would do little to enhance his appearance.

As he stepped toward the bar, he made a guess

that Sean Tyree's reason for going beardless was completely different from his own. The deep scar on the young man's cheek stood out like a vivid mark of Cain—yet he had made no attempt to cover it up with whiskers.

Was it because every time Tyree shaved in the morning he saw that scar and it served as an ugly reminder of how it had come to be?

Uneasily, Matt decided that could well be the case.

When he stepped up to the bar, Kitty finally looked in his direction and she came quickly around to greet him, a dazzling smile lighting up her face.

"Matt, I heard you were back in town," she said. "What happened out there?"

Matt shrugged, the words not coming easily to him. "It ended how I knew it would end, Kitty. There are three dead men over to the funeral parlor."

Kitty's hand lightly touched Matt's chest. "You're alive and that's all that matters to me." She tilted her head back, her searching eyes seeking his. "I was worried, Matt. I knew you were all alone and I was worried."

The marshal nodded slightly, saying nothing. He took Kitty's small hand in his own massive paw, a display of emotion that didn't come easily to him.

Over the years, he and Kitty had formed a bond that began and ended with friendship, neither of them yet willing to take the extra step that would move them beyond friendship and into love.

In the past, much had been spoken between them, but much more had been left unsaid. Matt had long since realized that they both knew Dodge was not the place for such talk. The words would inevitably come, but in a different town, in a different time. As to when and where, neither of them could guess.

As the perfumed smell of Kitty and her warm closeness made Matt's head swim, he told himself again that what they already had would suffice. There remained a gulf to be bridged between them, but not here and not now.

That was for the future—a future Matt could glimpse only occasionally through a mist of time and distance: Kitty and he always together, but moving like gray shadows, hazy, indistinct, without substance.

Matt smiled and said finally: "I came back, Kitty. As long as you're here, waiting for me, I'll always come back."

Kitty nodded, accepting what he had given her. "I'll be here, Matt. Depend on it."

The big lawman's attention moved beyond Kitty's bare shoulders to the bar.

Logan St. Clair was watching him, his shuttered gambler's eyes intent, but revealing nothing of what he felt or was thinking.

Matt moved around Kitty and stepped close to St. Clair and Sean Tyree.

"Welcome back to Dodge, Logan," he said. Then he added, making his point up front and in the open: "Staying long?"

Logan St. Clair smiled, knowing what motive lay behind the lawman's greeting. "Not long, Matt," he said. "Sean and I plan to stay around and play a little poker until the Texas punchers leave." His face hardened slightly. "You do remember Sean Tyree, don't you?"

Matt was spared the necessity of replying because Tyree stuck out his hand. "Good to meet you finally, Marshal. Last time I was here you were feeling right poorly."

Matt took the man's hand. "As I recollect, you weren't feeling so spry yourself."

The big lawman waited to see Tyree's reaction, but there was none, not so much a flicker of an eyelid. "I recovered, thanks to Logan here," he said smoothly.

Despite the terrible scar on his cheek, Sean Tyree was a handsome young man, Matt decided. His eyes were hazel, more green than brown, and he wore his auburn hair short, with just a hint of sideburns. His high-buttoned gray suit had an expensive English cut; his fine silk shirt was spotlessly white. He wore highly polished, elastic-sided boots and the watch chain that crossed his flat belly was made of thick gold links.

As far as Matt could tell, neither Tyree nor St. Clair carried a weapon, at least none that was visible.

About both men, there was an air of quiet, understated confidence, which perhaps came from wealth, yet Matt sensed they could be dangerous when roused.

"First herds are due in next week or the week after," Matt said, again testing the waters. "My deputy tells me Clint Stucker and his son, Cage, are bringing in six thousand head."

Matt had expected the names to strike a raw nerve in Tyree, but if they did, the man didn't let it show.

His face unchanged, Tyree asked: "What price are the buyers offering this year?"

"Eighteen dollars a head," Matt answered readily, but with the feeling that he was telling Tyree something he already knew.

Tyree was thoughtful for a few moments, then said: "Six thousand head will bring in a hundred eight thousand dollars. That's a lot of money"—then he added something that puzzled Matt—"especially if a man needed it real bad."

Instinctively, Matt felt that the calculation was also something Tyree had done before. But why? Was he, of all people, planning to buy the Stucker herd?

That didn't make any sense, and Matt dismissed the thought. Maybe Tyree was just idly speculating on the profits to be made in the cattle business. But why that extra bit about a man needing that kind of money bad?

The marshal had no answers, but he decided not to press Tyree or St. Clair further on how they felt about Clint and Cage Stucker. He knew he would just end up with even more unanswered questions and a bellyful of frustration. Both men were friendly and courteous, but closemouthed when it came to the Stuckers, and he let it go. At least for now.

After a few minutes of small talk, St. Clair and Tyree, accompanied by an elegant display of fine manners, made their excuses to Kitty about the sad necessity of leaving.

St. Clair gracefully bent over Kitty's hand and pressed it lightly to his lips. "You, dear lady, are a lovely distraction," he said. "But, alas, the gaming tables call."

To his surprise, Matt felt a sudden pang of jealousy, knowing full well that if he tried to kiss Kitty's hand like that he'd probably fall flat on his face.

For her part, Kitty giggled like a young girl and dropped St. Clair an equally graceful curtsy—and Matt's jealousy grew, surprising him even more.

After Tyree and St. Clair left, Kitty stepped behind the bar and found a bottle of good bourbon and two glasses. She nodded to a table by the wall and asked Matt: "Join me?"

Matt sat at the table, facing the door as was his habit, and Kitty poured drinks for them both. His mind working, the marshal glanced through the open doors, where the rising wind picked up a stray sheet of newspaper and sent it fluttering like a dove into the air. A townsman, nodding in the saddle, rode past and his horse's head tossed in alarm, the bit jangling, as the paper swooped close, then flapped to the ground. Unaware, the rider continued to doze.

Over at another table, Kitty's hostesses had reached some kind of agreement with the bald drummers and all four rose and headed for the stairs. The girls laughed and prodded the men up the steps, but the older of the two drummers glanced furtively over his shoulder. His eyes met Matt's and the man's face reddened and he quickly turned away.

Matt was ready to muse on the frailty of human nature, but realized Kitty was talking to him and gave her his full attention. ". . . one is an observation. The other—well, call it good old female intuition."

The marshal shook his head, his smile apologetic. "Sorry, Kitty. I was deep in thought and missed most of what you were saying."

"You're thinking about Sean Tyree, aren't you?"

Matt nodded. "Uh-huh, about him some. And other things."

Kitty sipped her whiskey, then laid the glass carefully on the table. "Sean Tyree is the subject of my observation."

"Oh, what about Tyree?"

"Just this, the young man was attractive to women before, but now, with that scar on his cheek, he's even more so. There will be very few ladies who will be able to resist him."

Matt smiled. "Does that include you, Kitty?"

Kitty did not return his smile. She shrugged her beautiful, naked shoulders and said: "I already have the man I want."

Matt accepted the sincerity of that, and asked: "And what's the good old female intuition part?"

"Matt, that young man has become rich with the passing years, but he's so eaten up with hate I believe he saved his money to use it as a weapon against the Stuckers."

The marshal shook his head. "I don't understand, Kitty. How would he do that? Clint Stucker is one of the wealthiest ranchers in Texas, or so he tells everybody. When it comes to money and the power it gives a man, he's got little to fear from Sean Tyree, or Logan St. Clair for that matter."

"I don't know what plans Sean Tyree has," Kitty said, her dark eyes troubled. "I do know that hate is eating at him like a terrible cancer. I saw it in him. I saw it in his eyes."

Remembering, Matt was silent for a few moments. Then he said: "I saw hate like that in Tyree's eyes once my ownself, but that was five years ago. I didn't see it tonight."

"Of course you didn't. Tyree has a gambler's eyes. Logan St. Clair taught him well."

"But you saw it."

Kitty nodded, and now she smiled, her long eyelashes fluttering like wounded butterflies. "When a man looks at a woman he desires, gambler or no, his eyes pretty much give away what he's thinking, no matter how hard he tries to keep that look corralled. In Sean Tyree's eyes I saw what I'd expected in those of a young man. But there was something else, something he usually manages to keep well hidden—a world of hurt and a dangerous hatred."

Kitty laid the tips of her fingers on Matt's big, scarred knuckles. "Be careful. Be very careful, Matt. I sense something terrible is about to happen."

Matt forced a grin. "Is that more of your woman's intuition?"

"Yes, it is," Kitty answered, half her lovely face in deep shadow. "And it's never once lied to me."

chapter 5

The Coming of the Herds

Drifting dust clouds rising into the clear Kansas sky signaled the arrival of the herds, plodding up the long, dry miles from Texas along the Chisholm and Western trails.

And with the cattle came the cowboys, young men who had never lived where churches stood, never once seen the dusty sunlight slant, colored, through a painted window, yet understood the beauty of God's creation better than any preacher, worshiping as they did in a vast cathedral roofed by the dim, quiet stars.

Wild as the cattle they nursed, yipping, whistling, swinging their lariats, they had driven the herds around mountains and mesas and by smooth-running streams, where sagebrush and greasewood flung their musky perfumes wide and far into the air.

Sitting forty-pound saddles that galled even their tough hides, straddling half-broke ponies, eating tin-can beans and salty, greasy bacon as smoky as sin, the cowboys had driven the herds through the mud and rain of storm-swept plains, heads bent against hammering rain and the mad symphony of the wind. They had crossed waterless wastelands, endless miles of scorching heat and dust, knowing that at any time they could find themselves in the middle of a prairie fire, quicksand or stampede.

Dirty, weary, often leaving behind a dead compadre in an unmarked grave along the trail, they rode on, herding the doggies north by the guiding light of a bright star, nodding in the saddle, dreaming of Dodge, the welcoming painted whore of the plains.

For the Texas puncher, Dodge, with its bright lights, whiskey and willing women, would make up for months of drinking the alkali water that gave him running sores and the beans that gave him the croup. For a week, or maybe just for a single day, he'd be rich, happily squandering his money, willing to stake his last dollar on the tumble of dice or the slender chance of drawing a fourth ace.

Young, wild and reckless, the cowboys were pouring into Dodge, and though the town rubbed its hands with glee, the hands of Matt Dillon and Festus were full contending with them.

With the governor's frantic letter lying forgotten on his desk, Matt patrolled the streets, stepping inside now and again to stroll through the crowded, roaring saloons.

Dodge was bursting at the seams. Broad-brimmed and spurred Texans brushed shoulders with farmers, sharp businessmen, real estate agents, land seekers,

Mexicans up from the border country, hungry lawyers, painted whores and respectable women in white sunbonnets and high-buttoned shoes of a certain pattern.

The cattle season was not fully set in, but Front Street was already jammed with cow ponies, express wagons going pell-mell, canvas-covered prairie schooners and farm wagons, all of them churning up clouds of yellow dust that sifted through every nook and cranny of the clapboard buildings and covered everything.

Over by the railroad tracks, the maze of corrals and feed sheds was filling up with cattle, and the wind brought the smell and swarms of bloated black flies.

The longhorns themselves, lanky and sleek, were much maligned but of excellent pedigree. They bore the blood of cows that had grazed the hills and meadows of Spain centuries before Francisco Vasquez de Coronado had come to Texas in search of *Quivira*, the fabled land where the apple trees bore fruit of solid gold.

Now, far from any meadow, jammed tightly together, their enormous horns clicking and clashing, the longhorns bawled and jostled, churning the ground under their feet to liquid mud.

And through all this noisy, gritty, grimy turmoil moved Marshal Matt Dillon, tall, determined and significant, courteous to all, but overfriendly to no one.

He made a couple of arrests for public drunkenness, and once buffaloed a liquored-up puncher who tried to draw down on him, but the first couple of weeks of the cattle season passed without a single shooting or knifing.

At the end of the second week came the first gun scrape after a couple of the whores at the Alamo got into an argument over the ownership of a silver ring. One of the doves, her talking done, aggressively unlimbered a pepperbox revolver and cut loose, missing her three-hundred-pound opponent, but slightly wounding a corset drummer who stood at the bar.

Matt was called and escorted the young lady to the calaboose. Next day she was fined three dollars for discharging a dangerous weapon within the city limits.

Mayor Kelley was willing to overlook little spats between whores, since the fines regularly levied on the girls for prostitution during the cattle season provided half of Dodge's revenue for the year.

The ladies were fined ten dollars a month and two dollars in court costs and keepers of brothels paid twenty dollars plus five dollars in costs. If the brothel sold whiskey, another five dollars' tax was added.

It was Matt's duty to collect these fines, and Mayor Kelley, a tough Irishman with more than a touch of larceny in his soul, would hear no argument on that point.

Another man in town was trying to get rich quick, but his method was to fleece the high-rolling cowboys.

Matt received complaints from several broke and angry punchers that the roulette wheel at Frank O'Hara's Saloon and Gambling Emporium was rigged.

The marshal investigated and discovered that O'Hara's chuck-a-luck tumblers and faro boxes were as crooked as a barrel of snakes and that the man's in-house gamblers were using marked cards. There was also evidence that O'Hara's girls, more hard-bitten than most, were rolling drunks.

On the surface, Frank O'Hara was a sleek, fat, jolly man, but when Matt met his truculent stare he found himself looking into the cold, emotionless eyes of a lizard.

O'Hara made the usual protests of innocence when Matt challenged him, but quickly admitted all and promised to mend his ways when the big marshal threatened to close him down.

Matt's brush with the saloonkeeper was routine law enforcement, something he had done many times before, and he thought nothing more of it. Yet his row with O'Hara would have later repercussions—in ways he could not have imagined.

Meanwhile Festus, who haunted the packed saloons and kept his ear to the ground, told Matt that Clint Stucker had not yet sold his herd, holding out for a better price.

The rancher had made the Alhambra Saloon his unofficial headquarters and was riding a winning streak at the poker table. Stucker had paid off most of his hands, keeping only ten, but these were not punchers—they were hard-eyed men hired for their skill with a gun, not a rope.

Cage Stucker was around, but he divided his time between the cattle pens and the herd of two thousand longhorns he was still holding on good grass south of Dodge.

Matt had not heard not a word about Sean Tyree and Logan St. Clair.

Then, as the third week of the cattle season began, Festus brought news.

Matt was in his office, struggling once again with paperwork, when Festus stepped inside, bringing with him a cloud of dust and the sound of tinkling pianos and raucous laughter from the saloons and dance halls along Front Street.

"Matthew," Festus said, getting right to the point of what he had to say, "I've been hearing talk about Logan St. Clair. And Cage Stucker."

Matt laid down his pen and looked up at his deputy. "All good, I hope."

Festus shrugged. "Depends on what you mean by good. I hear they're both crossing the Deadline and walking out with Becky Sharpe."

It took Matt a few moments before he remembered. "She's married, isn't she?"

"Sure is," Festus agreed. "Ol' Hank Sharpe is more'n twice Becky's age and keeps poorly. He's laid up in bed most of the time. That's the trouble when you're an old man with a pretty young wife. It's hard to keep her away from other men, especially when you're always flat on your back with a misery."

Matt nodded and picked up his pen. "Anything else, Festus?"

The deputy's disappointment showed. "Matthew, ain't that enough? Logan St. Clair and Cage Stucker are walking out with the same married woman. Ain't you going to do something about it?"

Matt shrugged. "What can I do? I'm paid to police the town, not the morals of its citizens."

"But . . . but, Matthew, they're crossing the Deadline."

"Are they wearing guns?"

"Not that I can tell."

"Then they're not breaking the law. So long as St. Clair and Stucker don't carry guns across the Deadline, walking out with Becky Sharpe is their business."

Festus scratched his jaw. "Well, it's all gonna end in trouble if'n you ask me. That Becky now, she's real purty, but she's a flighty little thing and I bet it pleases her to have a couple of handsome young men panting after her. I reckon she's playing one off against the other for what she can get."

Matt leaned back in his chair. There was no love lost between Logan St. Clair and Cage Stucker and both were skilled gunmen. At the edge of town, Boot Hill was full of men who'd been killed in gunfights over a woman.

What Matt had told Festus was true, neither man was breaking the law, but he decided maybe it was time to head off trouble before it came to a killing.

"Where is Stucker?" he asked.

"Last I saw him, he was heading over to the pens to check on his herd."

"And St. Clair?"

"He's over to the Alamo, playing poker with Doc Holliday and some other high rollers."

Matt rose, buckled on his gun belt and settled his hat on his head. "Festus, take care of things here," he said. "I'm going to have a word with Cage Stucker."

The deputy nodded, grinning. "I knowed you would. Gonna arrest him, Matthew?"

"For what? Like I said, Stucker hasn't broken any law. If I arrested every man in Dodge who walked out with a married woman, my jail would be full."

Matt stepped onto the boardwalk, glanced up and down Front Street, then made his way through the thronging crowds toward the cattle pens.

Day was shading into night, and above Dodge, the sky was streaked with streamers of jade, gold and scarlet. So far, the deepening amber twilight was being kept at bay by the flaring light from the windows of the saloons and dance halls. But soon full darkness, unnoticed, would arrive, filling the bottle-strewn alleyways with angled shadows, throwing a black veil over the plains, where the hungry coyotes would begin to call.

When Matt arrived at the pens, most of them were filled with mud-spattered, milling cattle. A clanking train eased along the railroad track, then lurched to a steaming halt, its whistle blasting.

Matt walked past dozens of pens, all of them full, then turned toward the tracks and the feed sheds. He stopped and studied the longhorns in a pen nearest the sheds. The crowded cattle all bore the Stucker Rafter S brand, but when he looked around, he saw no sign of Cage.

The marshal turned to retrace his steps back to Front Street, but stopped when a tall man leaning against a fence post asked: "Why are you looking over the Rafter S stock? If you're a buyer, the owner is Clint Stucker and he's over to the Alhambra."

Matt stepped toward the man, letting him see the star pinned to the front of his leather vest. "I want to talk to Cage Stucker," he said.

The man shouldered himself away from the post, so relaxed and self-assured his body seemed to move piece by piece, then slowly reassemble itself when he finally stood, straddle-legged, facing the lawman.

"You what passes for the law around here?" he asked. "What do you want with Cage?"

Matt was stung, but did not let it show. The man facing him looked like a hundred other two-bit gunmen he'd been seeing around Dodge for years. He carried two Colts in crossed belts, the holsters worn low on his thighs, a style wanna-be hard cases had adopted recently. The man's thumbs were tucked behind the belts, on either side of the buckles, and he was dressed in black pants and shirt and a high-crowned black hat. The only color about him was the scarlet bandana that hung loose around his neck, and the ivory handles of his guns.

The man was looking at Matt insolently; under his full mustache, a faint, mocking smile tugged at the corners of his mouth, showing prominent front teeth.

"My name is Matt Dillon and I'm the town marshal," Matt said evenly. "And what I want with Cage is my own business."

"I ride for Clint Stucker, so I'm making it my business," the man said. "My name is Johnny Lomax. Mean anything to you?"

Matt shook his head. "No. Should it?"

Lomax stiffened, his mouth thinning in annoyance. "Yeah, it should. It means plenty in Texas, and up here it means I come and go as I please."

"Fine with me," Matt said. "I have no problem with that, just so long as you're not breaking the law."

Lomax's pale blue eyes moved constantly, slitted and sly, like those of a rat, and now they glittered a warning in the shade of his hat brim. "Lawman, don't go letting that tin star give you any big notions. When I say I come and go as I please, I mean badge toters know to stay out of my way." The gunman's smile was mean, without a trace of humor. "See, that's an understanding I always reach with the local yokel."

"And if you don't reach an understanding?" Matt asked, feeling the anger rise in him.

"I always reach an understanding. The name Johnny Lomax"—the man touched the handles of his Colts—"and these guns kinda guarantee it."

Matt took a couple of steps toward Lomax and saw alarm flare in the gunman's eyes. Matt knew exactly what he was doing. By closing the distance between them, he had put Lomax at a disadvantage. An experienced killer, the man would know that if the range got too close this big lawman could take hits and shoot back, and he'd be unlikely to miss.

Desperately Lomax backed up, trying to open up some space between him and the huge, relentless marshal.

But Matt continued to crowd him. "Understand

this, Lomax," he said, stepping close to the gunman, his eyes hardening to the color of blue steel. "I've seen hundreds of your kind, cheap, little tinhorn wanna-bes. Say one more word and I'll take off those guns you're wearing and spank you with them like a redheaded stepchild."

"The hell you will," Lomax yelled. And he drew.

Later Matt would concede that Johnny Lomax was fast, very fast on the draw. But the man's guns had barely cleared leather when Matt's fist thudded into his jaw and sent Lomax reeling backward on rubber knees, his Colts dropping from suddenly nerveless fingers.

Matt didn't give the gunman a chance to get set. He stepped toward him and backhanded Lomax across the mouth with his left hand, pulping the man's lips against his teeth. Lomax crashed against the rails of the Stucker pen, startling the crowded longhorns so that they jumped away, bumping into one another, their eyeballs rolling white.

Matt went after Lomax again. He swung a hard left into the gunman's ribs, then took a step back and threw a roundhouse right that crashed into Lomax's cheekbone, splitting the skin wide open.

Lomax groaned and slid to the ground, blood trickling from his smashed lips over his chin.

Matt stepped beside the fallen gunman and slowly shook his head. As was the case with most men who lived by the gun, fistfighting was alien to Lomax. He'd figured Matt would try to match the speed of his draw—a punch to the chin was the last thing he'd expected.

"Always expect the unexpected, Lomax," Matt said, knowing his words were falling on deaf ears because the gunman was unconscious.

The big marshal grabbed Lomax by the collar of his shirt and dragged him back to Front Street, where horrified passersby hastily cleared a path for him.

As he dragged the groaning gunman toward his office, Matt heard someone say: "Hey, that's Johnny Lomax."

Matt knew that soon the word would spread around Dodge that Two-Gun Johnny Lomax, the feared Texas gunfighter, had let himself be buffaloed by a cowtown marshal.

It would be good for Matt's standing in Dodge as a tough and capable lawman, but he knew that in Lomax he had made himself a dangerous, deadly enemy. Now the only way the gunman would be able to salvage his wounded pride and badly damaged reputation would be to kill him.

Matt threw Lomax into one of the two cells in the jail behind his office. Festus turned the clanking key in the lock and said: "Matthew, that there's Johnny Lomax. He's killed a dozen men, they say. Now what in tarnation did he do to offend you that you'd risk your life to arrest him?"

"He talked too much," Matt said.

chapter 6

A Gambler Cashes in His Chips

Justice on the frontier was rough and ready at best, and next morning, much to Matt's disgust, Johnny Lomax was fined ten dollars and three dollars in court costs for assaulting a city police officer.

Clint Stucker paid the fine and one of his hands brought Lomax his guns and his horse.

Matt was standing near the courthouse door when Lomax came out, Clint Stucker's arm around his shoulder.

Lomax saw Matt and his eyes flashed his hatred. He threw off Stucker's arm, stepped beside Matt and snarled: "Next time you won't be so lucky, Dillon."

Matt nodded. "You know where to find me."

Clint Stucker, a man almost as tall as Matt but bigger in the chest and belly, stepped between them. "Johnny," he said, "you go stay with the herd outside of town. I'll tell you when to bring them in. Maybe a week. Maybe less if I find the right buyer."

Lomax looked from Matt to Stucker, made up his mind about something and nodded. "I'll go." He turned to Matt. "When I get back, I'll come looking for you."

"As I already told you, Lomax, I won't be hard to find."

Lomax gave Matt one last, lingering look, his pale blue eyes filled with menace. Then he stepped to his horse, swung into the saddle and galloped away.

"He will kill you, Dillon. You know that, don't you?" Stucker said.

"He can try," Matt answered.

Clint Stucker was a handsome man with yellow hair and mustache, only now, as he approached fifty, showing signs of gray. There was a hint of brutality about his thick-lipped mouth and his eyes were gray, without warmth, cold as chips of river ice.

"I hear Sean Tyree is in town," Stucker said, studying Matt closely as he gauged his reaction.

Matt nodded. "He's here, and so is Logan St. Clair."

"You tell them to stay away from my son and me, Dillon," Stucker said. "If they don't, we'll finish the job this time, on both of them."

His patience snapping, Matt said: "If a tinhorn like Johnny Lomax is the best you've got to offer, Stucker, my advice to you is to sell your herd to the highest bidder and haul your freight back to Texas."

Stucker was stung and it showed, his face blackening with anger. "You keep in mind what I just said. If those two-bit gamblers cause me and mine any trouble, they're dead men."

"I'm here to make sure that there's no trouble," Matt said. "While you're in Dodge, you and Cage keep your distance from Tyree and St. Clair, that's all."

"Will you tell the same thing to them other two?"

"I plan to."

"Just make sure you do, Dillon," Stucker snapped. He turned on his heel and stomped away, his spurs ringing.

Matt took off his hat, wiped off the sweatband with his fingers and glanced up at the cloudless sky. The burning sun was at its highest point, adding scorching heat to the misery of dust and the rank stench wafting from the cattle pens.

The way Clint Stucker was talking, he wouldn't bring in his remaining herd for another week. Could Matt keep the peace between Cage and Tyree for that long?

So far neither man had even acknowledged the presence of the other, but that could change in an instant.

Was Kitty's woman's intuition right? Was big trouble brewing?

Matt shook his head. As usual he had plenty of questions and no answers.

The marshal replaced his hat and stepped along the boardwalk toward his office. Apart from wagons and a few farmers and businessmen, the street was quiet; most of the cowboys were sleeping off last night's drunk. Dodge would drowse through the dusty heat of the day, ready to shake itself awake and come alive again at nightfall.

Like tired old whores, the saloons and dance halls, glittering, glamorous sin palaces by night, looked seedy and run-down in the harsh light of day. Paint was blistering and peeling from the false fronts, the timbers warped, curling away from the frames, revealing rusting nails. The red, white and blue bunting draped above the saloon doorways was covered in yellow dust, turning them a uniform shade of tan, and the windows were flyblown, smeared with coats of gritty dirt.

Matt felt the buildings crowd in on him, hot, close and stifling, making it hard to breathe, his boots thudding with a hollow sound on the uneven boardwalk.

Strangely restless, he changed direction away from his office and walked to the livery stable at the end of Texas Street. He saddled his horse and rode out of town, heading north toward Duck Creek.

Matt followed the creek as it swung east, riding through some pleasant, rolling country, until he reached Saw Log Creek, where he found welcome shade under a stand of cottonwood and willow at a bend on the south bank.

The marshal unsaddled his horse and watched him roll, then, when the bay settled down to graze, he stretched out under a tree, enjoying the cool, dappled shadows cast by the branches and leaves.

The wind stirred the buffalo grass and bees hummed among the wildflowers. A fish jumped in the creek, and above him, the thick branches of the cottonwood creaked in drowsy harmony.

Matt Dillon closed his eyes, his absence from Dodge tugging at his conscience. But he told himself that he'd done the right thing in taking a break from the town's intolerable heat, dust and clamor. Sometimes a man needs to ride out and find quiet, untroubled retreat in his own soul.

Matt dozed, then let himself drift into sleep.

A young antelope came to the creek to drink, then stopped, stiff-legged with alarm when it spotted the man stretched out under the tree. The little animal's head lifted, testing the wind. It took a single, hesitant step toward the creek. Then another. And another.

The antelope dipped its velvety muzzle into the water and drank, tiny ripples spreading away in growing circles from its mouth. After a while the pronghorn raised its head again, drops dripping from its muzzle, briefly glanced at the man under the tree, then turned and bounded away on silent hooves.

Matt slept on. . . .

The afternoon light softened and the day faded toward dusk and the pale lemon sky was streaked with bands of scarlet and gold. The wind rose, setting the leaves of the cottonwood to rustling, and the night birds began to call.

Matt stirred, then woke with start. How long had he been asleep? A glance at the darkening sky told him several hours. He rose, stretched, then saddled the bay and swung into the leather.

He felt rested and refreshed, at peace with himself.

But now it was time to get back. Dodge would be awake and painting her face.

The hands on the railroad clock in Matt Dillon's office were joined at midnight, but outside in the roaring, light-splashed night, Dodge was just hitting its stride.

A six-piece orchestra at the Long Branch noisily competed with tin-panny pianos from a dozen other saloons, filling the air with a jangling, tuneless cacophony of sound.

Drunken men, their voices hoarse with whiskey, yelled and whooped and hollered, the laughter of unbuttoned women ringing like silver bells, rising above the din.

Matt tried to ignore the racket, sighed and picked up the letter from the governor, giving it all his attention. A clean sheet of notepaper was spread out on the desk in front of him, and he held a steel-tipped pen in his huge, big-knuckled hand, a full bottle of black ink standing close by.

Matt laid the governor's letter aside, then, his tongue sticking out of the corner of his mouth in concentration, he carefully put his sputtering pen to paper and wrote in big, blocky letters: *DEAR GOVERNOR.*

The marshal eased back in his chair and held the paper up to the light of the oil lamp above his desk.

That, he decided, immensely pleased with himself, was a crackerjack start.

Festus had assured him that no matter the size of

the entourage, he was sure suitable accommodation could be found at any one of the half dozen livery stables in Dodge.

Matt laid the paper back on his desk and chewed the end of his pen, deep in thought. The clock on the wall now showed five minutes after midnight.

At twelve thirty, Matt had gotten no further than *Dear Governor*. He threw his pen down in disgust, instantly obliterating the carefully written salutation with a blot, and rose to his feet.

He put on his hat and buckled on his gun belt. It was time to make his rounds. His reply to the governor would have to wait.

Matt had just opened the door to step outside when he heard a shot, followed almost instantly by another.

Gunfire was not unusual in Dodge, but the direction of the two shots was—they had come from across the Deadline on the north side of the railroad tracks.

Matt stepped into the street and hurried toward the tracks. A few passersby on the boardwalks yelled out to him, asking what all the shooting was about. Matt ignored them and hurried on, his long stride eating up the distance.

He stepped across the tracks and off to his right saw a knot of men gathered around what looked like a body on the ground.

Here, across the Deadline, Matt found himself in a different world.

All the houses had been built carefully of brick or whitewashed pine and all had picket fences and vegetable gardens. Most boasted a fine carriage house and barn and a few even had detached servants' quarters.

Matt slipped the rawhide thong off the hammer of his Colt and slowed his pace as he approached the gathered men, taking time to assess the situation.

The moon lit up the scene ahead of him, and Matt took it in at a glance.

Cage Stucker, half drunk, a loose grin stretching his thick-lipped mouth, held a smoking gun in his hand, his arm hanging at his side. Three men who looked to be Rafter S riders stood beside Stucker, and one laughed and slapped the young rancher on the back just as Matt reached them.

The man on the ground was Logan St. Clair.

"He was going for his gun, Marshal," one of the riders said quickly as Matt loomed in front of him. He turned to one of his companions. "Ain't that right, Bill?"

"Damn right," the man called Bill agreed. "I saw him reach under his coat plain as day."

Matt ignored the men and kneeled beside St. Clair. The gambler's white shirt was stained with blood and his lips were white under his mustache. St. Clair had been shot twice in the chest, at so close a range the front of his shirt was still smoldering from burning powder.

St. Clair opened his eyes and looked up at Matt, death already sharpening his features, his skin gray. Slowly, with a tremendous effort, he reached down and pulled open his frockcoat. "Nothing," he whispered.

Then his eyes closed again and he was gone.

Matt rose slowly to his feet and looked over at Cage Stucker. "What happened?" he asked.

Stucker swayed unsteadily on his feet and giggled. "I wanted to brace him about walking out with my gal, but before I could say a word, he went for his gun. I shot him in self-defense." Cage turned to his hands. "Ain't that the honest truth, boys?"

The three hands mumbled their agreement, and Matt said: "This man was unarmed."

"Well, it sure didn't look that way to us, Marshal," one of the hands said. "His right hand reached under his coat. We all saw it plain."

Matt kneeled again and opened St. Clair's coat. There was a long silver case in the inside pocket. Matt retrieved it and stood. "He was reaching all right, but for his cigars."

Stucker shrugged, his eyes mean and ugly. "I guess smoking was real bad for his health."

The three hands guffawed, but Matt's face was set and hard. "Stucker," he said, "hand over your gun. I'm arresting you for the murder of Logan St. Clair."

Cage hawked and spat into the dust as Matt's feet. "Nobody takes my gun," he said. "There ain't a man alive I'd let take this here Colt from me."

There's a time for talking and a time for doing, and Matt decided the time for talking had just passed.

His hand blurred as he palmed his gun and hammered the barrel hard against the side of Stucker's head. The man staggered a few steps to his right, his eyes rolling white; then he collapsed in a heap on the ground.

Matt swung on the three Rafter S riders, but none made a move toward a gun. They kept their hands spread wide like their Colts were suddenly red-hot.

The marshal nodded to Stucker. "Pick him up and carry him over to the jail."

The men did as they were told, one at Stucker's shoulders, each of the other two supporting a leg. Led by Matt, the riders carried Stucker across the tracks and along Front Street.

A crowd gathered on the boardwalks and somebody yelled: "What happened?"

The man called Bill called out over his shoulder: "Logan St. Clair tried to draw down on Cage an' Cage shot him." He hefted Stucker's leg in his hands, adjusting his grip, then hollered again, breathing hard: "The Marshal buffaloed Cage an' for no reason a-tall."

A murmur ran through the crowd, some voices approving, others raised in condemnation of the marshal and his heavyhanded methods of dealing with prisoners.

Matt ignored the talk, knowing that when all the facts became known, Dodge would learn that St. Clair's death was cold-blooded murder and understand the right of it.

Festus, a shotgun in his hands and a worried look on his face, met Matt in the street. "Are you all right, Matthew?" he asked. "As soon as I heard there had been a shooting I came a-running."

"It's over, Festus," Matt said. "Logan St. Clair is dead and I've charged Cage Stucker with his murder." He nodded behind him. "St. Clair's body lies just over the tracks yonder. Round up some men and carry him to Percy Crump's funeral parlor."

Festus fell into step alongside Matt. "Matthew," he said, "I only got one thing to say—you just told me it's over, but it ain't. I've got a feeling this killing is only the beginning."

Suddenly weary, Matt snapped. "Festus, go do like I told you."

The deputy's wounded eyes searched Matt's face, wanting to talk more. But Matt, his voice softer, ended it. "Festus," he said, "just . . . just do like I said."

Festus, gauging the marshal's mood, nodded. "Right away, Matthew."

Matt watched his deputy hurry away toward the tracks, calling out to men on the boardwalk to follow him.

Later, with the still unconscious Cage Stucker locked in his jail, Matt tossed the keys on his desk and slumped into his chair, his head in his hands.

He didn't want to admit it, even to himself, but Festus had been right.

This wasn't over, not by a long shot.

Sean Tyree would see to that.

chapter 7

The Gathering Storm

After a hurried inquest conducted by the county coroner, the trial of Cage Stucker for murder was scheduled for two weeks hence, the Honorable Simeon T. Walker, the federal circuit judge, to preside.

At Matt's request, bail was refused, since the marshal deemed Stucker a flight risk who could light a shuck for Texas before justice was done.

Sean Tyree, looking drawn and worn, the scar on his pale cheek more stark than ever, ignored all the excited talk going around Dodge about Stucker and quietly made funeral arrangements for Logan St. Clair.

He spoke to no one but Percy Crump, made no accusations, laid no blame—and Matt thought all this made the man even more menacing, like a smoldering volcano ready to erupt.

Tyree had packed away his cards, dice and gambler's finery; he had changed into range clothes, a sweat-stained black hat, a blue shirt and blue canvas pants held up by wide leather suspenders. His boots were of the finest quality, handmade in Abilene by the famous Thomas C. McInerney, but, to Matt's relief, the young man did not carry a gun.

Clint Stucker had brought in his last herd, and the ten Rafter S gunmen were in Dodge, including Johnny Lomax, all of them telling anybody who would listen how Logan St. Clair had gone for a gun and that Matt Dillon had secretly palmed the weapon so it would look like the gambler was unarmed.

Most vocal of all was Lomax, the pale-eyed gunman spreading the rumor that Matt, St. Clair and Tyree had been in cahoots, running a protection racket to fleece the owners of the saloons and dance halls.

"An' then he said you laid off the Long Branch only because you and St. Clair was both sparkin' Miss Kitty," Festus told Matt as they sat in his office drinking coffee ten days before Cage Stucker's trial. "Matthew, you better tell Lomax to shut his gopher trap afore he gets folks' thinking turned around the wrong way, especially the mayor an' them hardshell Baptists across the tracks."

Matt shrugged. "Festus, I think the folks in Dodge know me better than that. Oh, they might listen to what Lomax and the others are saying, but I doubt they believe a word of it."

Festus shook his head, his uncertainty showing. "Well, I sure hope so, Matthew. For all our sakes."

But Matt was less confident than he pretended. Lies like those that Lomax was spreading could hurt. Folks might get to thinking that there was no smoke without fire and such talk might prejudice the jury in Cage Stucker's favor.

And there was the problem of Sean Tyree. The young man wasn't carrying a gun, but he was no doubt annoyed at what the Rafter S hands were saying about his friend's killing. If there was an angry showdown between an unarmed Tyree and Johnny Lomax, there could be another murder in Dodge.

Matt left Festus to feed the complaining Cage Stucker his breakfast beef and beans, and walked down to the Long Branch, his first stop on what would turn out to be an eventful morning.

Even at this early hour, the saloon was busy, with elegantly dressed Northern meat packers talking beef and prices with booted and spurred ranchers, pasty-faced gamblers squaring their decks and preparing for bed, a sprinkling of businessmen from across the tracks drinking three fingers of bonded bourbon with their morning coffee and a few cowboys, hungover and hurting, nursing beers as they counted the few coins in their pockets and contemplated the error of their ways.

As always, Kitty Russell looked fresh and lovely, the long, smoky hours she'd spent greeting customers at the bar seemingly having had no effect on her. She wore a plain morning dress of gray wool that clung to every generous curve of her body; her hair was pulled back with a red ribbon. Even without her usual makeup she was a beautiful, desirable woman and the sight of her made Matt's breath catch in his throat.

Matt greeted the men he knew, then followed Kitty to a table, where Sam the bartender brought them coffee. Kitty poured cream into her cup, held the silver jug up to Matt, a question in her smile, but the marshal shook his head.

"I drink it the way it comes," he said.

"One day you'll have cream in your coffee, Matt," Kitty said. "And that's the day I'll know you're a changed man."

Matt grinned. "Ready to settle down, you mean?"

"Something like that," Kitty said.

"You'll be the first to know. In the meantime, keep the cream jug handy."

For a few minutes, Matt and Kitty made small talk, but the marshal could see the woman had something on her mind, something more important than the heat and flies and the merits of Eddie Foy's rendition of "Kalamazoo in Michigan" at the Comique.

Finally, Kitty got round to it. "Matt," she said, her eyes troubled, "I've got something to tell you."

"Figured you had, but I was biding my time." Matt smiled. "Let me hear it."

Doubt showed in Kitty's face and she said: "Maybe none of it's important."

"Let me hear it anyway."

Kitty poured them both coffee, dabbed a loop on her thoughts and said: "Amos Wright from the telegraph office was here last night and he said—"

"Does Amos Wright ever keep anything secret?" Matt interrupted. "I swear, give him half a chance and he'll bend your ear into a bow knot."

"Maybe so," Kitty continued, "but what he told me was interesting. Well, I thought it was interesting." The woman sipped her coffee, then carefully replaced the china cup on its saucer and said: "Amos told me that Sean Tyree had sent off a pile of wires. One was to a lawyer in El Paso, a man named Jenkins, and there were six or seven others."

Kitty leaned across the table. "Amos couldn't remember all the names but he did recall two of them. One was to"—Kitty's nose wrinkled in thought—"oh yes, a man called Nathan Price and the other to someone by the name of Jenness."

"Steve Jenness?"

Kitty nodded. "Yes, that's it. Steve Jenness."

"And you say he sent out six or seven wires?"

"That's what Amos said." Kitty's eyes searched Matt's face. "Matt, have you heard those names before?"

Matt leaned back in his chair, a sigh escaping his lips. "Steve Jenness is a gunfighter out of Smiley, Texas. He ran with Wes Hardin and the Clements boys and the rest of that hard crowd during the Sutton-Taylor feud. After that, he drifted to Cheyenne, where he wore a badge for a couple of years. They say he's killed a dozen men. I don't know if that's true or not, but by anybody's standard, Steve Jenness is a handful."

"And Nathan Price?" Kitty asked.

"High-stakes gambler. Mostly works the saloons in

New Orleans and the riverboats. He's been in shooting scrapes and I recollect him being mentioned as a close friend of Logan St. Clair. Apart from that, I've heard nothing else about him."

Matt drank his coffee, deep in thought. He would talk to Amos Wright to confirm his suspicions, but he was willing to bet that Tyree had sent those wires to named and belted men, revolver fighters of reputation, all of them top-tier guns like Steve Jenness and Nathan Price.

But why?

Did Tyree think Cage Stucker would be found not guilty at his trial? If that happened, did Tyree plan to administer his own brand of justice, with a half dozen of St. Clair's gun-handy friends backing him up? Or if Cage was found guilty, did Tyree reckon he still had an old score to settle with Clint Stucker?

The questions were troubling, and as usual, Matt had no answers.

Well, there was one thing for sure—

"Well, there's one thing for sure, Matt," Kitty said, reading his mind, as she had an uncanny habit of doing. "Those wires can only mean trouble."

Matt nodded and rose to his feet. "Kitty, this is my town and I plan to keep a lid on whatever might happen. If Jenness and Price and the others ride into Dodge, I'll tell them to drift—and fast."

Kitty looked up at Matt, her beautiful eyes taut with fear. "Be careful, Matt. Be very careful."

The big marshal nodded. "Kitty, I won't sit with my back to any windows, trust me."

As he turned to leave, Kitty's voice stopped him

in midstride. "Matt," she said, "woman's intuition, remember?"

"I'll remember," the marshal answered.

"And there's one more thing," Kitty said. "Doc Holliday told me that Clint Stucker's luck has run out over to the Alhambra. Doc says Stucker is losing big just about every night."

Matt nodded, saying nothing, storing that information in his memory. He stepped out of the saloon into the warm morning sunlight, yet he felt a sudden chill. And that bothered him because he didn't know why.

At the telegraph office, Amos Wright confirmed Matt's worst fears. Apart from the lawyer in El Paso, Sean Tyree had sent six one-word wires, all to named men.

That word was *COME*.

"And will they come, Marshal?" Wright asked, his eyes eager. "I mean, here to Dodge?"

Matt saw no reason to lie. "Amos," he said, "I'm willing to bet those men are already on their way."

When Matt left the telegraph office, he saw Quint Asper, the town blacksmith, hurrying toward him. Asper was a handsome, dark-haired man, huge in the shoulders and arms, the veins standing out on his massive biceps like a ship's cables.

As was his habit, Asper, a sociable man, wiped off his right hand on his worn leather apron and extended it toward Matt. "Nice to see you again, Matt," he said. "You don't stop by the forge to shoot the breeze so often these days."

Matt took Asper's hand, his smile apologetic. "Been keeping real busy, Quint."

The blacksmith nodded. "I know how it is. I've been busy my ownself. Seems like every cow pony in Texas is in Dodge and they will keep throwing shoes."

Matt waited, knowing Asper had something to tell him. The blacksmith got right to the point. "Strange thing, Matt. Young Sean Tyree rode up to the forge early this morning, setting a big ghost hoss."

"Quint, a man rides a white horse, it's his business. It doesn't make him strange."

The blacksmith shook his head. "That ain't the strange part. The strange part is he asked to borry a hammer and a nail."

Matt shrugged. "He could be building something, a shed maybe."

Asper allowed a look of exasperation to cross his face. "Matt, think about it—you don't build a shed with one nail. You don't build anything with just one nail."

"Well,. then he's hanging up a picture. A man needs only one nail to hang a picture."

"Matt," Asper said, his patience thinning, "he took the hammer and nail and rode out of town." The blacksmith waved a hand toward the plains. "Ain't nowhere out there to hang a picture."

"You gave him the hammer?" Matt asked, stating the obvious because he could think of nothing else to say.

Asper nodded. "Sure. And he said he'd bring it back tomorrow."

"He rode out of town. In what direction?"

"North," the blacksmith said. "And before you ask, he didn't tell me where he was headed."

"Well, Quint, thanks for the information. I have no idea what it means, but I'll study on it some."

"Glad to be of help," the blacksmith said. Asper walked away, shaking his head, mumbling to himself. "This sure has me buffaloed . . . one nail . . . hanging a picture. . . ."

Matt watched the blacksmith go, trying to make sense of what Asper had just told him but drawing a blank. Finally, his head bent in thought, he turned his steps back along Front Street, planning to go back to his office, but the events of the morning were not yet over.

Matt looked up from his dust-covered boots and saw Clint Stucker, flanked by Johnny Lomax, riding toward him, the rancher's face like thunder.

The two men reined up when they were a few yards from Matt, and Stucker leaned forward in the saddle, his thick finger jabbing angrily in the marshal's direction.

"Dillon," he said, "know this. If the verdict at Cage's trial is guilty, I won't let you hang my son."

Anger flaring in him, Matt snapped: "Stucker, that's for a jury to decide, not me."

"I've said my piece, Dillon," Stucker roared. "Try to take my boy to the gallows and the streets of Dodge will run red with blood."

Matt made no reply, his contempt for the huge rancher obvious.

"Damn you, you set this whole thing up, Dillon,"

Stucker yelled, his raised voice attracting the crowd of onlookers he'd been hoping for. "Where's the gun you took off St. Clair's body and hid away?"

Matt took a step toward Stucker, his fists clenched. "I'm not going to stand here in the street and argue with you, Stucker," he said. "But I'll say this one thing, and then you'd better let it go. Logan St. Clair was unarmed when Cage shot him."

"The hell he was," Johnny Lomax hollered, glancing around at the crowd, trying to enlist their approval. "Three men saw him reach for the gun inside his coat. But you took it, Dillon."

"Lomax," Matt said, flat and low, his anger barely controlled, "you're a damn liar."

The gunman looked like he'd been slapped. His hand dropped to his holstered Colt, but Stucker quickly reached across and stopped him. "No, Johnny. I don't want two men in jail accused of murder."

Lomax, his eyes ugly, said: "Boss, after I gun Dillon, who's gonna arrest me?"

"I will."

The voice came from Matt's right, and Lomax's head whirled, all his pent-up rage suddenly ready to vent itself on this new target.

His Honor Mayor James H. Kelley stood on the boardwalk outside the Long Branch, his legs spread, a shotgun in his hands, the barrels steady on Lomax's belly.

Even Lomax, a gunman who fancied himself to be all horns and rattles, quailed at the sight of a scattergun, especially in the hands of someone like the short, stocky and determined mayor of Dodge, a man known to have no backup in him.

Kelley shifted the glowing cigar in his mouth and said in his soft Irish brogue: "Now you two fine gentlemen be riding along. We'll have no more yelling and shouting and disturbing the peace, distracting a man from his breakfast in the morning."

Matt could see the wild want-to in Lomax's eyes. But the gunman knew that if he made the slightest move toward his Colts, Kelley would cut loose and blow him out of the saddle.

It was Stucker who ended it. "We'll be riding on, Mayor," he said, swallowing his pride. "We want no trouble with the law."

"Ah," Kelley said, "you're a lovely man, Clint Stucker." He motioned with the shotgun. "Now be off with you and be about your business."

Stucker kicked his horse forward, pausing alongside Matt long enough to say: "You keep in mind what I told you, Dillon. There will be none of my flesh and blood hanged in Dodge."

He spurred his horse, the animal's flank bumping hard against the marshal as he passed. Lomax followed after him and glanced down at Matt as he rode by, cold death in his pale gunman's eyes.

"I'd say you've made a couple of enemies there, Matt," Kelley said, sliding the butt of the shotgun under the right armpit of his fashionable tweed coat. "I sense there could be trouble ahead from those two."

Matt nodded. "Seems that way." He smiled at the mayor. "Thanks."

"Think nothing of it, me boy," Kelley said. "Only too glad I could help."

The mayor jerked a thumb over his shoulder toward the door of the Long Branch. "I was sitting in the saloon, having me morning cigar and bourbon, when I heard all the commotion in the street. I saw you being braced by them two Texans, so I borrowed Sam's shotgun and . . . well, here I am and there you are."

"Thanks again," Matt said.

Kelley waved a dismissive hand. "Just keep this thing bottled up, Matt. If the Cage Stucker trial ends in a hanging sentence, if need be I'll bring in the army to make sure justice is done."

"You won't need the army," Matt said. "I can handle it."

Kelley nodded. "Then see that you do."

The mayor turned to step back inside. But he stopped and swung around on the marshal. "Matt," he said, his brown eyes flashing, "do something about the stray dogs like I told you. Hell, man, the streets are full of curs." The mayor's eyes shifted from Matt to an alley across the street. "Damn it, look, there's one of the flea-bitten critters right now."

Kelley swung the shotgun to his shoulder and triggered both barrels, and people turned in alarm as the *boom*! of the gun echoed along Front Street. "Did I get him?" Kelley asked, taking the smoking gun from his shoulder, his short-sighted eyes peering intently across at the alley.

Matt shook his head. "You missed him, Mayor."

"Well, damn it all," Kelley snapped. He shook his

head then turned on his heel and stomped back into the Long Branch.

Festus came running up the street a few moments later, puffs of yellow dust spurting out from under his flying boots. "Matthew," he gasped, "what's all the shooting about?"

"The mayor cut loose with a shotgun at a stray dog," Matt said. "And missed."

"Too bad," Festus said, scratching his hairy cheek.

"No, it isn't," Matt said. "It wasn't a dog. It was Clem Mitcham's pet donkey."

But Mayor Kelley was not quite finished with Matt. Later that afternoon he told him Logan St. Clair's funeral was scheduled for the next morning, and because Matt was the senior representative of the law in Dodge, it would be appropriate for him to attend.

Matt would have done so anyway. He didn't know St. Clair well, but by all accounts the gambler was an honorable man who had deserved a better fate than to be shot down in the street by a drunken killer.

The morning of St. Clair's funeral dawned bleak and gray. Storm clouds, driven over the high peaks of the Rockies toward the Kansas plains by a keening wind from the west, hung low over Dodge, and now and then a sullen rain spattered against the window of Matt's office.

The oil lamp was still lit over Matt's desk when he shrugged into his slicker and jammed his hat firmly on his head.

Festus watched him intently, then said: "Young

Cage is complainin' about his beef an' beans again, Matthew. Says he wants a change: bacon and eggs for breakfast this morning."

"Does he know we're burying Logan St. Clair today?" Matt asked, hesitating in the doorway.

"Sure does," Festus answered. "And he still wants his bacon and eggs."

"Then give him a change, Festus. Just the beans, no beef."

The deputy laughed and slapped his thigh. "Yoowee! That's sure gonna make ol' Cage madder than a rained-on rooster. He'll throw them beans right at my head, you know. Just like he done last night."

Matt shrugged. "If he does that, he doesn't eat."

The rain was starting up in earnest when Matt stepped onto the boardwalk. Huge drops hammered against his slicker, drumming hard on his hat as he walked, head bent against the wind, toward the cemetery.

Logan St. Clair would not lie in Boot Hill. There was a second graveyard reserved for those who died with clean sheets on the bed—and this is where Sean Tyree would bury his friend.

When Matt walked under the wrought-iron arch above the cemetery gates, he saw that the mourners were few.

Sean Tyree, hatless, stood beside the grave next to a tall, skinny preacher, a man from the other side of the tracks named Reverend Saunders. Percy Crump, long-faced and solemn, was there in his official capacity as undertaker, and four of his men stood ready to lower St. Clair's mahogany-and-brass coffin into the grave. Kitty Russell, the hood of her black woolen cloak pulled over her head, stood close to Tyree.

Despite the sadness of the occasion, Matt permitted himself a slight smile. Kitty was running true to form. She always appreciated good customers, especially a high roller like Logan St. Clair, and mourned their passing.

There were no others. Matt had heard St. Clair had many friends, but it seemed mighty few of them were in Dodge.

When Matt stepped up to the graveside, he removed his hat and nodded to Kitty, then to Tyree. The young man glanced briefly at him with vacant eyes, seemingly unaware, then looked back down with a fixed, steady gaze into the yawning, muddy depth of the grave.

Matt realized that Sean Tyree was suffering grief that went into a heartrending sorrow that cast a hundred shadows, each one darker than the other.

As was the custom at that time in the West, over his range clothes Tyree wore a voluminous black mourning garment, no doubt supplied by Percy Crump. The teeming rain had plastered Tyree's hair to his head, drops trickling like tears down the terrible scar on his cheek.

Reverend Saunders turned to Matt, a question in his brown hound-dog eyes.

Matt shook his head. "There will be no others."

Saunders sighed, opened his Bible and said: "Then let us begin."

Head bowed, Matt listened to Saunders intone the service for the dead. The preacher's voice was flat and sonorous. He was a man going through the motions, mouthing empty, meaningless phrases by rote to bring scant comfort to the living.

No day is a good day to bury a man, Matt thought, the preacher's words now dropping like rocks, falling short before they reached his ears, but this day was one of the worst.

The rain lashed down in sheets, drumming on the lid of the coffin, and the wind tossed the branches of the wide oaks growing around the cemetery, scattering leaves, sending flocks of startled crows flapping skyward. Somewhere toward town a horse whinnied and then a dog barked until a man's angry voice yelled the animal into silence, followed by a curse and the slamming of a door.

The preacher's sermon came to a finish, and at a discreet signal from Crump, his men each picked up an end of a rope and slowly began to lower the coffin into the grave. The hole was narrow, and it took several minutes for the coffin to bump and scrape its way to the bottom.

Kitty dabbed tears from her eyes with a tiny lace handkerchief, then picked up a handful of wet soil and threw it into the grave. Matt did the same thing. Kitty stepped beside Tyree and gently placed her hand on his shoulder. As though he hadn't noticed, the man did not acknowledge her. All his attention was fixed on the grave and the coffin heavy with what had once been Logan St. Clair.

After one last, lingering look at Tyree, Kitty turned on her heel and walked away, and Matt followed after her. When he reached the outskirts of town, Matt turned and looked back. Tyree was still standing beside the grave, though the work of Percy Crump and his men was long since finished and they were all gone.

"Matthew, doggone it, he's still there, just a-standing beside that grave." Festus Haggen helped himself to coffee. "I tell you, Matthew, it boogers me 'cause it jest ain't natural."

Matt glanced at the clock. It was almost ten thirty. Sean Tyree had now been standing at St. Clair's graveside for sixteen hours.

"All he does is stand there, looking down at where they filled in the hole." Festus shook his head. "It ain't natural, I tell you."

Matt rose and stepped to the door. The rain had stopped a couple of hours earlier, but not before turning Front Street into a river of mud. But at least it had laid the dust and the air smelled fresher and cleaner.

Cowboys came and went along the street, mud thrown up by the hooves of their ponies spattering to the tops of their new, high-heeled boots. The saloons were going strong and the crowds were in full voice, the pianos tinkling, the notes swirling around Dodge like tiny shards of broken glass.

"You gonna bring him in, Matthew?" Festus had

stepped to his side. The deputy looked longingly over at the Long Branch, his tongue running over dry lips.

Matt sighed. "I guess I'd better. He could die of hunger if he's there much longer."

Festus looked around him, at the crowding darkness beyond the bright lights of town. "It's getting late, Matthew. Ain't you afeered of ha'ants an' sich?"

Matt smiled. "Festus, the dead can do you no harm. Only the living can do that." He crossed the office and found his hat. "I'll go speak to him. Keep an eye on the prisoner."

Festus nodded. "I'll be sure to do that, Matthew. But first I figured I'd step over to the Long Branch and see what's going on. You know, keep the peace like I'm supposed to."

"The Long Branch looks peaceful enough to me." Matt smiled.

The deputy scratched his hairy jaw. "Looks can be deceiving, Matthew. There could be all manner of law breaking going on over there."

"Well, go ahead, then," Matt said. "But make sure you're back here in a half hour to check on the prisoner."

Festus gave a little hop and clapped his hands in glee. "I'm on my way, Matthew."

Matt watched his deputy pick his way across the muddy street, then found a spare lamp and checked the wick and oil level. He stepped onto the boardwalk and made his way toward the cemetery.

Away from the lights of the town, the graveyard

was in inky darkness. A few tattered clouds scudded across the face of the moon and the branches of the oaks, stripped of most of their leaves by the wind, were raised like skeletal arms in prayer.

Matt found shelter by the cemetery gate and after several tries and a burned thumb managed to flame the oil lamp. He raised the lamp above his head, a circle of pale yellow light dancing in front of him, and made his way to St. Clair's grave.

Sean Tyree was still there, head bent, the black mourning garment billowing and flapping around him.

Matt stepped beside the man, saying nothing, remembering Tyree as he'd once been: a shaggy-haired boy in homemade buckskins riding a barebacked paint pony, his head full of dreams. In the past five years Tyree had come a long way, but maybe the dreams were all gone.

"Sean," Matt said finally and gently, "it's time to go back."

The lamp cast Tyree's face in light and shadow, but the vicious scar on his cheek stood out deep and deathly white. The man kept his head bowed and did not turn in Matt's direction. The marshal realized then that Tyree's grief had given way to an ominous depression, that the blood in his veins was running black.

"It's time to go back, Sean," he said again, more firmly.

Matt experienced a few moments of doubt, thinking that Tyree would not answer. But the man's head slowly turned and his grim mouth opened.

"Let me be, Marshal," he said. "I've been handed a bitter cup and I plan to drain it to the dregs."

Matt felt a sudden jolt of foreboding as he met the burned-out cinders of Sean Tyree's eyes.

He was looking into hell.

chapter 8

Another Notch for Johnny Lomax

When Matt returned to his office, Festus was back from the Long Branch, smelling of whiskey, no doubt having taken advantage of Kitty's openhanded generosity, since the deputy never seemed to have any money.

"Well?" Festus asked as Matt stepped inside.

"Well what?" Matt asked, laying the lamp on his desk.

"You know dang well what, Matthew. Did you bring Tyree back?"

Matt shook his head. "He's drinking from a bitter cup, like other people around here I could name."

If the deputy was chagrined, he didn't let it show. "So what do we do now?" Festus asked.

Matt shrugged. "Nothing. Tyree will come back when he has a mind to."

The lamp flame above Matt's desk trembled in a

breeze coming through a crack in the door, its light gleaming on the blue barrels of the rifles and shotguns in the gun rack, glowing with a mellow, honey-colored luster on the pine floor and walls.

"How's the prisoner?" Matt asked.

"Complainin' as usual," Festus replied. "Says he wants to talk to you, by the way."

"I'll talk to him," Matt said, "though I doubt he has anything to say that I want to hear."

The marshal opened the door that led to the two iron-barred cells at the rear of the office and stepped through. One cell was vacant. Cage Stucker was in the other, stretched out on the bunk.

"You wanted to talk to me, Stucker," Matt said.

The man rose and put his hands on the bars. "Yeah, Dillon, I want you to let my pa bail me out of here."

Matt shook his head. "Not a chance. You might hightail it back to Texas."

"Now why the hell would I do that?" Stucker asked, his eyes ugly. "I know and you know that a jury will never convict me of murdering Logan St. Clair. Why all the fuss anyhow? What's one two-bit gambler more or less?"

"Stucker, if you don't know the answer to that question by now, you'll never know it."

A sneer twisted Stucker's thick lips. "My pa will never let me hang."

"So he told me," Matt said.

"Then you'd better heed his warning," Stucker said. "That is, if you want to go on breathing."

Matt thought that through, then said, his voice flat

and deadly serious, "Get this into your thick skull, Stucker. If the jury finds you guilty of murder and your pa tries to stop me hanging you, I'll gun you. Then him."

Stucker sniggered. "Big talk, Dillon, but I think Johnny Lomax will have something to say about that."

"It won't make any difference to you," Matt said. "One way or another, you'll be dead."

Stucker's suddenly white face gave the lie to his pretended bravado. "Don't count on it, Dillon. Don't even count on living too much longer your ownself."

As though he hadn't heard, Matt asked: "Anything else you need?"

"Yeah, I asked that stupid deputy of yours to bring me the makings and he didn't do it. I haven't had a smoke in days."

Matt didn't smoke himself, but he knew how tobacco hunger affected some men who were much addicted to it, especially the Texas drovers who had picked up the cigarette habit from Mexican vaqueros. "I'll see to it that Festus brings you tobacco and papers," he said, a small act of kindness from a man who could never bring himself to take pleasure in the suffering of others, even a lowlife like Cage Stucker.

"And I want bacon and eggs!" Stucker yelled as Matt closed the door behind him.

"Is that what he wanted to talk to you about, Matthew?" Festus asked. "Bacon and eggs?"

Matt nodded. "That and other things. He says he asked you to bring him the makings."

The deputy opened a drawer on Matt's desk and

brought out a tobacco sack and papers. "Got them right here, but ol' Cage has been so ornery, I didn't give them to him."

"Well, go give them to him now, Festus," Matt said. "If he doesn't smoke, he'll only get ornerier."

"Whatever you say," Festus said, rising to his feet, picking up the sack. "But if it was up to me, ol' Cage would be going without."

Matt smiled. "You're a hard man, Festus Haggen." He rubbed his stomach. "Maybe it's all this talk of bacon and eggs, but I'm hungry all of a sudden my ownself. I think I'll mosey on down to the Sideboard and see what's on the chalk board."

"Ma Prescott has a right nice roast sirloin and boiled potatoes," Festus said, hesitating at the door to the cells. "Had me some for breakfast."

"Sounds good," Matt nodded. "I'll try it."

Despite the late hour, the Sideboard was filled with cowboys suffering the pangs of the whiskey hunger, and a few meat packers and buyers sat hunched over at tables, drinking coffee and talking business.

Matt found an empty table by the wall and Ma Prescott, a fat, jolly woman who had buried seven husbands, served him. The marshal took Festus' advice and ordered the roast beef and potatoes, adding a glass of cold buttermilk.

When the food arrived, it was good, and Matt ate hungrily.

He'd just finished his meal and eased contentedly back in his chair, when he heard the shots. Two of them, so very close together the untrained ear would have taken them for one.

Every eye in the restaurant turned to the big man wearing the star, seeing what he would do. Taking his time, Matt wiped his mouth on his napkin and rose. He fished in his vest pocket for a coin, but Ma Prescott shooed him toward the door.

"Pay me later, Marshal," she said. "Sounds like maybe you've got police business to attend to."

Matt nodded his thanks and stepped onto the boardwalk. A clerk in a too-tight suit, plug hat and high, celluloid collar ran toward him, his face alight with excitement.

"You. What's going on?" Matt asked, grabbing the man's arm.

"Johnny Lomax just k-k-killed a cowboy at the Alamo," the clerk said, stuttering his agitation. "I got to go tell my wife. What a lark!"

When Matt stepped into the saloon, a crowd had gathered around a body on the floor. Johnny Lomax, his thumbs in his gun belt, thin lips peeled back in a grin, stood to one side; several Rafter S hands were yelling and slapping him on the back.

"What happened here?" Matt asked, his eyes slanting cold and hard to Lomax.

One of the hands said quickly: "It was a fair fight, Marshal. Johnny here—"

"Not you," Matt snapped. He pointed to a man in the crowd, a buyer judging by the expensive cut of his broadcloth suit and thick gold watch chain, the fob a Masonic square and compass. "You tell me."

The man looked uncomfortable and more than a little scared. His tongue touched his top lip and his eyes darted nervously from Matt to Lomax and back again.

"Let me hear it," Matt said.

"I'll tell you what happened, Marshal."

A rancher Matt knew and liked, a whip-thin, grizzled veteran of a dozen trail drives named Tom Johnson, stepped forward.

Johnson nodded to the dead man. "That there's Jim Talbot. He was eighteen years old and come up the trail with a herd from Brownsville." Johnson turned to Lomax, his eyes hard and unafraid. "He was a good kid, always laughing, never did anybody no harm, and he rode drag on the trail without complaint."

"How did it happen, Tom?" Matt asked, gently prompting the man.

"Lomax over there teased the youngster about his freckles, asked him if he'd been weaned from his mama's teat yet. Young Jim took it for as long as he was able. Then something inside him snapped and he drew." Johnson, a hard man made harder by a hard life, trembled, and Matt knew it was from rage and not fear. "Young Jim's gun hadn't even cleared the leather when Lomax put two bullets into him."

"It was a fair fight," Lomax said. "The kid drew down on me."

"Everybody here see that?" Matt asked, looking around at the crowd. "Did the boy draw first?"

Not a single voice was raised to say it happened

any different, though Matt felt a hostile current of anger directed at Johnny Lomax.

For his part, the gunman was unconcerned, his face flushed, a gleam of triumph in his eyes. "You got no case against me, Dillon," he said. "And you ain't gonna buffalo me and drag me off to your jail like you did Cage Stucker."

No matter what his own feelings were, Matt realized that as far as the law was concerned Lomax had acted in self-defense. But the marshal and everyone else in the saloon knew the man had murdered a green, unskilled kid only because he wanted to add another notch to the handle of his Colt and bolster his reputation as a dangerous gunman.

But the law was the law and Matt had it to uphold.

An impotent rage in him, the big marshal said: "Somebody, get Percy Crump."

"I'll get him," Tom Johnson said. "I owe young Jim and his folks that much."

When Johnson left, Matt kneeled beside the dead cowboy. Jim Talbot looked even younger in death, like he was asleep in the bunkhouse, a scattering of freckles across his nose and cheeks, yellow hair tumbling over an unlined forehead.

Lomax had twice hit the youngster in the breast pocket of his shirt, the bullets only an inch apart. Jim Talbot must have been dead when he hit the floor.

Matt rose to his feet, the crowd parting as Percy Crump arrived. The undertaker shook his head and whispered, "Tut-tut-tut," under his breath, then took the tape measure from around his neck and went to work.

Matt looked over at the grinning Johnny Lomax, wanting to gun him real bad.

But he fought down his anger, even when Lomax, an arrogant grin on his face, asked: "Well, Marshal, are you planning on arresting me?"

The words didn't come easily to Matt, each syllable sticking tight in his throat like a rock. "The kid drew first. Everybody here saw it. I have no legal cause to arrest you, Lomax."

Matt turned on his heel and walked out of the Alamo, the gunman's mocking laughter following him.

Since the Stucker herd arrived in Dodge, two men had died.

How many more must there be before all this was finished?

Matt knew only time would answer that question.

And when it came, the answer would be written in blood.

chapter 9

The Hanging Judge

The morning after the Lomax killing, Mayor Kelley stomped into Matt's office, chewing furiously on his cigar as he always did when he was excited or agitated.

Without preamble, the stocky Irishman perched on the corner of Matt's desk and said: "Bad business last night, Matt. There's been way too much killing in Dodge of late."

Matt's temper flared. "Don't you think I know that? Johnny Lomax shot in self-defense and maybe fifty people saw it. It was murder, all right, but I had no legal cause to arrest him."

Kelley sighed. "I'm not blaming you, Matt. But all this shooting and killing has to stop. The king of Russia's son might be visiting soon, and I don't want him having to step over dead bodies to get to his hotel."

The mayor shifted his cigar from one corner of his mouth to the other. "Anyhow, Tom Johnson is paying to have the Talbot kid's body shipped back to Texas. He says his folks wouldn't want the boy to lie in foreign soil."

"Jim Talbot was just eighteen, and Lomax goaded him into a fight," Matt said, the words tasting bitter on his tongue. "The kid was no gun hand. He didn't stand a chance."

"Well," Kelley said, sighing deeper, "like you said, it was self-defense and there's an end to it." Mischief glowed in the mayor's shrewd eyes. "But at least I have some good news to impart."

Matt's smile was thin. "I could use some about now."

"Just an hour ago I got a wire saying that Judge Simeon Walker has been taken right poorly and will not be on the bench for Cage Stucker's trial." Kelley took the cigar from his mouth and studied the end closely. "Guess who's taking his place."

Matt shook his head, saying nothing.

"Judge Micah Merriweather." Kelley waited for Matt's reaction, but got only a blank look, and his disappointment showed. "You haven't heard of Judge Merriweather?"

"Can't say as I have," Matt answered.

"Micah Merriweather was a prosecuting attorney at Judge Isaac Parker's court in the Indian Territory," Kelley explained patiently. "It was his prosecutions back in seventy-five that got six outlaws hanged at the same time on the same gallows. I remember a couple of them. Edward Campbell. I knew him. He was a black man convicted of killing two people after he caught his wife in bed with another man. And one of the others was James Moore, a no-account murderer and bank robber."

Matt leaned forward in his chair, his interest kindled. "Do you think Merriweather will be a tougher judge than Simeon Walker?"

"No doubt about it, me boy," Kelley said. "Judge Merriweather has political ambitions and the loudest part of his platform is his desire to rid the West of outlaws and the likes of Johnny Lomax and Cage Stucker. He calls gun-toting gentry like them two murdering scum." The mayor's smile was thin, without amusement. "Merriweather learned his trade at Parker's knee and like ol' Isaac himself he's a hanging judge, depend on that."

Kelley rose to his feet. "Matt, I thought your case against Cage Stucker was mighty thin. But with Micah Merriweather on the bench, well, who knows? It could go badly for Stucker, real bad."

Matt had not known who Micah Merriweather was, but apparently it was a name known to many of the citizens of Dodge because the news spread around town like wildfire.

And it very quickly came to the ears of Clint Stucker.

The big rancher burst into Matt's office, a frown on his face, his eyes red veined with anger. "Dillon," he said, his voice harsh and demanding, "I want to talk with my boy!"

Matt rose to his feet, standing a head taller than Stucker. "You have that right," he said.

Stucker was taken aback. He had expected an argument. Now, to feed his wrath, he retreated into bluster. "Then lead the way, damn it. Time is a-wasting."

Matt opened the door to the cells and Cage immediately sprang to the bars, clenching the iron with white-knuckled fists. "Pa," he said, tears starting in his eyes, "Dillon told me about Judge Merriweather." Cage's face was very white. "He'll hang me, Pa."

"Nobody's going to hang you, boy," Stucker said. "I've sent to Kansas City for a lawyer, the best money can buy." The rancher reached through the bars and grabbed his son by the front of his shirt. "Now quit your sniveling and act like a man."

"But he'll hang me, Pa," Cage whined. "Remember, it was him that got Frank Carson hung down to the Indian Territory."

"Carson was different. He rode for us but he wasn't kin," Stucker said. "And he made the mistake of ravaging and strangling a sodbuster's wife. The best lawyer in the world couldn't get him off with that, not when Merriweather packed the jury with twelve long-faced pumpkin rollers who wanted Carson dead."

Cage dashed tears from his eyes. "Don't let them hang me like they done Carson, Pa."

Stucker took a step back from the bars, his face like thunder. "You're soft, Cage, like your mother was soft. But you're my blood, and by God, nobody hangs my blood."

Without another word, the rancher turned on his heel and brushed past Matt. The marshal followed him into the office, and Stucker stood waiting for him at his desk.

Stucker opened his mouth to speak, hesitated, then carefully began to reach into the pocket of his canvas ranch coat. He stopped in midmotion and said: "Dillon, I'm bringing a pistol out of here. I'll do it real slow, so don't go making any mistakes."

Matt's hand dropped to the butt of his Colt. "Ease it out gentle, Stucker. If I see anything I don't like, I'll gun you."

The rancher grunted and did as he was told. Holding the handle by two fingers, he came up with a Smith & Wesson Pocket .32 and laid the little gun on the table.

Just as carefully, Stucker reached into the inside pocket of his coat and produced a thick wad of bills. These he laid alongside the revolver.

"That's a thousand dollars, Dillon, more money than you've ever seen in one place at one time in your life," Stucker said. "More money than you make in a year as a tin-star lawman."

A frown gathering between his eyebrows, Matt asked: "What do you want from me, Stucker?"

"That money is yours," the rancher answered. "All you have to do is stand up in court and say you made a mistake. Tell the judge you found this .32 in Logan St. Clair's waistband but in all the excitement clean forgot about it."

"And that's all, huh? Make a liar out of myself."

"Hell, you've lied before, Dillon. We all lie."

"I don't, Stucker," Matt said evenly. "And I've

never wanted anything bad enough in my life to steal it. So pick up your money and get out of here."

"Damn you, Dillon, my boy's life is at stake."

"Stucker, Cage should have thought some about that himself when he murdered Logan St. Clair."

His face dark with fury, Stucker swept up his money and dropped the Smith & Wesson back into his pocket. "This isn't over, Dillon," he snarled, his eyes ugly. "Not by a long shot."

Stucker stormed to the door, then stopped and whirled to face Matt. "Don't go sitting by any windows, Dillon," he said.

Anger flaring in him, Matt asked: "Is that a threat, Stucker?"

The rancher shook his head. "The hell it's a threat. It's a fact."

Stucker jerked open the door and stormed outside, slamming it hard behind him.

No sooner had Stucker left than Festus came in, shaking his head, a worried look on his face. "I just passed Clint Stucker, Matthew," he said, "and he looks as mad as the buzzard that circled my mule for half a day one time afore he realized she was just asleep."

Matt smiled. "He's mad all right, ever since he heard Judge Micah Merriweather will be on the bench at his son's trial."

"Heard that my ownself. Folks say Merriweather is a statute wrangler who plans on being president one day. I hear he's as tough as a trail-drive steak and he don't take kindly to guns and gunfighters."

Festus poured himself coffee from the pot on the stove and perched on the corner of Matt's desk. "Matthew, I got a favor to ask. Do you recollect that well I dug for the widder Brady? Well, she sent her boy into town to tell me it's plumb dry again and I should get out there and dig it deeper."

"I don't see a problem so long as you're back here by dark," Matt said.

"I plan to leave at sunup, the day after tomorrow," Festus said. "That way I can get the well dug and be back in Dodge afore things start a-poppin'."

Matt nodded. "Just make sure you hit pay dirt this time."

"Heck, Matthew, I did the last time. But the widder Brady and them seven young'uns of hers must go through a sight of water, an' why I don't know."

Festus stepped to the door and threw the grounds from his cup into the street. When he returned he said: "Matthew, I nearly plumb forgot. Miss Kitty wants to talk to you. Says it's kinda important."

A few minutes later, Matt left his office and crossed the street toward the Long Branch.

It was still an hour shy of noon, but already hot. A sultry wind stirred up dust devils that spun wildly for a few moments before collapsing in a puff of dust and the few cow ponies standing hipshot at the saloon hitching rail hung their heads, drowsing amid clouds of flies. Tethered in the thin shade thrown by the Long Branch was a smart-looking fringe-top surrey, a big American mare in the traces, a rare and expensive rig not often seen this side of the tracks.

The stage from Hays had just pulled in, and five gray-faced, exhausted passengers were heading toward the Great Western Hotel, working kinks out of their backs as they dragged along bulging carpet-bags.

Owen Lacey, a cheerfully profane man with a gray beard down to his belt buckle, was up on the box and he yelled a friendly greeting to Matt as the marshal passed. Matt waved to the driver, then stepped into the comparative coolness of the Long Branch.

Kitty and Sam the bartender had their heads together, deep in conversation, when Matt strolled up beside them. Kitty saw the big marshal and smiled. She reached under the bar and hefted a basket onto the polished mahogany counter.

"What's that?" Matt asked.

"That," Kitty said, "is a picnic basket." She smiled again, more sweetly this time. "Where are you taking me, Marshal Dillon?"

Not being much of a hand for picnics, Matt had it in mind to try to wriggle out of it, making the excuse that because of his duties he couldn't leave Dodge. But the heart-stopping sight of Kitty in a pink gingham dress, with a straw bonnet hanging on her shoulders, made him hesitate—and that was all the opening the woman needed.

"Well?" Kitty asked. "Or does a girl have to throw

herself at your feet before you'll take her on a picnic?"

Matt's shoulders relaxed. He smiled and threw up his hands. "All right, I surrender, Kitty. Now I set down and study on it, I recall there's a place up on Saw Log Creek that I always figured was a real pretty spot." He glanced at the basket. "What do you have in there?"

"Some cold fried chicken, bread rolls, a bottle of wine . . . and, oh yes, a peach pie."

Matt nodded. "The peach pie clinches it. I guess we're picnicking."

Kitty had rented the fringe-top surrey from a livery stable across the tracks and Matt took the ribbons when they drove out of Dodge and headed north toward the Saw Log.

Above them the sky was cloudless blue and the land lay around them sweet and green from the recent rain, bright with patches of blue, yellow and pink wildflowers.

Kitty took off her bonnet and leaned out from under the surrey's canopy, her eyes closed, letting the sunlight bathe her face, and Matt, watching her, all of a sudden found it hard to breathe.

The mare stepped out right smartly as Matt followed Duck Creek, then swung a little east along a dusty wagon track that led to the Saw Log. The buffalo had all but vanished from the plains, but on both sides of the road wallows cratered the ground, mute monuments to mark their passing.

When Matt and Kitty arrived at the creek, the place was exactly as the tall marshal remembered from a few days before, a stand of cottonwood and willow, the grass under them dappled by leafy shadow, rippling water chuckling nearby over a bed of sand and pebbles.

Matt stepped out of the wagon and gave Kitty his hand. He nodded to the spot under the cottonwood where he'd fallen asleep and said: "Over there. It's a shady place for a picnic."

Kitty looked around her. "Oh, it's beautiful," she said. She stood on tiptoe and kissed Matt's cheek. "You're so clever, Matt, remembering this place."

"I guess that's because I knew I'd bring you here one day, Kitty," the big marshal said. Then he blushed. Such talk never came easy to him.

But Kitty didn't seem to notice his confusion. She ran over to the cottonwood and sat, her dress spreading elegantly around her. She patted the ground next to her. "Come sit here, Matt. And bring the basket. I'm getting hungry."

Matt loosed the mare from the traces and let the horse graze. He unbuckled his gun belt, hung it on the seat of the surrey, then fetched the picnic basket.

For the next hour he and Kitty ate and drank and talked, two people completely at ease with each other, comfortably close, reminiscing about days long gone and the shared experiences that went with them.

Not for the first or the last time, Matt thought Kitty the most beautiful woman he had ever seen. And as he always did, he wondered what she saw in him.

Matt licked his finger and caught up the last crumbs of peach pie from the plate as the bright day began to shade into late afternoon, the shadows lengthened and the shimmering light began to die around him.

He rose and put the horse into the traces, then stepped over to Kitty and gave her his hand.

The echo of a shot racketed across the flat grasslands, and a startled, exclamation point of dust kicked up between Matt's feet. He pulled Kitty upright and pushed her behind the cottonwood, just as another bullet slammed into the tree trunk, then another.

"Stay here," Matt said, waiting to see Kitty nod. When she did, he made a dash for the surrey, bullets smashing into the ground around him.

A puff of gray smoke drifted from a rise about two hundred yards away. Matt grabbed his gun belt, slid the Colt from the leather and thumbed off two quick shots in that direction. The hidden gunman was well out of revolver range, but he wanted to keep the bushwhacker's head down and let him know he wasn't shooting at a scared pilgrim.

The marshal fired again, sprinted back to the cottonwood and dove behind the trunk. He got up on one knee, his Colt cocked and ready.

But there were no more shots.

A haze of dust soon lost in the twilight and a distant hammer of hooves told Matt that the bushwhacker was gone.

Kitty rose and brushed leaves and grass off her dress. "Who was that?" she asked, her voice unsteady, a strand of hair falling over her forehead.

Matt, his face grim, eased down the hammer of his Colt and shoved the gun into the holster.

"Kitty, I had an offer from Clint Stucker today," he said. "He just told me I should have taken it."

chapter 10

Matt's Hand Is Forced

When Matt and Kitty rolled into Dodge, the town was coming alive, the lamps lit along Front Street, jets of blue gas already glowing on the walls of the crowded saloons.

Matt dropped off Kitty at the Long Branch, then drove the surrey to the livery stable across the tracks.

He walked back to his office and checked on Cage Stucker. The man lay on his bunk and was surly and uncommunicative. He glanced at Matt with baleful, belligerent eyes, the planes of his face somber and brooding, like he'd been thinking some highly unpleasant thoughts.

For his part, Matt had nothing to say to Stucker either. He walked back into the office, unbuckled his gun belt and hung it on a hook on the wall.

It was time to make another stab at replying to the governor.

But when Matt took up his pen, the words wouldn't come. Too many thoughts were crowding into his head, demanding his attention.

Someone had tried to kill him today, or at least badly scare him, and the bushwhacking could only have been masterminded by Clint Stucker. But how could he prove such an accusation?

After ten minutes, Matt gave up all ambition to write, threw down his pen and rose to his feet. He stepped across the room and slid his Colt from the gun belt. He shucked out the spent shells, then reloaded from the cartridge loops and buckled the gun around his hips.

It was time to have a talk with Clint Stucker.

When Matt stepped inside the Alhambra, the saloon was packed with cowboys, gamblers, buyers and the usual assorted riffraff of the frontier, shifty-eyed drifters who had no visible means of support yet always seemed to have money to spend. A dozen girls in red, yellow and blue silk dresses mingled with the men, their bare shoulders revealing the swell of milk-white breasts, generous hips swaying as they walked. All the women were young and they were pretty enough, but in the calculating, hard-eyed way of fallen angels; their forced laughter rang false, like the flat, tuneless pealing of cracked bells.

Clint Stucker sat at a gaming table, playing poker with three other men. One, by the expensive cut of his frockcoat and the confident way he handled the cards, was a professional gambler. The other two were ranchers like Stucker, men who had suddenly found themselves in the money after selling their herds, coming off years of barely getting by on hard-scrabble, two-by-twice ranches where the grass was thin and the profit margin even thinner.

Such men won and lost money with equal aplomb, often dropping every cent they had at the table, returning home to Texas with empty pockets to face the tears and recriminations of their worn-out, hollow-eyed wives.

Among all this crowd, one man stood out: a tall, thin towhead who had the small of his back pressed against the bar. He was dressed in the dusty, nondescript range clothes of the typical Texas cowboy, but Matt recognized the breed. This was no thirty-a-month ranch hand. He was a fighting man, drawing warrior's wages from Clint Stucker, and the Remingtons on his hips, worn low and butt forward, were not for show.

Matt stepped to Stucker's table, his spurs ringing, and stood looking down at the huge rancher, saying nothing.

Stucker glanced up, and his lips peeled back from his lips in a snarl.

"What's this, Dillon, you arresting a man for playing poker now?"

The marshal shook his head. "Just want to ask you a question, Stucker. I want to know if you or one of your boys took a ride today."

Stucker half rose in his chair. "What the hell are you talking about, Dillon?"

Matt's voice hardened, his dislike of the big, arrogant rancher plain. "Somebody tried to kill me today, Stucker, out on Saw Log Creek. Kill me or scare me real bad. Would you know anything about that?"

"You accusing me?" the rancher demanded, anger flaring, quick and bloodshot, in his eyes.

Carefully, keeping his tone even, Matt said: "Not accusing. Asking."

"When did this happen?" Stucker asked.

"Just before sundown."

"I was here at sundown." Stucker waved a hand around the table. "Ask any of these men."

The gambler looked up at Matt, his glance guarded and careful, hands still as sculpted white marble on the table in front of him. "He was here at sundown, Marshal."

The two ranchers nodded agreement, and Stucker said: "There. Now you know, Dillon. So get the hell away from me."

Stucker bent his head to his cards, but Matt wouldn't let it go. "How about your boys, Stucker? Where was Johnny Lomax? And come to that, where was the yellow-haired hombre over there holding up the bar? He looks a mite dusty to me, like he just got in from a long ride."

The towhead pushed himself off the bar, his blue eyes hard under his hat brim. "You heard Mr. Stucker," he said. "He told you to beat it."

Matt glanced at the man, then studiously ignored him, saying to Stucker, "Well, where was he?"

Before the rancher could answer, the gunman took a step toward Matt, his confidence very apparent in the relaxed, easy way he held himself. "Why don't you ask me that question?" he said.

This time Matt didn't even look at the man. "Well, Stucker," he said, "I'm waiting for an answer."

Stucker looked up at Matt, a slight smile playing around his cruel mouth. "Don't mess with Elliot, Dillon. You're no kind of match for him."

The saloon had gone quiet, as the crowd stopped carousing to watch the drama unfolding at Stucker's table. The piano player struck a few last, faltering notes; then he too lapsed into silence. Rising from his stool, the man looked warily around the room, then moved away on cat feet from any possible line of fire.

Suddenly the *tick, tick, tick* of an overhead fan, unheard before, was now very loud in the expectant stillness.

"I'm still waiting for an answer, Stucker," Matt said. "Where was your boy over there around sundown this evening?"

Stucker could have smoothed it over, bluffed and blustered his way out of it, but he chose not to.

"Why don't you ask him?" he said, his smile widening into a malicious grin.

"Yeah," the man called Elliot said, "why don't you ask me, Marshal?"

Matt nodded. "All right, where were you—"

"I know the rest," Elliot interrupted, " 'around sundown this evening.' Well, it ain't none of your damn business."

One of the saloon girls giggled and a man cursed

as he nervously tipped over his drink, the glass falling with a loud clunk onto the floor.

The eyes around Matt were eager. The crowd, many of them already half drunk, was enjoying the excitement, and quiet bets were already being placed on which of the two men facing each other was the faster.

Matt's words dropped like pebbles into a still pool. "You have a choice, Elliot. Answer me here or in a cell. It's up to you."

The gunman's pale gaze slid to Stucker, asking a silent question. He got his answer when the rancher looked up at Matt and said: "Don't even think of drawing on Tam Elliot, Dillon. He's killed more men than you have fingers."

Stucker was enjoying this. His face wore a smug expression and he obviously believed he had caught Matt wrong-footed. Now the big lawman would either have to draw and be gunned down or turn his back and slink out of the saloon.

Either way, Clint Stucker would come up a winner.

But as it happened, it was Elliot who pushed it.

"Dillon, you ain't taking me to no cell and I don't intend to answer any of your damn fool questions." The gunman's relaxed pose stiffened, ready for the draw. "Now what are you going to do about it?"

Matt drew. But the muzzle of his flashing Colt came only as high as Stucker's temple. Taken aback, his guns already clear of the leather and leveling, Elliot hesitated.

"Stucker," Matt said quickly, "call your boy off or I'll scatter your brains all over the table."

The rancher's face paled and he ran a tongue over suddenly dry lips. "You're a sworn lawman. You won't pull the trigger."

"Try me," Matt said, his voice harsh and merciless.

Stucker thought it through, then said tightly: "Tam, put the Remingtons away." He turned in his chair and looked at the gunman. "You'll get your chance some other time."

Slowly, reluctantly, Elliot dropped his guns back into the leather, his blue eyes on fire.

"Now," Matt said, pressing the muzzle harder against Stucker's temple, "tell him to unbuckle and shuck the gun belt."

Stucker's body went rigid. "Do as he says, Tam. He's just crazy enough to kill me."

Of all the causes that conspire to cloud a man's judgment, pride is the worst. And Tam Elliot's touchy gunman's vanity would not let him back down and step away.

"The hell I will," he yelled, and his hands streaked to his Remingtons.

Elliot was unbelievably fast, but Matt's gun was already up and level. As Elliot cleared leather, Matt shot him in the chest. A woman screamed as the gunman crashed against the bar, sudden crimson blood bubbling between his lips. Elliot recovered and fired as Stucker and the others at the table dived for the floor. One bullet splintered the pine at Matt's feet, the other split the air next to his right ear. Matt fired again, the blue Colt bucking hard and high in his hand. Elliot screamed his fury as he was hit a second time. He tried desperately to bring up guns that suddenly seemed too heavy for him. Matt fired, fired again, then watched the gunman double over and crash to the floor.

Stucker got his elbows on the table and began to clamber to his feet, his jowly cheeks ashen.

He looked up at Matt, then over at the fallen gunman. "You killed him," he said, shaking his head, unable to believe the evidence of his own eyes. "You killed Tam Elliot."

Matt ignored Stucker and pushed his way through the gaping crowd that had gathered around Elliot's body. The marshal got down on one knee and pulled the gunman onto his back. Elliot's eyes were wide-open but he was already looking into infinite darkness. A wisp of something green was caught in the buckle of Elliot's gun belt and Matt carefully removed it.

The marshal stood and studied what he'd discovered. It was part of a single blade of buffalo grass, just a couple of inches long.

Matt stepped to Stucker's table and dropped the piece of grass in front of him. "Stucker, that was caught in Elliot's buckle. Seems to me he was lying on his belly, and when he rose, he pulled a piece of grass with him." Matt's eyes bored cold and hard into Stucker. "No buffalo grass grows in Dodge, but there's plenty out on the rises by Saw Log Creek."

His face gray, Stucker picked up the fragment of grass and twirled it thoughtfully in his fingers. He was silent for a long time. Then he said: "Dillon, if Elliot tried to kill you, it was none of my doing." He looked up at Matt. "If I feel my boy's life is at stake,

I'll burn your jail down around your ears and gun you if I have to, but I don't hold with bushwhacking a man."

Stucker was still in a state of shock at the death of Tam Elliot, and his guard was down, his eyes revealing exactly how he felt.

Matt looked into those eyes and saw confusion, uncertainty . . . and a trace of fear.

It dawned on Matt then that someone had given Elliot the order to kill him, but it hadn't been Clint Stucker.

But if not Stucker, then who?

chapter 11

Festus Disappears

Matt Dillon reserved a year-round room at the Great Western Hotel that he seldom used, preferring to bunk down in his office, especially now that Cage Stucker was his prisoner.

He woke to see Festus placing the coffeepot on top of the newly lit stove.

"Morning, Matthew," the deputy said. "I reckon she'll bile real soon."

Matt rose and stomped into his boots. He ran a hand over his unshaven chin and found soap and a razor, then poured water into a basin from the pitcher.

While Matt shaved, looking at himself in a small steel mirror hanging on the wall, Festus studied him closely, restlessly hopping from one foot to the other, wanting to say something.

"Speak, Festus," Matt said, carefully edging his

sideburns. "I can tell when you've got something sticking in your craw."

The deputy scratched his own hairy jaw and said: "I'm sorry I missed all the excitement last night. I was over to the other side of the tracks where you always send me, though why I don't rightly understand."

Matt shrugged. "You know that's the mayor's idea, Festus, not mine." He turned and looked at his deputy, drying his face with a scrap of towel. "Seems to me you'd have missed it anyway. It happened almighty sudden."

Festus rose and looked at the coffeepot. "She's a-biling," he said. His shrouded eyes slanted to Matt again. "They say Tam Elliot killed ten men, most of them down on the border country. He was one of the fastest around. That's what they say."

Matt nodded. "He was fast all right, and he was game."

"You think he was the one who tried to kill you and Miss Kitty?"

"Uh-huh, I believe Elliot tried to kill me," Matt said. "But I don't think he was interested in harming Kitty."

"Clint Stucker behind it, Matthew?" Festus asked.

Matt shook his head. "No, Stucker didn't give the order."

Puzzlement showed on the deputy's face. "But . . . but if'n it wasn't Stucker, then who was it?"

"I don't know the answer to that," Matt said, rolling down the sleeves of his shirt. "But I surely intend to find out."

Matt stepped to the door, opened it and looked outside. The night had shaded into a pale lilac dawn, the lemon sky banded with purple, and Dodge was already slumbering.

Far down Front Street, a tall figure emerged from the Alhambra, staggered a little and was soon lost in darkness. A few cow ponies stood at hitching rails and a buckboard rattled past, the driver's head bent and nodding as though he was asleep.

Down by the cattle pens a steam train chugged slowly along the track. The locomotive's whistle sounded, a haunting widow-woman's wail that spoke briefly of aching loneliness and loss before it vanished into the stillness.

A skinny calico cat slid along the wall of Matt's office, looked up, saw the tall marshal and hissed like a snake. Matt smiled at the cat, but the animal turned and ran, its tail forming a question mark, querying the newborn morning about the identity of the huge, two-legged creature who blocked its path.

Matt stepped back inside and closed the door. Festus was standing by the coffeepot. "She's biled, Matthew," he said. "Should I bile her some more?"

"Smells good," Matt said. "I reckon it's ready enough."

Festus found two cups and poured coffee for them both. "I got to drink this and then be on my way to the widder Brady's place," he said.

Matt sipped his coffee and nodded. "That's right. You've got a well to dig."

"Be back well afore dark, Matthew—count on it."

Festus left a few minutes later, riding his mule

along Front Street, where the rising sun was slowly washing out the angled night shadows from the alleys and corners of the buildings.

Matt watched his deputy leave, poured a cup of coffee for Stucker and walked back to the cells. Cage Stucker was asleep and Matt rattled the cell door. Stucker's head swiveled to Matt and the marshal said: "I'm heading down to the Sideboard for breakfast. You want me to bring you anything?"

Without lifting his head, Stucker answered: "Yeah, bacon and eggs. And a half dozen biscuits."

"I'll see what I can do." Matt reached down through the bars and placed the cup on the floor. "Coffee," he said.

"That ain't coffee. It's vile swill," Stucker said.

Matt shrugged. "Take it or leave it."

When Matt walked into the restaurant, there were only a few people eating. A couple of drummers in celluloid collars and cuffs sat in earnest conversation with a saloon girl who had traded her silk for a demure gray morning gown, and a couple of cowboys sat at another table hungrily wolfing steak and eggs.

All eyes turned to the marshal, the story of Tam Elliot's shooting now known to everyone in Dodge. Matt read the eyes of the other diners, their forks stopped halfway to open mouths. The drummers, from back east, were looking at him in outright horror, seeing him only as a man of violence in a violent land they could never understand. The saloon girl's painted eyes slanted to Matt, as cold, hungry and calculating as those of a wolf, watching him, sizing him up as a bedmate, ready and willing to bathe in his reflected glory as a dangerous gunfighter should he as much as crook a finger in her direction. The girl turned in her chair, facing the marshal, her shoulders back, upthrust breasts displaying the goods on offer.

The cowboys, who had seen shooting and sudden death before, glanced at Matt when he stepped inside, then looked quickly away, wanting no truck with gun-slinging lawmen.

A perverse sense of humor tugging at him, Matt smiled at the drummers and the two men flushed and nervously lowered their eyes to their plates. He touched his hat brim to the girl, and she eagerly returned his smile, her teeth flashing small and white in a scarlet mouth.

"Going to be another hot one," Matt said to no one in particular as he took his chair. "Shaping up that way."

None of the men made any comment, but the girl's smile widened and she fidgeted in her chair, preparing to get to her feet.

Matt gave the girl a slight shake of the head. The young woman's eyes widened in surprise, then she pouted in disappointment and turned quickly away from him.

The marshal sighed, ordered steak and eggs from Ma Prescott and asked her to prepare a plate for his prisoner. "He wants bacon, eggs and maybe a half dozen biscuits."

Ma, her face flushed with steam from the kitchen, sniffed. "Too good for him if you ask me." She dabbed at her eyes with the corner of her apron.

"That Logan St. Clair was such a nice man, and so handsome."

When Matt finished eating, he got Stucker's plate from Ma, covered in a red-checked napkin.

"There it is, Marshal," she said. "And much good may it do him."

Matt paid his bill, then walked back to his office, gingerly carrying the plate by the rim because the bottom was so hot it burned his fingers.

He had no idea why he was doing this for Cage Stucker, and if someone had suggested to him that it was just a random act of kindness on his part, he would have scoffed at the very notion.

Stucker needed a change from beef and beans—that was all.

Matt stepped into his office and walked back to the cells. "Grub's up, Stucker," he said.

Stucker rose from his bunk and took the plate, the coffee Matt had brought him still sitting untouched on the floor.

"Four eggs, about a half pound of bacon and plenty of biscuits—just like you ordered," Matt said.

Lifting the plate to his nose, Stucker peeled away the napkin and sniffed the food suspiciously. As Matt turned, the man swore and hurled the plate at the bars of his cell. The plate shattered into a hundred pieces and bacon, egg yolk and biscuits splattered over the walls.

"I can't eat that garbage," Stucker yelled. "It's cold."

An icy rage in him, Matt looked down at the food scattered over the floor of Stucker's cell.

"That's all you're getting to eat until your trial, Stucker," he said. "I advise you to start picking it up or you'll be mighty hungry."

Night fell on Dodge, but Festus had not returned. Matt was worried. It was unlike his deputy to be late in reporting for duty. Festus was not overconscientious about his appearance, and his personal hygiene left much to be desired, but in matters relating to his work, he was a model of dependability.

The clock on the office wall showed five after eight when Matt opened the door, hoping to see Festus riding Ruth along Front Street, full of apology and the widow Brady's soda cracker pie.

The street was busy with riders and wagons, but there was no sign of the deputy.

Matt stepped to the edge of the boardwalk, peering through the dust kicked up by the constant procession of horses—and was about to turn away when he made out the rangy silhouette of a saddled mule plodding along the street toward him.

From long habit, Ruth stopped at the office hitching rail and stood three-legged, her head down, taking no interest in what was going on around her.

Matt stepped beside the mule and immediately noticed the note pinned to her saddle. He took the scrap of paper, stepped into the light cast by an oil lamp outside his office and read.

Shaking his head, unable to believe what he was seeing, Matt scanned the penciled scrawl a second time.

DILLON—IF YOU WANT TO SEE YOUR DEPUTY ALIVE AGAIN TELL THE JUDGE LOGAN ST. CLAIR WAS CARRYING A GUN.

There was no signature and the note had been written on a page torn from a tally book carried by every cowboy and rancher.

Matt stepped beside Ruth and ran a hand over her saddle. It came away clean. There was no blood.

Festus Haggen wasn't the sort of man to let himself be kidnapped without putting up a fight, so he must have known his abductor and trusted him.

Did Festus trust any of Clint Stucker's gunmen?

Matt rubbed his chin, thinking it through. That was unlikely. His deputy had a low opinion of Johnny Lomax and the rest of the Stucker warriors and would have hauled iron before any of them got close enough to capture him.

Who else would want Cage Stucker to get away with cold-blooded murder?

Matt could think of no one.

Deeply troubled, he led Ruth to the livery stable, unsaddled the big mule and threw her some hay and a bait of corn.

Tim Rawlins, a talkative man who had left an arm on the field at Shiloh, worked at the stable. He stepped out of his office, saw Matt and stepped to his side, his thin face framing a question.

"Say, Marshal," he said, "I always wondered why ol' Festus favors a mule over a hawse." Rawlins shrugged. "Been meaning to ask him but never seemed to get round to it."

Matt, hurt spiking at his belly, forced a smile. "Way Festus tells it, when he was with the Texas Rangers, a buckskin horse throwed him one time. After that, he set right down on the notion to ride a mule."

Rawlins shook his head. "He's a strange one, that Festus." He looked around. "Say, where is he?"

Unwilling to lie, Matt compromised. "His duties have him all tied up at the moment. But he'll be in to check on Ruth."

A puzzled expression crossed Rawlins' face and he opened his mouth to speak. But Matt, anticipating another question, quickly sidestepped the man and hefted his saddle and bridle from the rack.

A few minutes later, he swung onto the bay and headed out of Dodge, clattering over the wooden bridge spanning the Arkansas before swinging south toward the widow Brady's place a couple of miles north of Mulberry Creek.

Maybe he could find Festus before his abductors had a chance to hide him away.

But in the dark, in wide-open country, that was a big maybe.

Matt followed the old military wagon road, twin tracks bare of grass, cutting due south across the prairie directly toward the west bend of the Mulberry.

The moon bathed the land around him in silver light, and the wind rippled the tall bluestem grass like waves on a troubled sea. Yucca plants grew here and there on each side of the road, spikes of snow-white flowers blooming among their sharp-pointed leaves.

Matt kept the bay at a steady lope, constantly searching the way ahead for any sign of a struggle.

As he neared Mulberry Creek a few shallow hills rose from the flat, bluestem giving way to the shorter, tougher buffalo grass on their crests, where the soil was thinner and drier.

The widow Brady's place lay at the foot of one of these hills, a log cabin with a barn, pigpen and corral, surrounded by yucca and a few struggling red cedars.

When Matt reined up outside the cabin, oil lamps glowed in each of the two windows, and smoke from the chimney rose gray against the dark sky.

"Hello the house!" Matt hollered.

A few moments passed; then the door opened a crack and the twin barrels of a shotgun poked out. "What do you want?" A woman's voice, hesitant and slightly scared.

His voice soft so not to alarm the woman any further, Matt said: "Mrs. Brady, I'm Matt Dillon, city marshal of Dodge. I'm looking for my deputy, Festus Haggen."

"Why you looking for him?" Mrs. Brady asked, her voice now strident. "He's a lazy good for nothing who can eat his weight in groceries."

"Sounds like Festus, all right," Matt said. "But his mule came back to Dodge without him and I'm some worried."

The door creaked open and the widow Brady stepped outside, a couple of youngsters clinging to her skirts. She looked up at Matt, saw the star on his vest and lowered the shotgun.

"I swear," she said, "that deputy of yours ain't scared of hard work because he can lay right down beside it and sleep like a pup."

"He was supposed to dig a well for you, Mrs. Brady," Matt said.

"Supposed to is right. He ate me out of house and home, then dug my dry well a couple of feet and called it quits. Said his back was killing him."

"What time did he leave?" Matt asked.

The woman shrugged her thin shoulders. "Oh, I don't know exactly, maybe a couple of hours before sundown." Mrs. Brady's face showed sudden concern. "Marshal, nothing bad has happened to Festus, has it?"

Matt didn't want to burden this woman with his problems. She had enough of her own with her passel of young'uns and no man to do for her.

"I don't know, Mrs. Baker," he said. "I sure hope not." He leaned forward in the saddle. "If he got throwed from his mule and is hurt, he might show up here. If he does, you send your oldest boy to Dodge and let me know."

"I sure will, Marshal," the woman said. "Festus is a shiftless no good and so lazy he has to prop himself up to spit, but I guess he has his good points."

Matt hid his smile. "I guess he has, Mrs. Brady." He touched his hat brim. "So long, ma'am, and if he shows up, be sure to let me know."

The marshal wheeled his bay and headed back to Dodge.

Cage Stucker's trial was in two days time and he had to find Festus by then.

But no matter what happened, one thing was certain—he would not change a single word of his testimony.

chapter 12

Cage Stucker Meets the Judge

For the next two days, Matt Dillon kept at it. He was in the saddle at daybreak, looping around Dodge in ever-widening circles, hunting for his deputy. He explored every creek and shadowed rise, but it seemed Festus had vanished from the face of the Earth.

Matt got the same blank stare and slow shake of the head from every farmer he spoke to, and the soldiers at Fort Dodge who knew Festus said none of their patrols had sighted hide nor hair of him either.

On the morning of Cage Stucker's trial, Matt was out long before first light, but he met with the same result and finally rode back to Dodge dusty and weary, his concern for the deputy growing.

He was determined not to change his testimony at Stucker's trial, which was scheduled for two o'clock, but did that mean he'd be signing Festus' death warrant?

It was a heavy burden, and it lay harsh and accusing on Matt's conscience, giving him no peace.

When he returned to his office, Kitty showed up a few minutes later, strain showing on her sleepless face. "Did you have any luck, Matt?" she asked.

The big marshal shook his head. "No. I saw nothing moving but the wind on the grass."

Kitty's eyes were troubled. "Matt, the talk around town is that Festus has lit out, that he doesn't want to be in Dodge if Cage Stucker is sentenced to hang."

Stepping to his desk, Matt opened a drawer and passed Kitty the note he'd found on the deputy's saddle. "Does that look like he lit out?"

The woman read the note and angrily crumpled it in her hand. She was silent for a few moments, then asked: "Is it really so terrible?"

A frown gathered between Matt's eyebrows. "I don't understand. Is what so terrible?"

Kitty took a deep breath, uncomfortable about saying what had to be said. "Is it so terrible that Cage Stucker walks free? I'd gladly trade that murderer's life for the life of Festus."

Matt looked like he'd been slapped. "Kitty, you want me to lie?"

"Don't think of it as a lie, Matt. Think of it as a way of saving Festus Haggen."

Matt glanced at the clock on the wall. It was still two hours until the trial opened.

He turned to Kitty, feeling not anger, but an odd

kind of sadness and a vague sense of loss. His fingers strayed to the badge pinned to his vest.

"When I accepted this star, I understood that I was being asked to uphold the law, no matter the personal cost to me, no matter the sacrifices I'd have to make. The star itself is a piece of tin worth about two-bits, but I don't measure its value in money. To me its real worth is in what it stands for, and it stands for law, order and above all truth. Truth has no special moment of its own—it's now and it's always."

Matt touched Kitty lightly on the back of her hand. "Sure, I can go on the stand and lie, but then I'll take off this star and never put on another. Maybe a lie will save Festus' life, but at the same time I'll be spitting on everything I hold worthwhile and there will be no going back from that, Kitty, not ever."

The woman's eyes searched Matt's face, looking for something, and then she found it. "High-flying sentiments, Matt, but I can boil them down to just one word: pride. You'll let Festus die, not because of truth or duty or whatever else you say you hold sacred, but because of your own selfish, pigheaded pride."

Kitty turned on her heel, her eyes tearing, and walked quickly to the door. Matt reached out to hold her, but she wrenched herself away from his grasp. "Don't touch me, Matt," she said. "Please don't touch me ever again."

Kitty threw open the door and stormed outside, slamming it shut after her. Matt stood for a long moment, looking at the door, willing Kitty to come back and open it and run into his arms.

It didn't happen.

Finally Matt sat at his desk and buried his face in his hands.

Was Kitty right? Was he letting Festus die because of his own selfish pride, an emotion that had about as much value as a strutting rooster crowing on a dung heap?

The marshal's fingers strayed to the star on his vest.

All he had to do was take off the scrap of tin before he went to court.

Then he could lie under oath, not as a sworn lawman but as a private citizen.

Matt's eyes strayed to the clock on the wall. His moment of truth was approaching fast . . . and he had a decision to make.

Next to a hanging, a murder trial was one of the grand entertainments on the frontier, eagerly anticipated as a gala occasion, and folks would gather from miles around to see the show. By one o'clock, farm wagons were rolling into Dodge from all points of the compass, the men dressed in their Sunday-go-to-meeting clothes, stern wives sitting beside them in demure calico gowns and new straw bonnets.

Even the jaded denizens of Dodge made the effort and rolled out of bed at this early hour, yawned and dressed and headed, eyes bleary, for the courthouse.

Matt, wearing his star, shackled Cage Stucker and

brought him into the front office. A barber, at Clint Stucker's expense, had shaved the man for the occasion and trimmed his mustache and hair.

Cage watched with sullen eyes as Matt loaded shells into his Greener and waved the shotgun toward the door. "Let's go," he said.

Matt pushed Stucker outside, the young rancher blinking against the sudden afternoon sunlight, and the two walked solemnly to the courthouse, the marshal pushing his way through crowds of gawking bystanders.

The court had quickly filled up with spectators, but so many people had gathered to watch the proceedings that they spilled onto the boardwalk and the street outside. A couple of clerks were appointed as runners, to keep those standing outside informed, minute by minute, of what was happening inside.

When Matt led Stucker into the court, the jury was already seated. The marshal glanced over at the twelve men, all solid respectable citizens from across the tracks.

But these were bankers, businessmen and store owners, their living more or less dependent on the Texas cattlemen, and they were unlikely to convict unless the evidence against Cage Stucker was overwhelming.

Uncertainty tugging at him, Matt unshackled Stucker and directed him to a chair beside his lawyer, then found one for himself close by.

Becky Sharpe was in court, dressed in black and prettily pale, reveling in the spotlight, playing up her role of the bereaved lover. The young woman was crying, making a fuss, wailing that she was undone, her Mexican maid constantly holding a vial of smelling salts to her upturned freckled nose.

Becky kept crying out, "Oh, my Logan," before collapsing into more tears, her eyes nevertheless slanting every now and then toward the staid jurymen and the eager, craning spectators, judging their reaction.

Matt realized that Becky Sharpe's performance had already begun to prejudice the jury. The expression on the faces of the twelve men ran from annoyance to outright disgust with a few stops in between. After all, this was a married woman—with an invalid husband no less—and such grief over the death of an illicit lover was unseemly to say the least.

Cage Stucker's lawyer, a tall, spare, balding man named John Powell, wore pince-nez glasses on a black cord and he peered over the rims at Becky Sharpe, his spectacles catching the light, a slight smile playing around his thin mouth.

To Matt, Powell looked like a gaunt bird of prey, and like the marshal, he knew the effect the woman's grandstand performance was having on the jury and it seemed to please him immensely.

His Greener between his knees, Matt glanced around the courtroom. The three gunmen who were with Cage the night he killed St. Clair sat beside Clint Stucker and Johnny Lomax. Shorn of his guns, Lomax looked somehow smaller and incomplete, but there was no underestimating the malice and pure hatred in the looks he directed at Matt, his eyes burning like jets of blue gas. There was no sign of Sean Tyree.

"All rise."

The clerk of court and the bailiff led the way for His Honor Judge Micah Merriweather.

Merriweather looked like an ancient Roman patrician, not flesh and blood but a man carved out of a block of marble. He was small and wizened, and there was a sour, pinched look about him. The thin skin stretched tight over his high cheekbones was red veined from the harsh downstroke of the razor, and a scraggly goatee framed a narrow gash of a mouth. His black eyes were hard and intolerant, as bright as those of a bird, darting everywhere, missing nothing.

When Merriweather was seated, Becky Sharpe's performance grew wilder. The woman cried and moaned and called, "Logan," even more than she'd done before.

The judge watched her for a few tense moments, like a hawk ready to pounce on a chicken, and finally roared for the prosecuting attorney.

The prosecutor, a young up-and-coming lawyer named Charles Gray, gulped and rose to his feet, a forefinger running around the inside of the celluloid collar, which suddenly seemed too tight for him.

Merriweather pointed his gavel at Becky Sharpe. "Is that creature a material witness to the alleged crime?" he asked.

Gray gulped again and shook his head. "No, Your Honor. She was . . . uh . . . the paramour of the deceased."

Merriweather turned in his seat. "Bailiff, remove that woman!"

Becky, fainting into the bailiff's arms, was taken

from the courtroom, her cries fading as the doors were closed behind her.

"Now, Mr."—Merriweather quickly flipped through some papers on his bench—"ah yes, Mr. Gray, this court is now in session and you may proceed."

Charles Gray called City Marshal Matthew Dillon as his only witness.

Matt took his seat in the witness stand beside Merriweather's bench, and the judge ordered him to take the oath.

After this was done, Gray rose to his feet, but Matt stopped him in his tracks.

"Your Honor," he said, "before we proceed, I should tell you that my deputy has been missing for the last two days and I found this note on the saddle of his mule."

"On his mule?" Merriweather said. "My word, but that's passing strange."

Matt nodded, not knowing if Merriweather thought the note strange or the fact that a deputy marshal of Dodge City rode a mule. He passed the scrap of paper to the judge and the man scanned it briefly. "And will you change your testimony, Marshal Dillon?" he asked.

"No, sir," Matt answered, his voice firm. "Not a single word of it."

"I thought not," Merriweather said, nodding his approval.

A ripple of puzzled talk ran through the courtroom as John Powell sprang to his feet, his pince-nez glinting. "May I see the note, Your Honor?" he asked.

The judge passed over the piece of paper and Powell read it. "This means nothing," he said. "This could have been written by anyone, even the marshal himself in an effort to prejudice the court. I demand any reference to it be stricken from the record."

Merriweather thought for a few moments, then turned to his clerk. "Strike any reference to this note from the record. It has no bearing on the case."

Powell smiled and went back to his chair and was soon in earnest, whispered conversation with Cage Stucker.

Under Gray's questioning, Matt related the events leading up to the murder of Logan St. Clair.

"And did you find a weapon on the dead man?" Gray asked.

"He was unarmed," Matt replied.

"But you did find something on his person, did you not?"

"Yes, a silver cigar case."

Gray stepped to his table and held up the case. "Is this the object in question?"

Matt nodded. "Yes, it is. I believe St. Clair was reaching for a cigar when Cage Stucker shot him."

"Objection, Your Honor!" Powell interrupted. "That is speculation on the part of the witness."

"Objection sustained," Merriweather said. "Strike the remark from the record."

"You found no revolver anywhere on Logan St. Clair's person, Marshal?" Gray asked.

Judge Merriweather, his voice edged by annoyance, snapped: "Mr. Gray, the witness has already said the victim was unarmed. The court sees no purpose in belaboring the point."

"I just wish to make it clear to the jury that the marshal found no weapon of any kind on St. Clair's body," Gray said.

"I'm quite sure, Mr. Gray, your point has already been made," Merriweather said. "Give the jury credit for some intelligence and proceed."

After a few more questions about the arrest of Cage Stucker, Gray asked Powell if he wished to question the witness.

"No questions," the lawyer said, and again surprised whispers broke out among the spectators.

One by one, Powell called the three Stucker gunmen to the stand.

And all three swore that Logan St. Clair stopped Cage Stucker by the railroad tracks and loudly demanded, with much foul, abusive language, that he stay away from Becky Sharpe.

Each of the gunman declared that Cage was in fear of his life and that when St. Clair suddenly reached inside his coat, Cage drew and fired. And all implied that Marshal Dillon had bent over St. Clair's body and removed an object from his waistband, possibly a small revolver.

Gray challenged all three witnesses, but the gunmen had been well coached and stuck firmly by their story.

The alleged removal of a revolver was speculation, and this testimony was duly removed from the record. But when Matt looked over to the jury, their eyes were on him, some of them hostile, others speculative, and he realized that the damage had been done.

After the last witness, Merriweather directed the jury to retire and consider a charge of murder in the first degree against Cage Stucker. Also, as dictated by city ordinances, the lesser misdemeanor of discharging a firearm north of the area known as the Deadline, delineated by the railroad tracks.

Dusk was falling and lamps were lit inside the courthouse when the jury filed out to consider their verdict.

They shuffled back into the jury box just fifteen minutes later, none of them meeting Matt's eyes.

"Gentlemen of the jury," Merriweather asked, "have you considered your verdict?"

The foreman, a plump banker called Hazlitt, replied for all. "Yes, we have, Your Honor. We find the defendant, Cage Stucker, not guilty of murder, but guilty of unlawfully discharging a firearm north of the Deadline."

Clint Stucker and his gunmen rose to their feet and whooped and hollered, slapping each other on the back. Cage Stucker turned to Matt, grinning, his eyes glinting in triumph.

The crowd in the courtroom began to argue loudly among themselves, and the racket didn't cease until Merriweather loudly banged his gavel and yelled for silence.

"Another outburst like that and I'll clear the court," he said, his thin mouth pinched, anger flaring in his eyes.

He looked down at Cage Stucker and said: "The defendant will now rise."

Stucker stood, still grinning, and looked around

the court. He waved to his father and Johnny Lomax and raised his arms in victory above his head.

"Mr. Stucker," Merriweather snapped, "this is a court of law. Please disport yourself accordingly."

Chastened, Cage dropped his arms, his grin slipping, and stood facing the judge, Powell at his side.

Merriweather was silent for a few long moments, as though composing himself; then he said, the anger in his voice barely controlled: "It is my firm belief that the late Logan St. Clair met his death by being shot down and cold-bloodedly murdered by you, Mr. Stucker. But the jury has seen fit to find otherwise and that is their prerogative."

His eyes filled with a burning contempt, Merriweather added: "According to Dodge City ordinance number one-twenty-six concerning the reckless use of firearms, I hereby fine you three dollars for the unlawful discharge of a revolver north of the Deadline."

The judge sighed, shook his head and banged his gavel. "This court is now dismissed."

As the Stuckers celebrated with the noisy well-wishers crowding around them, Matt Dillon sat, his head bowed.

Just two thoughts were uppermost in his mind.

Where was Festus?

And where was Sean Tyree?

chapter 13

Dark Vengeance

Matt returned to his office, placed his shotgun in the rack and threw the clanking shackles into a trunk near the door to the cells.

A few minutes later he walked to the livery stable through the thronging crowds on the street, most of them cowboys celebrating Cage Stucker's acquittal, and saddled the bay.

He rode south again, toward the widow Brady's place, but saw no sign of Festus.

Making a wide loop, he rode east as far as Coon Creek, then forded the Arkansas where the river narrowed around the sand banks at Miles Crossing, and rode north to the Dry Basin country before swinging west.

As Matt rode out of the shallow, mile-wide sinkhole that was the basin, the iron rails of the Santa Fe railroad glittered in the distance, heading northeast toward the stockyards and meat-packing plants of distant Chicago.

Nothing moved in that endless land as the marshal swung back in the direction of Dodge. He had ridden far and wide for hours but had seen no other living soul.

The day had grown hot, and sweat stained the front of Matt's shirt. The bay, usually tireless, was slowing down, his head hanging, and once or twice he stumbled, his nose almost pecking into the grass.

Matt found shade under a stand of stunted red cedar, unsaddled the bay and let him roll. The horse stood and began to graze and the marshal fetched his back up against a thin tree trunk and rested, his hat dangling loose in his hands.

He had seen nothing of Festus, and now doubt began to cloud his mind. Was the deputy still alive, or had he been killed to keep his mouth shut about the identity of his kidnappers?

Matt shook his head, refusing to consider that possibility. Most times, Festus didn't look like much, but he was tough as an old bootheel and a hard man to kill.

The marshal rose from his uncomfortable seat and looked around him, at the flat miles of grass stretching away in every direction, ending in haze a vast distance away where the blue vault of the sky met and married the green earth.

Unless his bushwhackers had him stashed somewhere in Dodge, a possibility Matt considered unlikely, Festus was somewhere out here. But in all this limitless wilderness, the question was where.

Matt wiped sweat from his hatband, then settled the hat back on his head. Suddenly he was eager to get back to Dodge. Maybe even now Festus was sitting in the marshal's office, drinking coffee, still stewing about being taken so easily and vowing bloody revenge on his captors, with his boots propped upon the desk.

Maybe. But Matt had the uneasy gut feeling that this would not be the case.

He had searched high and low for his deputy and found not even a trace of the man. Where the hell was he?

His frustration evident in his clenched fists and the grim line of his mouth, Matt looked up at the sky as though trying to find the answer there. But the sky turned a blank face to him, revealing nothing, unconcerned with the petty problems of mortal men.

Matt saddled the bay and headed back to Dodge. The wind was driving from the south, hot and relentless, flattening the front of his wool shirt against the hard-muscled planes of his wide chest and shoulders.

He would try again tomorrow. And the next day and the day after that. He would keep trying until he found Festus and the men who had taken him. This he vowed.

When night fell on Dodge, Clint and Cage Stucker and most of the Rafter S hands were celebrating at Ham Bell's Varieties Saloon, where George, the least belligerent of the fighting Masterson brothers, tended bar.

Matt didn't expect any trouble, since the Stuckers

were in an expansive mood, treating all and sundry to drinks. The girls at Ham Bell's were said to be even prettier than the ones at the Long Branch, and the beer was always iced, served in frosted mugs, the bonded whiskey straight up and undiluted.

Ham Bell's was a place for whooping it up, not fighting, and Matt briefly considered letting well enough alone and steering clear of the place.

But the nagging worry at the back of his mind was the whereabouts of Sean Tyree. The man had not been present in court, but he had no doubt heard about the verdict by now and it could hardly have pleased him.

Prodded by a sense of unease, Matt rose form his desk and buckled on his gun belt.

Maybe he should stroll over to the saloon and just check on things.

Outside, the air was heavy, close and hard to breathe, thick darkness crowding in from the flatlands, only here and there being kept at bay by the dancing orange light of the guttering oil lamps along Front Street. The night was oppressively hot, the kind of stifling heat that makes animals restless and men irritable, and the lack of traffic on the street was unusual, like an omen. Or a warning.

Matt kept to the boardwalk until he was opposite Ham Bell's; then he crossed the street, his boots kicking up little puffs of dust.

A piano was playing in the saloon, almost drowned out by the roar of drinking men and the laughter of women. The stained glass doors constantly slammed open and shut as people came and went, their faces flushed, grinning, their eyes shining like cats in a dark alley.

Matt stepped, unnoticed, inside. George Masterson, magnificently mustached and pomaded, a diamond stickpin in his cravat, was lost behind the press of men and women crowding to the bar.

The marshal stepped to the wall beside the door and stood, his arms folded, watching.

Cage Stucker was at the bar, the three hands who had testified at his trial beside him. The faces of all four men were reddened by whiskey, and Cage held a blond girl in a tight blue satin dress in one arm, bending his head between slugs of his drink to kiss her open, willing mouth.

Johnny Lomax sat at a table with Clint Stucker and a few other hands, sharing a bottle, their eyes on Cage. They whispered to one another, laughed and pointed when the young rancher's hands wandered over the girl's breasts and hips.

For the most part, the crowd seemed bent on having a good time and there was no sign of trouble. Cage was occupied with the girl and obviously had his mind on other things besides violence.

Matt was about to call it a night and leave . . . when a door opened and hell stepped into Ham Bell's saloon.

Out of the corner of his eye, Matt saw the back door of the saloon open quickly and then close. He thought nothing of it and was ready to turn away when a flash of black drew his attention.

Sean Tyree stood just inside the door, still wearing the black mourning garment, but the voluminous broadcloth was pulled back to clear the guns in crossed belts around his slim hips.

The young man's face had tanned in recent days, making the livid white scar on his cheek stand out like a vicious claw mark. His eyes under the brim of his black hat burned hot, like coals.

"Stucker!" Tyree yelled.

Cage looked up and saw Tyree at the door, and his face drained of color. He roughly threw the girl away from him and she stumbled, crashing onto her back across a nearby table, scattering cards, glasses and poker chips. The startled players jumped to their feet in alarm.

Cage Stucker's hand flashed for his gun, his draw lightning fast. The three gunmen with him were a split second behind, frantically clawing leather as Tyree fired, the shots from his Colts very close together, sounding like a thunderous drumroll.

"No!" Matt yelled, moving toward Tyree, aware of time slowing down around him, like he was running through a deep vat of molasses.

The first of Tyree's bullets hit Stucker in the mouth, smashing through his teeth before blowing out the back of his head, a spraying scarlet-and-gray fan of blood and brain haloing around him.

Tyree's guns hammered, sowing death and terror. One of the Rafter S gunmen went down, coughing blood. Then another dropped. The third, a young redhead, two-handed his long-barreled Colt to eye level, fired, missed, then screamed as he was hit hard in the center of his chest.

Johnny Lomax was on his feet, his guns clearing

leather, coming up fast. He fired, but the dying redhead staggered in front of him and took the bullet in his belly. Lomax cursed, kicked the man away from him and fired again. Tyree shot back at the same instant. Lomax's bullet chipped wood from the doorjamb near Tyree's head, but Tyree's shot burned across Lomax's upper left arm, drawing blood. The gunman yelped and turned away, his face gray, unwilling to believe he'd been hit.

Matt was closer now. He lunged for Tyree, but the man spun on his heel and stepped through the door, slamming it shut behind him.

Matt struggled with the door, pulled his gun and ran outside.

The alley behind the saloon was dark. Matt ran, but his foot rolled on an empty bottle and he stumbled and fell. The big marshal picked himself up, rubbed a hurting knee, then ran again, following the sound of Tyree's pounding feet in the gloom.

Ahead of Matt, a gun flared orange and a bullet whined past his head. He fired at the gun flash, fired again and ran, determined to keep Tyree in sight.

The alley opened up on a narrower, even darker passage between the saloon and the hardware store next to it. Matt, limping, stumbled down the alley and hobbled out onto Front Street.

He saw Tyree about thirty yards away, the mourning garment billowing like the wings of a great bat as he ran. Matt raised his Colt, snapped off a shot, but Tyree kept on going.

The marshal followed, his bruised knee slowing him down. Tyree disappeared from sight as he suddenly darted into the darkness alongside the Dodge House Hotel and Billiard Hall. It looked like a planned move, and Matt suspected that was where Tyree had stashed his horse.

The big marshal punched the spent shells from his Colt and reloaded from his cartridge belt. He walked to the corner of the hotel, peering into the darkness that lay beyond the lamp-lit front porch. There was no sound but the rustle of the wind. Matt stepped deeper into the alley, the guttering oil lamps briefly painting the right side of his face with amber light before the darkness swallowed him.

"Tyree! Sean Tyree, come on out of there!"

No answer. Somewhere in the Dodge House an open screen door banged back and forth in the wind and a woman called out in her sleep and then fell silent.

"Tyree!"

The hollow echo of Matt's voice mocked him, and he cursed softly, but long and passionately.

Slowly, aware of the soft chime of his spurs, Matt walked alongside the long, high wall of the hotel, favoring his aching left leg, every nerve in his body tense and waiting.

Something moved in the darkness, a bottle chinked and Matt stopped in his tracks, his Colt coming up fast, hammer back and ready.

A soft meow and the same calico cat Matt had seen a few days before ran toward him, pulled up at the last moment, hissed in alarm, then turned and ran back the way it had come.

As the marshal's hammering pulse slowly faded

from his ears, he silently cussed cats in general and that little calico in particular.

Beyond where Matt now stood, the hotel threw a wedge of thick shadow across the waste ground between it and the closed, dark-windowed New York millinery store next door. A scrap of paper fluttered across the dusty street and caught on Matt's boot. He kicked the paper loose, then walked deeper into the shadows.

"That's far enough, Marshal. You've given me no cause to drill you."

The whispered voice emerged from the shadows. Tyree's voice.

"Sean," Matt said, "throw down your gun and come out real slow. There are four dead men back at Ham Bell's and it's all of your doing."

Matt heard Tyree's soft, joyless chuckle. "Stucker and the rest were informed well beforehand. I gave them the chance to draw." A heartbeat pause, then the man added: "They got more of a chance than they gave Logan St. Clair."

Matt had no inclination to argue the finer points of the law in a dark alley. "Tyree," he said, "I'm not here to talk about the right or wrong of what happened. I'm coming after you, and if I'm put to it, I swear to God I'll gun you."

Matt took a step deeper into the alley; then Tyree said: "Wait, Marshal, there's something you should know. I—"

Horsemen galloped along the street and Matt turned and watched them rein up at the hotel, a cloud of yellow dust kicking up as high as the withers of their mounts. "A couple of you men check that alley."

It was Clint Stucker.

Matt heard feet pound away in the darkness and he yelled: "Tyree, stop!"

"He's in there!" Stucker called out.

Horsemen crowded into the alley, guns drawn, as hoofbeats hammered behind the hotel, then began to fade into the distance.

"After him!" Stucker yelled. "Don't let him get away!"

"No!" Matt hollered, stepping into the path of Stucker and his men.

But five riders galloped past him, a grim-faced, cursing Stucker in the lead. The rancher led his men around the corner of the Dodge House and guns banged, then the sound of pounding hooves became lost in the silence of the night.

Above him, Matt heard windows fly open and the heads of hotel guests appeared, loudly demanding to know what in blue blazes was going on and what was all the shooting about.

Matt ignored the angry, shouted questions, turned on his heel and stepped back onto Front Street.

People were running in and out of Ham Bell's place, and he watched the frockcoated, cadaverous form of Percy Crump hurry like a flapping vulture toward the saloon.

The marshal walked slowly toward the saloon, his head bent in thought. Sean Tyree had been about to tell him something before Clint Stucker showed up with his riders.

But what?

Could it be that he knew something about Festus' disappearance?

And if he did, would Clint Stucker let him live long enough to tell what he knew?

Come sunup, Matt decided, he would seek answers to those questions.

chapter 14

A Line Is Drawn

When Matt arrived at Ham Bell's saloon, Cage Stucker and two of his gunmen were dead. The third, a gut-shot redhead, would not last until morning, predicted Percy Crump with a melancholy expression and a professional shake of his head.

Matt looked over a scene of bloody carnage.

The shattered face of Cage Stucker looked like broken stone, stark and ugly in death, and the two dead gunmen lay in widening pools of blood, Colts still clutched in stiffening hands.

The young redhead was breathing his last on a pool table, trying to bear an agony that was beyond bearable, cursing Sean Tyree and cursing the day he was born. The blonde in the blue dress pushed a wisp of hair from the dying man's forehead and whispered something to him. The redhead bared his teeth against a sudden shock of pain and made no answer.

Matt brushed Percy Crump aside and stepped beside the gunman. The man turned scared eyes to Matt, tried to say something, then gurgled deep in his throat and was gone.

Percy Crump stood at Matt's shoulder. "I always know," he said, looking down at the dead man. "If put to it, I could give you the hour and the minute and maybe even the second." Crump was silent for a few moments, then added: "Yes, maybe even the very second."

Matt ignored the undertaker, busy with his own thoughts. Sean Tyree, lightning fast with his guns, had killed four men in the space of as many seconds. Matt decided that when he caught up with Tyree, if he ever did, the young man would be a handful.

Matt returned to his office, bunked down and caught a few hours' sleep. He was awake before first light, drank some cold coffee, then walked to the livery stable. He rode the bay back to the office, looped the reins to the hitching rail and stepped back inside.

The marshal took a .44.40 Winchester from the rack and thoughtfully fed rounds into the chamber.

Twelve miles north of Dodge, near the bend of Bison Creek, lay Horse Thief Canyon, a deep gully carved out of Dakota sandstone by water that in ancient times flowed toward the Smoky Hill River.

The canyon rose like a ruined fortress out of the surrounding flatland, its steep, grass-covered sides sculpted by wind and rain into fantastic shapes that the Cheyenne and Pawnee revered as gigantic, petrified bears and wolves. Matt had ridden far, but had seen nothing of Festus—but what better place to hide a man than the canyon?

The big marshal nodded, blaming himself for not riding to the Horse Thief earlier.

Now he intended to remedy that lapse.

Matt stepped outside and shoved the Winchester into the boot. Above him the awakening sky was pale blue, building clouds to the north tinted lilac, gold lace fringing their edges.

The marshal tested the wind, smelling distant rain. Above him a red-tailed hawk cried out, hovering on still wings, then called again and slanted away from him, gliding toward the dark banks of the Arkansas.

Matt put his foot in the stirrup and was about to swing into the saddle when he heard the thud of hooves on the road behind him.

He turned and saw Stucker and his riders come in, all of them bent over in the saddle, a tired, dispirited posse covered in dust and defeat.

It was Johnny Lomax who saw Matt first. The gunman's head jerked up and he leaned over and whispered something to Stucker. The big rancher's eyes swept to Matt, and he swung his horse toward him.

Stucker, his hard, brutal face lined by exhaustion, reined up a couple of yards from Matt, his eyes harsh and accusing.

"Which side will you take, Dillon, now the ball has opened?" he asked.

Matt smiled. "I take it you didn't find him?"

"We'll find him," Lomax answered. "We'll find him and we'll hang him."

"Which side will you take?" Stucker asked again.

"The side of the law," Matt replied.

Stucker chewed on the end of his mustache, then shook his head. "There is only one law here, my law, the law of blood for blood. Sean Tyree murdered my blood, and by God I'll see him kick at the end of a rope for it."

Matt stood, looking up at Stucker, the bay's reins in his hand. Dodge was still in darkness, the shadows thick, brooding and long. "Go back to Texas, Stucker," he said. "Go home to your ranch. There's already been too much killing here."

Stucker's eyes caught fire and he waved a hand toward his riders. "Me and these men here, we plan to get fresh horses and head out again." He leaned forward in the saddle. "Step between us and Tyree, Marshal, and we'll kill you."

The line had been drawn and Matt accepted it as such. "Stucker," he said, slowly, so the man would hear and understand every word, "if you take the law into your own hands and harm Sean Tyree, I'll hang you." Suddenly angry, he took a step toward Lomax and the Stucker gunmen. "That goes for all of you, every man jack of you."

"Big talk," Lomax said, his voice flat and hard, his urge to kill easy to read. "No matter what happens, Dillon, no matter who else dies, no matter who else hangs, you and me will have it out. It's getting so I can no longer abide breathing the same air as you."

The man's finger stabbed at Matt. "Soon, very soon, I'll gun you."

Matt's smile held a hint of malicious humor. "How's your arm, Johnny boy?" he asked.

Lomax stiffened in the saddle, his face stricken. His hand streaked for his gun, but Stucker reached out and stopped him. "Let it be, Johnny," he said, his eyes on Matt. "Just . . . let it be."

The rancher looked down at Matt, his growing hatred for the marshal writ large on his face. "I've drawn the line, Dillon," he said. "Here in Dodge, you're the law. Out there"—Stucker waved a hand toward the plains—"you're nothing. Nothing! Take the side of the man who murdered my blood and you'll die just as surely as night follows day."

"Know one thing, Stucker," Matt said, matching the man's anger. "In Dodge or out there on the flat grass, I'll uphold the law."

The big rancher nodded. "Then so be it. Dillon, from this moment on, consider yourself my mortal enemy and a walking dead man."

Matt stood for a few moments, watching Stucker and his riders head toward the livery stable, then swung into the saddle.

He had to find Sean Tyree. And fast.

Matt rode north across the plains as the day brightened around him. Horse Thief Canyon was almost due north, but he had no intention of leaving a trail that could easily be followed.

Clint Stucker and Johnny Lomax were his sworn enemies and they would not rest until he and Sean

Tyree were dead. He understood fully the danger that lay in Johnny Lomax. The gunman had been stung by Tyree because he had underestimated the man. Matt knew that he would not make the same mistake twice.

The marshal rode into Duck Creek, splashed through shallow water for a mile or so, following the bed of the creek east, then climbed out and headed north again.

Several times he paused on the crest of shallow rises, checking his back trail. He saw nothing.

Saw Log Creek lay ahead of him; then he must cross six miles of flat, open country before fetching up to the canyon.

Wishful of hot coffee but having none, Matt gave the bay his head, loping through bluestem and Indian grass that reached a height of five feet in places. Yucca grew here and there, a valuable plant to the Cheyenne, who used the roots as soap, the tough leaves for basket fibers.

As he had done at Duck Creek, Matt rode down into the bed of the Saw Log and followed the creek east for a couple of miles. Finally he rode out of the creek and swung to the northwest. After a mile or so, he came upon a wild horse trail and he followed it until the narrow path ended at a small blue lake bordered by a few willows and cottonwoods.

Here Matt watered the bay and rested, working the kinks out of his back, bending and straightening his leg, stiff from the tumble he had taken behind Ham Bell's saloon.

Rain clouds were gathering to the north, building

one on top of the other like gigantic gray boulders, and Matt heard a distant rumble of thunder.

He unrolled his slicker from behind the saddle and shrugged into it, and not a moment too soon. Rain pattered on the grass around him, drumming against his hat, kicking up startled Vs of water all over the surface of the lake. The wind rose, rippling the grass, and the bay tossed his head, enjoying the coolness that came with the breeze, his bit jangling.

Matt, a man who had once spent much time in wild, lonely places, stood, his face upturned to the rain, letting it beat down on him, smelling its sweet, clean fragrance, like the newly washed hair of a beautiful woman. He had long grown accustomed to the comfortable, settled life of Dodge, yet few men knew and loved the wilderness as much as Matt Dillon did. And he could go back to it if that was what fate dictated, moving through mountains and pines like an Indian, leaving no mark, taking only what he needed, his needs small at that.

Maybe now, as he grew older, he would like a woman to share it with him, showing her the plants she could eat, and those she couldn't, and others that provided excellent medicines. He could teach her how to build a shelter and a fire and how, with only a knife, to survive anywhere.

Matt's head lowered, the progression of his thoughts leading to Kitty. He pondered the gulf that had opened up between them. A quick, keen sense of loss stabbed at him but he shook his head, clearing his mind.

There would be time enough to think of Kitty

when all this was over, a time to come together . . . and heal.

Matt gathered up the reins of the bay and swung into the saddle.

Right now he had to consider what lay ahead. Was Festus in Horse Thief Canyon? Was Tyree?

And if Tyree was there and all talk failed and it came down to the speed of the draw, was Matt fast enough to shade the younger man?

Time would tell . . . and that time was coming soon.

chapter 15

The Riddle of Horse Thief Canyon

Matt rode up on the Horse Thief from the south. Sentinel Rock, a tall spire of weathered sandstone, marked the entrance to the canyon, red cedar and a few stunted oaks growing at its base.

The marshal reined in the bay and sat for several minutes, carefully studying the canyon. The rocky walls were steep, roughly cut and shaped by rain and wind, here and there large sections of cliff broken away by water seepage and its seasonal freezing and thawing.

Grass, mostly buffalo and grama, grew on top of the rusty brown and gray canyon walls. Within the canyon, shadows lay dark, and there was no sound but the snake hiss of the rain.

As Matt sat his horse, studying the layout of the canyon, the storm continued on its way east. The clouds parted and the rain drizzled, then slowly pattered to an end. The sun broke through, shining hot and bright, and the shadows began to flee from the canyon floor.

Matt kicked the bay forward, alert and ready, his eyes scanning the canyon and the land around him. Nothing moved but the grass and the branches of the trees and there was no evidence that anyone had been here.

He rode closer, then reined in his horse when he caught the glint of something metallic in a cedar break at the bottom of the canyon's right wall.

Matt studied the spot, and when the wind rustled among the tree branches, he caught it again, just a brief glimpse of metal catching the sun.

The marshal slid the Winchester from the boot and cranked a round into the chamber. He swung the bay toward the cedars, keeping the horse to a walk, his rifle across the saddle horn.

When he was about fifty yards from the cedars, Matt swung off the bay and removed his slicker, draping it over the back of the saddle.

The rifle held across his chest, he stepped cautiously toward the clump of trees.

There! He saw it again—the sudden flash of metal in the sun. Aware of how nakedly out in the open he was, Matt sprinted for thirty yards as fast as his hurting knee would allow, then dropped onto his belly, the Winchester coming up to his shoulder.

"You in the trees!" he yelled over the sights. "Come out with your hands raised or I'll cut loose with this here rifle."

There was no answer.

Matt looked around him, feeling the sun hot on his back, the grass under him still wet from the rain. He watched a couple of jays glide into the cedars, rustle noisily among the branches, then finally settle down to roost.

Had there been a man in there, lying in wait, the birds would have spotted him and flown quickly away.

Matt rose to his feet, still wary, his senses clamoring. He moved forward, all his attention riveted on the cedars and the thick, concealing grass growing around their trunks.

When he was a few yards from the cedar break, the jays suddenly fluttered out of the trees, scattering leaves, and Matt's rifle came up fast, his eyes desperately seeking a target.

There was none, just the trees as they'd been a moment before, still and quiet, their branches moving gently in the wind.

The big marshal let his hammering heartbeat return to normal; then, angry with himself for being spooked so easily, and feeling more than a little foolish, he stepped into the cedars.

Within a few moments he found what he was looking for.

Pinned to the trunk of the thickest of the trees a twenty-dollar double eagle caught the sunlight, the gold shimmering. A single blacksmith's nail fixed the coin to the trunk.

Matt lowered his rifle. This was why Tyree had asked Quint Asper for a hammer and a single nail. But what was the coin's significance and why had

Tyree nailed it here, in a remote wilderness canyon miles from Dodge?

He had no answer to that question; nor did he ponder it.

Now it was high time to enter the canyon and see if Sean Tyree was still there.

Matt unbuckled his spurs and hung them on the cedar, then moved on silent feet toward the canyon entrance.

Stepping slowly and cautiously, he walked into the canyon, steep walls rising on either side of him. There were many small spring pools scattered around the canyon floor, some of them noisy with croaking bullfrogs, and deer and coyote prints were everywhere.

Just a few years before, this place had been a watering hole for buffalo, but now the great shaggy animals were all gone and the deer had moved in to take their place.

Here, deep within the canyon, it was quite dark, the air so cool it was almost cold after the heat of the sun. Stepping carefully, Matt walked deeper into the canyon. After a few yards, his eyes busy scanning the tops of the walls, he almost stepped right on top of a drowsy rattlesnake. The startled animal coiled quickly, shook its tail in warning, then rapidly slid away from him, figuring that in this instance retreat was preferable to a fight.

Matt watched the snake go, again hearing his heart thud fast in his ears. That had been close and not an experience he cared to repeat anytime soon.

Two hundred yards into the canyon, he found a

cave, a shallow opening in the rock to his left, about four feet above the floor.

Was this where Tyree was holed up?

Moving slowly and carefully, the big marshal stepped closer to the cave. He maneuvered around a boulder so his rifle could cover the entrance, the rock providing shelter should Tyree open up on him.

Matt's eyes scanned the cave mouth. But there was no movement.

"You in the cave, let's see you come out with your hands up and empty!" he yelled, aware that he might be talking to himself.

"Matthew . . . is that you?"

It was Festus' voice, thin and quavering, but unmistakably that of the deputy.

"Festus, are you all right in there?" Matt hollered.

"I'm fine, Matthew. But I sure need a drink."

"You need water?"

"Hell no," Festus cried, "I don't need to go pizening my insides. I mean whiskey."

"I got none of that," Matt yelled back. He hesitated for a few moments, then asked: "Where is Tyree?"

"Matthew, how did you know it was that young feller what took me?" Festus asked.

"Saw his calling card on a tree back there. Where is he?"

"Gone, Matthew. He got on his hoss and took off when he saw you a-coming."

Matt stepped closer to the cave and looked up at the entrance. "Festus, this is a box canyon. He can't have gotten far."

"You're wrong about that, Matthew," Festus said.

"There's two ways out. You came in one of them and young Tyree left by t'other."

"Hold on. I'm coming up there," Matt yelled.

The marshal climbed into the cave. Festus, bound hand and foot, sat with his back against the rock wall. He looked tired and even hairier than usual, but as far as Matt cóuld tell, he was unhurt.

"Are you all right?" Matt asked.

The deputy nodded. "Sure. Young Tyree took real good care of me. I always had plenty of grub, that is if'n a man has a hankering for beans an' peaches."

Matt got his pocketknife and quickly cut the deputy free. Festus rose, rubbed his wrists, and his tongue touched his top lip. "You certain you didn't bring no whiskey, Matthew?" he asked. "I could sure use a snort or two about now."

Matt shook his head. "Sorry, Festus. I didn't bring a drop."

Disappointment clouded the deputy's face; then he smiled. "Well, anyhoo, thanks for finding me. It was sure lonesome here by times an' at night the canyon is right spooky, made me think of ha'ants an' sich, especially on account of how young Sean wore a black funeral cloak all the time." Festus shook his head. "That can clabber a man's blood, let me tell you."

Tyree had obviously left in a hurry. His coffeepot was still smoking on the coals of a small fire, and cans of food were stacked against the cave wall.

Matt found a cup and poured himself coffee. It was black and strong, the way he liked it, and he drank it gratefully.

"Tell me what happened, Festus," he said finally.

"Not much to tell, Matthew," the deputy answered, scratching a hairy cheek. "You recollect I left early in the morning to go dig out the widder Brady's well."

Matt nodded. "I talked to her. She says you're not afraid of hard work."

The deputy smiled and nodded. "Ain't that the honest truth. Anyhoo, after I got the well dug, I headed back to Dodge on account of how it was crowding up to dark, an' that's when I met young Tyree on the road.

" 'Howdy, Sean,' says I, and he says howdy right back, as nice as you please, Matthew. Then he draws his gun so fast I don't even see his hand move an' he buffaloes me. Hits me right acrost the side of my head. Next thing I know, I'm tied hand and foot over the rump of Tyree's hoss and he brings me here."

Matt poured himself more coffee, his face troubled. "I'm trying to figure out the why of all that, Festus. Tyree left a note on the saddle of your mule, told me to change my testimony at Cage Stucker's trial or he'd kill you. What did Tyree think he had to gain by helping Stucker get away with murder?"

Festus' eyebrow crawled up his forehead like a hairy caterpillar. "You mean, you ain't figured that out yet, Matthew?"

Matt shook his head. "That's why I'm asking you."

"Because ol' Sean didn't want Cage to hang. He wanted to execute them his ownself, with a six-gun an' up close and mighty personal like they done to Logan."

"And he did," Matt said, his voice as bitter as the dregs of coffee in his cup. "Tyree stepped into Ham Bell's saloon last night and shot down Cage and the three who were with him the night Logan St. Clair died."

Festus whistled between his teeth. "Now the fat's really in the fire. I bet right now Clint Stucker is out looking for that young man."

"He is, and Stucker says he plans to hang him." Matt's eyes searched Festus' face. "Do you think Tyree will light a shuck out of Kansas now Cage is dead?"

Festus shook his head. "Him? Not a chance. Tyree told me he still has a score to settle with Clint Stucker. I reckon he won't light out until Clint is six feet under like his son."

For a few minutes Matt squatted by the fire, deep in thought. The revenge Tyree was planning had something to do with the double eagle nailed to the cedar trunk. But how would he use the coin as a weapon against Stucker and his gunmen? Matt thought it through, but could not come up with an answer.

Finally, still baffled, he rose and doused the fire with the contents of the coffeepot, sending up a small cloud of hissing steam. "I guess we'd better head back to Dodge, Festus, and try keeping a lid on this thing before it blows."

The deputy's gun belt and Colt were stashed at the rear of the cave. Festus buckled the belt around his waist, a frown gathering between his eyebrows.

"Matt," he said, "I got to ask—did you change your testimony at Cage's trial?"

The marshal shook his head. "No, Festus, I didn't."

Festus considered Matt's answer for a couple of moments, then said, "You done right, Matthew."

"Tell that to Kitty," Matt said.

chapter 16

Dawn of the Gunfighters

Matt and Festus rode double into Dodge just as night was falling.

Festus was anxious to check on Ruth, so Matt rode directly to the livery stable. Festus fussed and fretted over the mule for a while, narrowly avoiding an ill-tempered kick for his pains; then he and Matt walked back to the marshal's office.

The saloons were crowded, and down by the railroad tracks, cattle were being loaded onto boxcars, their bawling and the pounding of hooves on wooden ramps loud enough to be heard all over town.

Although the usual laughter and the sound of jangling pianos drifted through the saloon doors, Matt sensed a tenseness in the air, as though the recent rash of killings was weighing heavy on the town. It seemed like Dodge was holding its breath, waiting to see what happened next.

As Matt and Festus reached the office, Clint Stucker's dust-covered posse came in from the plains. The seven men rode past in a sullen silence, every eye turned to Matt, hard and accusing, the warning plain.

Festus scratched his chin, thoughtfully watching Stucker and his tired riders tie up their mounts outside the Alhambra. "Matthew, I reckon those ol' boys ain't never gonna catch Sean Tyree if'n he don't want to be caught," he said.

"Maybe," Matt said. "But they'll widen their loop every day and pretty soon they're going to find Horse Thief Canyon."

"Could be," Festus said, a twinkle settling in his eyes. "And maybe that's exactly what Tyree is planning on."

As Stucker and his riders stomped into the Alhambra, Festus shifted his attention to the Long Branch, and Matt saw the whiskey hunger on his deputy's face.

Smiling, Matt dug into his pocket, found a dollar and spun it to Festus. "That will get you started. I have a feeling that Kitty's going to be so glad to see you, she'll supply the rest."

Festus grinned and touched the dollar to his hat. "I'm on my way, Matthew. If'n you need me, you'll know where to find me."

Matt watched Festus hurry across the street and step inside the saloon. Then he turned and walked into the office, sat at his desk and, as he'd done so many times recently, picked up his pen. It was time to take another stab at answering the governor's letter.

Matt had no sooner drawn a sheet of paper close to him than the door burst open and Festus stormed in, his face a stiff mask of worry.

"Matthew," he said, his voice tight and breathless, "I got news, all of it bad."

Matt laid down his pen and rose to his feet. If Festus had given up his whiskey to hurry back to the office, what he had to say must be important.

"Let me hear it," Matt said. "I'm kinda getting accustomed to bad news."

"Steve Jenness is in town," Festus said, laying it right on the line without any preamble. "And Nathan Price is with him. That's not all. I hear tell there's maybe three or four other strangers rode in today, none of them cowboys."

"Gunfighters?" Matt asked.

Festus nodded. "That's their stamp."

The marshal stood for a few moments, trying to absorb what Festus had told him. Of them all, Jenness was probably the most dangerous, by all accounts a skilled and deadly gunfighter who didn't know the meaning of fear. The gambler Nathan Price was no bargain either.

"Heard something else," Festus said.

Despite the worry nagging at him, Matt smiled. Festus was a man who kept his ear to the ground and Dodge could keep mighty few secrets from him.

"I heard," the deputy continued, taking Matt's silence for a go ahead, "Clint Stucker hasn't sold his herd yet, but he's losing big at the poker table. Doc Holliday is over to the Long Branch and he told me Stucker is gambling like a desperate man. But dang it all, the harder he tries to win, the more he loses. Doc says at that rate he'll go broke fast."

Matt nodded. "Doc should know."

The information Festus had brought about Stucker was interesting, but Matt tucked it away at the back of his mind. Steve Jenness and the others were a more immediate and pressing concern.

"Where are Jenness and Price?" Matt asked.

"Over to the Alamo," Festus answered. "Minding their own business, Doc says."

The Alamo was one of the quieter saloons in Dodge. It had no music or girls, but boasted a plush parlor furnished with deep leather chairs and sofas where a man could enjoy at his leisure fine cigars and the best whiskey and brandy in town.

Matt got his hat and settled it on his head. "I think I'll go have a talk with those two."

Festus took the Greener from the wall, broke it open, checked the loads and snapped the shotgun shut again. "I'm coming with you, Matthew," he said.

"Put the scattergun away, Festus." Matt smiled. "I said talk, not fight."

"But, Matthew . . ." The deputy's face revealed his concern.

Matt patted Festus on the shoulder. "Go back to the Long Branch and get your drink. I just plan on having a pleasant conversation with Steve Jenness."

"Matthew, are you sure?"

"I'm sure. Now go and have a little fun like I told you, Festus. You deserve it after being hog-tied in a cave for so long."

The deputy cast a last, longing glance at the Greener. "Well, if'n you're sure . . ."

"I'm sure." Matt grinned. "Now go."

When Matt walked into the Alamo, the bar was full, but there were no punchers in sight. The clientele was mostly businessmen from the other side of the tracks, cattle buyers and a few of the more prosperous ranchers. The parlor was separated from the bar by a wooden partition and Matt stepped toward it, nodding now and again to men he knew.

The marshal rounded the partition and there was no doubt that the two men sitting at a table, their backs to the wall, were Steve Jenness and Nathan Price.

Both were dressed in black broadcloth frockcoats of the best quality, spotless, boiled white shirts and string ties. Neither wore guns. The younger of the two—Matt guessed it was Price—sported the flowered vest of the professional gambler, and when he looked up at the tall marshal, his eyes suddenly became guarded and wary.

Matt stepped up to the table and looked down at the two men. "My name is Matt Dillon," he said. "I'm the city marshal of Dodge."

Jenness rose to his feet, extending his hand. "Marshal, your reputation precedes you, sir. My name is

Steve Jenness and this is my . . . uh . . . associate Nathan Price."

Matt took Jenness' hand. The man had a direct, open smile that hid nothing. Or so it seemed. Price was less direct, his startling blue eyes shifting from Matt's face to the star on his vest and back again.

Before he dropped Jenness' hand, the marshal took a few moments to study both men.

Jenness looked to be in his mid-forties; gray was showing in his black hair at the temples. He had hard golden brown eyes, high, wide cheekbones and a bronze cast to his skin. Matt suspected Jenness had Indian blood in him, maybe, judging by the high cheekbones, Comanche or Kiowa.

Nathan Price was a study in contrast. His hair was corn silk yellow, his eyes sky blue and penetrating. He looked like a man drawn in on himself, not one to easily reveal what he felt or thought.

Both men wore the full, sweeping mustaches then in fashion and both carried themselves well, confident, self-assured . . . but with a concealed undercurrent that Matt identified as an all too ready capacity for violence.

There was no doubt in the marshal's mind that both these men were dangerous, and when put to it, they'd be deadly—and almighty sudden.

Jenness graciously waved Matt into a chair, and when the marshal was seated, he asked: "Now how can we help you, Mr. Dillon?"

Matt pretended an apologetic smile. "Oh, just the usual questions I ask when I meet men of reputation like yourself and Mr. Price." He paused, his voice hardening a little. "Why are you in town and how long are you planning on staying?"

Jenness' laugh was genuine, his eyes shining with amusement. "Well, Marshal, you certainly are forthright." He glanced over at the stone-faced Price, then said: "We plan on paying our respects at the last resting place of our friend Logan St. Clair."

"And then?" Matt asked.

"Why then we'll drift." He turned to Nathan Price again. "There's nothing to keep us in Dodge City, or indeed in Kansas, is there, Mr. Price?"

Price shook his head, his eyes steady on Matt. "No, not a damn thing."

Matt knew he was getting less than the truth, but he had little reason to run these two gunfighters out of town. Visiting a friend's grave was hardly a crime.

"The cemetery is just to the north of town." Matt said. "As far as I know, there is no headstone." He paused, then said, "I guess Sean Tyree hasn't had time to put one up yet."

Matt waited to see Jenness' and Price's reactions to Tyree's name, but the faces of both men were poker-player blank, revealing nothing.

Jenness leaned over, picked up his glass and sipped his whiskey. He very carefully laid the glass back on the table, then said: "Logan set store by Sean Tyree. That young man is already rich, but he'll go far and make his mark one day." His fingers strayed to his cheek. "Great pity about the scar, though."

Matt had not gotten the reaction he was looking

for, so he changed the subject. "I guess you'll visit the cemetery tomorrow."

Jenness nodded. "Ah yes, tomorrow. Myself, Mr. Price and a few others. Then we'll bid your fair city adieu."

Matt rose to his feet, an imposing figure almost seven foot tall in his boots and hat, a strong, robust man, not easy to take down. "There's a train out at ten in the morning and an eastbound stage at noon. I'd appreciate it if you gentlemen catch one or the other."

Jenness nodded. "Your suggestion is most gracious, Marshal. And we'll give it our due consideration." The gunfighter's eyes, glowing like those of a hawk, found Matt's and locked on them. "Now is there anything else we can do for you?" He spread his hands, his voice apologetic. "As you can see, Mr. Price and I are at our cigars and brandy."

A strange sense of defeat pulling at him, Matt shook his head. "No, that's about all I want to say." He turned to step away, then stopped. "By the way, Mr. Jenness, when I talked about the train and stage, it wasn't a suggestion. It was an order." Matt touched the brim of his hat. "I'll bid you good night, gentlemen."

The marshal left the Alamo and walked back to his office.

He had laid it on the line for Jenness and Price, yet he had the feeling the gunfighters were determined to ignore his order to get out of town. And how many more named gunslingers were around? That was something he needed to find out and fast.

And there as one more thing, Matt decided.

Festus had been right—it was time to take the Greener down from the rack.

chapter 17

Grave Matters

Matt was awake well before dawn. He washed and shaved, then hurried to the livery stable, saddled his horse and rode though a dark, sleeping town.

After giving it some thought, Matt had left the shotgun behind, but he carried field glasses, dusty from lack of use, but important for what lay ahead.

Clint Stucker and his riders would be out on the plains soon, continuing their hunting for Sean Tyree, and Matt planned to keep them well away from Jenness, Price and the other gunfighters who had descended on Dodge.

If need be, he'd ride with Stucker to avoid a shooting war and trust that Jenness' professional courtesy—by long tradition extended from one gunfighter to another—embraced cowtown marshals and that the man would not mark him as a target.

Matt left the bay at the gates of the cemetery, where six other horses were already tied to the hitching rail.

It seemed the mourners had already gathered.

The marshal stepped through the gates and turned in the direction of St. Clair's grave. Darkness lay thick around him but a horned moon was nudging aside the last stars of night and the sky was brightening from black to cobalt blue. Out on the flat grass, a coyote yipped its hunger and the wind whispered among the branches of the oaks lining the path that led to St. Clair's grave.

Ahead of him, Matt caught the glow of an oil lamp and he left the path and walked toward the pinpoint of light, slipping the rawhide thong from the hammer of his Colt.

When he fetched up to the grave, six silent men stood around the newly turned earth, their heads bowed, an oil lamp guttering at their feet, flaring a shifting orange light on their pants and boots.

Jenness looked up when he saw Matt arrive, but no sign of recognition showed on the man's wide, cigar store Indian face and he bowed his head again.

Matt recognized Nathan Price, as immobile and still as a pillar of rock. Three of the other men he did not know, but a fourth, a young man of medium height with long jet-black hair hanging to his waist could be the Wyandotte Kid.

As Matt remembered, the Kid had an Irish miner father and a Wyandotte Indian mother. Like Steve Jenness, he'd been a hired gun in the murderous

Sutton-Taylor feud and had later drifted north into the Indian Territory, where he'd made a name for himself as a gunfighting deputy marshal for Judge Parker.

The Kid had recently killed a named gunman in Guthrie and had the reputation of being a dour, dangerous and difficult man to handle.

Matt looked around at the still, silent sentinels standing around the grave, the hollows of their eyes pools of darkness, and decided that Logan St. Clair had made some mighty unusual friends.

These men were not mourners in the accepted sense of the word—these were warriors paying their last respects to a fallen comrade they regarded as one of their own.

As the night began to die around him, shading toward a gray dawn, Matt saw that the six men were armed. All had guns belted around their hips except Price who preferred the gambler's mode of carry, a Smith & Wesson Shofield .45 in a shoulder holster of soft leather hanging under his left arm.

Suddenly wishful of the Greener standing oiled and ready in the rack at his office, the marshal thought briefly of hauling iron and ordering the mourners to drop their gun belts. But almost as soon as the thought entered his head, he dismissed it.

If all he'd heard about the Wyandotte Kid was true, the man was wild, reckless to the point of madness. He might just say the hell with it and draw. The fight would then become general and men would die. Matt figured he could shoot two or three of the gunfighters, but he too would be killed, and that would solve nothing and maybe make the situation a whole lot worse.

Trying to find a way out of his problem, Matt was about to tap Jenness on the shoulder and take the man aside, when he saw the Wyandotte Kid's hard black eyes slide to the dirt road that ran outside the cemetery gates.

Matt turned, following the Kid's fixed, malevolent stare. Clint Stucker and his gunmen were riding past, one of them with his hand to his mouth, stifling an early-morning yawn.

The Wyandotte Kid stepped around Matt and walked closer to the gate, his right thumb tucked inside his cartridge belt, close to his gun.

Johnny Lomax, riding in the lead beside Stucker, turned his head, saw the Kid and turned away. Then his head snapped back again, his body stiffening in stunned recognition.

The Kid had eyes only for Lomax. The two men glowered at each other as Stucker's cavalcade trotted past, as though both were reliving some ancient wrong. Lomax turned in the saddle, his hostile gaze still reaching out to the Kid. He remained like that, right hand supporting himself on the cantle of his saddle, until he reached a bend of the road and disappeared from sight.

Matt watched the dust kicked up by the riders settle, then glanced at the Kid. Lomax and the Wyandotte Kid knew each other. Maybe they'd fought on the same side in some forgotten range war or had clashed as enemies. However it had happened, the sight of the Kid had deeply disturbed Lomax, and he was not a man easily shaken.

Jenness and the others had also seen Stucker's men, and now they ended their vigil, Price hurriedly crossing himself. One by one, they stepped away from the grave.

Like Price, Jenness had swapped his broadcloth finery for nondescript range clothes: brown canvas pants, wide suspenders drawn up over a blue woolen shirt, spurred boots and a battered black hat. He wore a single holstered Colt, the hard rubber handle worn smooth from much use, and an identical revolver was shoved into his waistband.

Matt stepped in front of Jenness. "Now you've paid your respects, you'll remember what I told you about the train."

The marshal had laid it on the line, and the predatory, hawk eyes of Jenness revealed that he understood. "And like I told you, Marshal," he said. "I'll take it under advisement."

Gone was the gracious tone of last night, and in its place the gunfighter's voice was harsh and cold—the voice of a man who had made up his mind about what he planned to do and would not be turned from it.

Jenness brushed past Matt, but when the marshal loudly called his name, he stopped in his tracks.

The gunfighter turned slowly, his hand close to his Colt, and Matt said: "Jenness, leave Stucker alone. If you go after him, I'll stand in your way and stop you." He took a step closer to the man. "I plan to arrest Sean Tyree and the law will take it from there." Matt's voice softened just a little. "Don't you see it? With Sean in custody, he'll be safe from Stucker and his men."

Jenness thought that through. The Wyandotte Kid, his black eyes unreadable, stepped beside him. Finally Jenness said: "Sean will hang in this town."

Matt shook his head, a sense of urgency prodding him. "I doubt that. A jury could see it as a fair fight. After all, Tyree did give Cage Stucker a chance to draw. I can testify to that."

Jenness was unmoved, his face an expressionless mask, like a slab of carved mahogany. "Sean will hang in this town. One way or the other, by the law or by lynch law, he'll hang." The man paused for a couple of heartbeats, then said: "I don't intend to let that happen."

Desperately, Matt tried another tack. "Jenness, Cage Stucker is dead. The murder of Logan St. Clair has been avenged. Now it's time to let it go."

"The man who bred him, who made him what he was, still breathes," Jenness said. "I saw him ride past, and even from where I stood, I smelled the rotten stink of him." The gunfighter spoke without passion, an iciness in him. "Clint Stucker is the one who threw the double eagle on Sean Tyree's bed as the boy lay close to death. He has yet to atone for that." Jenness traced a line down his left cheek with his forefinger, his thick nail pressing hard, leaving a livid welt. "There are scars that never heal."

Matt stood, facing the gunfighters who crowded around him, confused memories of blood, bullets and buckskin spinning around in his head. He was all out of words, and even if he could hunt down more, Steve Jenness and the others would not listen to them.

In the end, Matt stepped aside and let Jenness and the others go to their horses. He watched them ride out, heading due north, away from the direction taken by Stucker and his gunmen.

Matt walked to his bay and stroked the horse's head. "Well, Buck, I did my talking and now it's all done and it didn't do one bit of good." He smiled. "What do I do now, boy, huh? What do I do now?"

The big horse shook his head, jangling his bit, and Matt laughed. "As uncertain as I am, aren't you, Buck, big feller?"

The laughter quickly fled from the marshal's eyes and burned out on his lips. He swung into the saddle. Even though his authority ended at the city limits, he could do no good hanging around Dodge. Out there, on the flat grassland, was where the trouble was brewing and that was where he had to be.

Matt Dillon rode out after Stucker, for the first time in his life feeling alone . . . and vulnerable.

chapter 18

Blood on the Long Grass

Matt rode through the dawning morning, the sky above him pale blue, streaked with red and gold. The recent rain had brought new life to the prairie and thick carpets of pink and yellow wild-flowers spread out in every direction, nodding to one another like polite dowagers in the breeze.

Stucker and his riders had left a trail across the grass that was easy to follow and Matt stopped now and then to check the land around him with his field glasses. Once, to his south, he saw a small herd of antelope grazing along the rim of a buffalo wallow and when he was still a couple of miles east of Saw Log Creek the high-strung bay reared as a jackrabbit jumped up between his legs and zigzagged away in panic.

Stucker was heading due east, but after his tracks

crossed Saw Log, they took a swing to the north, heading toward the rolling country around the south fork of Buckner Creek.

Matt followed, passing an isolated farm, where a faded woman in a faded dress stood at the door of her cabin, dull-eyed and unsmiling. Matt waved as he rode by but the woman ignored him, then turned on her heel and stepped back inside.

This time better prepared for a long ride, the marshal chewed on a strip of the beef jerky he'd packed in his saddlebags, his glasses to his eyes, wondering at Stucker's movements.

The horse tracks scarring the grass curved toward Buckner, and just three miles beyond lay Horse Thief Canyon. Had Stucker, or maybe the shrewd Johnny Lomax, worked out Sean Tyree's location, the only logical hiding place in a flat, featureless sea of grass?

Matt swept the land around him with the field glasses. He saw no sign of Jenness and the other gunfighters, though once he thought he saw dust rise to his east, just a fleeting glimpse before it was gone.

Antelope, he told himself, or maybe a big buck deer on the move.

When he reached Buckner, the muddy bank was churned up where Stucker and his men had stopped to water their horses. The tracks then led out of the creek and headed northeast, angling directly toward the canyon.

A sense of urgency prodding him, Matt chewed down some jerky and followed Stucker's tracks. He cleared the creek, headed out onto the flat and spurred the bay into a run, so close now he could see and taste the dust kicked up by the horses of the riders ahead of him.

He rode past a sharp bend on the Buckner, a wider stretch of the creek lined with cottonwood and willow, and followed as the tracks ahead swung sharply to the north. Now there was no doubt in Matt's mind—Stucker was headed directly for Horse Thief Canyon.

But Clint Stucker never reached it. Not that day.

As the first rattle of gunfire echoed across the prairie, Matt reined in his horse hard and the big bay, unused to such treatment, reared and angrily tossed his head. A thick cloud of dust kicked up from the horse's prancing hooves as a second drumbeat thunder of gunfire shattered the hushed silence of the plains.

Fighting his rearing horse, Matt reached under his knee and yanked the Winchester from the scabbard. After a few moments he got the bay settled down, then spurred in the direction of the guns.

Matt's view of what was happening ahead had been blocked by a stretch of bluestem standing almost six foot high. He charged through the long grass, the long stems whipping at him—and rode into a scene of carnage.

Two of Stucker's riders were down, their blood staining the grass, and a third swayed in the saddle, ashen with shock, scarlet spreading wet and thick over the left shoulder of his shirt.

Johnny Lomax was in the saddle rapidly levering

and shooting his rifle, but looking beyond the man, Matt could see no target. Clint Stucker sat his horse off to one side, his face strained and unbelieving, a smoking Colt in his hand.

Matt slowed his horse, set his rifle upright on his thigh and rode to Stucker.

"What happened here?" he asked.

Lomax had stopped shooting and he rode alongside Stucker. "What happened? Man, can't you see what happened? We were bushwhacked." Lomax pointed out a slight rise about fifty yards away. "They were up there, hidden by the grass, and when we got close, they cut loose on us."

Stucker was silent, looking around him, his eyes wild, trying to comprehend what had just happened.

Apart from Lomax, only two of Stucker's men were unhurt. The gunmen sat their horses close together, looking just as bewildered as Stucker, but considerably more scared.

"Who were they?" Matt asked. "Did you see them?"

"I sure saw one of them," Lomax said. "There's no mistaking that long hair. It was the Wyandotte Kid." The gunman spat. "I should have gunned that damn half-breed a long time ago."

Stucker looked at Matt, blinking, like a man coming out of a sleep. "Dillon, was this any of your doing?" he asked.

"None of my doing," the marshal answered. "I'd hoped to prevent this."

Lomax's face twisted into a sneer. "Seems to me

you were right cozy with the Kid and Steve Jenness and them this morning. Dillon, I'm calling you a damned liar."

Matt's anger flared, but his voice was even as he said: "Lomax, when you call a man a liar, you better stand ready to back it up."

The gunman's eyes narrowed, his teeth drawn back from his thin lips, wanting to draw real bad. But Matt's rifle was pointed right at his belly and it took some of the fight out of him. "Not now, Dillon," he said finally, his fast breath slowly settling. "I'll back it up some other time."

"Damn you, Lomax," Matt yelled, his already overstretched patience snapping. "Let me see you back it up now."

"Johnny!" Stucker quickly rode between Matt and Lomax. "Let it go. I can't afford more dead men, not today." He turned to Matt. "Johnny didn't mean nothing by that. We're all on edge and men say things they don't mean when they're on edge."

Matt eased back, his flaming anger settling down to a red-hot smolder. He nodded toward Lomax. "Let me hear him say it."

The gunman's face was defiant, his tense body primed and ready, but Stucker, seeing it, spun on Lomax, the harsh, commanding tone of his voice leaving no room for argument.

"Say it, Johnny. It's only words and words don't matter a damn."

Lomax stiffened. He shook his head, his snake eyes on Matt like those of a cobra ready to strike.

The gunman was very close to the draw, a fact not

lost on Stucker. The rancher's gun swung up, steady on Lomax's chest. "Say it, Johnny, or by God I'll kill you my ownself." His tone became softer, wheedling. "It's words, Johnny. Only words."

Lomax thought it through for a few long seconds; then the hell slowly left his eyes and the fires burned down. "I didn't mean nothing by it," he said, a hesitant, reluctant whisper.

"See," Stucker said to Matt, "Johnny didn't mean nothing by it." His eyes met the marshal's. "Now who were those bushwhackers? I want names."

"No names, Stucker," Matt said, a twinge of meanness curling sharp in his gut. "But I will tell you that all of them are good friends of Sean Tyree."

Stucker looked like he'd been slapped. He opened his mouth to speak, shut it, then spun angrily on his remaining riders. "You two put Jed and Frank on their horses. We'll take our dead back to Dodge."

One of the men kneed his horse close to Stucker. "We'll do as you say, Mr. Stucker, but when we get to Dodge we want to draw our time."

"You're yellow, Wilson," Lomax hissed between clenched teeth. "You and Simms over there, plumb yellow."

The man called Wilson nodded, his face relaxed. "You could say that, Johnny, but it was Steve Jenness standing by that grave this morning and no mistake. Me and Simms want no part of him. I saw Jenness kill a man in Lampasas one time and he's pure poison."

"Hell, I'll take care of Jenness," Lomax said. "Then he won't be around to scare you no more."

Wilson was as calm as before. "Maybe you can take him, Johnny, maybe you can't. But me and Simms don't plan on sticking around long enough to find out, not after what happened here today."

"Then go and be damned to ye," Stucker yelled. "When we get back to Dodge, I'll pay you what's owed. Then get the hell out of my sight."

Later Matt drew his bay aside as Stucker led out his dead. Two men lay facedown over their horses and the wounded man swayed in the saddle, his face gray from shock and pain.

Johnny Lomax took up the rear and he turned to Matt as he left, his pale blue eyes full of malice and hate—the eyes of a born killer and a dangerous, unforgiving enemy.

After Stucker's melancholy cavalcade was gone, their dust drifting in the breeze, Matt rode to the top of the rise, where the Wyandotte Kid, Jenness and the others had lain in wait. There were empty cartridge cases scattered around and a half-smoked cigar. But when Matt raised his glasses to his eyes and swept the plains stretching away from him, he saw nothing.

It was as though the gunfighters had vanished off the face of the Earth. Matt reached behind him, fumbled around in his saddlebags and found another strip of jerky. He chewed thoughtfully, his attention on Stucker.

The rancher had been leading his men when Jenness and the others opened up on them. Stucker was a big man, out in front and an easy target. Yet not a single bullet had even come near him. Jenness and the others were expert marksmen, unlikely to pass on an opportunity like that.

Unless—Matt nodded to himself—unless Stucker had not been hit because Jenness wanted him to remain alive.

The question was why.

The marshal looked up at the sun-seared, bright blue bowl of the sky, all shadow of the night gone as if the darkness had never been.

Matt found no answer to his question writ large across the sky. But this he knew: Stucker was not bulletproof, so it seemed that Sean Tyree was planning a different fate for the rancher, something far worse than death itself.

Matt had no idea what that fate might be.

But right now he would not want to be walking in Clint Stucker's boots.

Matt rode north toward Horse Thief Canyon, his Winchester ready across the saddle horn.

The sun was at its highest point in the sky and around him bees hummed among the wildflowers—a lazy, drowsy drone that Matt did not allow to distract him from his watchfulness.

Ahead of him the canyon was bathed in sunlight, few shadows showing on its craggy walls. As far as Matt could tell, the place was deserted. And this opinion was confirmed when he saw a small whitetail doe stop warily at the canyon entrance, then, gaining confidence, trot inside.

Matt sat his horse, his glasses sweeping the canyon. First he scanned the sheer walls before moving down to the entrance, where his search lingered. Nothing stirred, and the doe had not come out again.

A lifting breeze sent a cool shaft of air through the heavy heat of the afternoon as Matt took the glasses from his eyes and kneed the bay forward at a walk.

He dismounted when he was still a hundred yards from the canyon and went the rest of the way on foot, taking advantage of every scrap of cover he could find.

The canyon lay silent, keeping its secrets.

But one thing was different from before.

Matt stepped to the red cedar by the entrance and looked over its trunk. The double eagle was gone, and only a narrow hole remained in the bark where the nail had been.

Matt lowered his rifle, thinking it through.

Sean Tyree had removed the gold piece, and that could mean only one thing—the young man felt the final reckoning was near.

Tyree had already planned his showdown with Clint Stucker, and it was coming very soon.

Matt shook his head, a coldness in his belly. However all this ended, he knew the last chapter could only be written in the blood of dead men.

chapter 19

A Gathering of Evil

The next seven days passed without incident, and Matt was kept busy with town business.

Down by the loading pens, a cowboy was gored in the belly by a longhorn and was taken to Fort Dodge to be treated by an army doctor, though there was little hope that the man would live. Another cowboy got drunk in the Long Branch and then decided to shoot up the moon. Matt arrested the man, and the next day, contrite and suffering from a massive hangover, the puncher was fined two dollars and thirty cents in costs for disturbing the peace. A couple of drummers got into a fistfight over the charms of a woman at the Alhambra. Matt banged their heads together, ending the scuffle, but made no arrests.

On the morning of the seventh day there was an Indian scare.

A fat farmer and his even more enormously fat and perspiring wife rode into town, several arrows sticking out the back of their wagon. The couple yelled to everyone who would listen that a hundred wild Cheyenne were after their scalps.

Matt did a little detective work and traced the "Indian attack" to a prank by the Masterson boys and Doc Holliday. He warned the contrite practical jokers that any repeat would see them on the next stage out of town, and all fervently promised to change their wicked ways.

Then, later that afternoon, Festus brought much more serious news. Clint Stucker was hiring guns.

"Matthew, he's signed up maybe three dozen already, and him and Johnny Lomax are looking for more," Festus said, his eyes troubled.

Matt was irritated. "Where is he finding these men? Who are they?"

Festus breathlessly rattled off some names, and Matt grew more irritated by the moment.

None of the men Festus mentioned were gunfighters. They were some of the no-account border trash who migrated up from Texas every year with the herds, dance hall loungers, saloon scroungers and billy-club artists who prowled the dark alleys with rats' eyes, preying on drunks. All were work-shy but willing enough to cut any man, woman or child in half with a shotgun for fifty dollars.

Matt shook his head. "Stucker thinks that riffraff will stand against Sean Tyree and Steve Jenness and the rest?"

Festus scratched his cheek. "Well, Matthew, ol'

Clint is keeping them boys well likkered up and he's feeding them right. Got girls off the line visiting their camp most nights too. I reckon he feels what his men lack in quality, they'll make up for in numbers. There is a right passel o' them, and who knows? With enough whiskey in them, they jes' might fight."

Festus frowned; then his face cleared and he said: "Oh yeah, an' I almost forgot. Stucker has offered a bonus of five double eagles to the man who brings him Sean Tyree's head."

"Where are they?" Matt asked, an unfocused anger growing in him.

"A mile or so east of town," Festus answered. "They're camped on the south fork of Duck Creek. Got tents an' cooks an' all sorts of home comforts."

Matt was silent for a few moments, his mind busy. Moving his men outside of Dodge had been a shrewd move on Stucker's part. Matt had no authority to ride out to the creek and order them to disband—that was a job for a United States marshal. But it would take at least a week for the marshal to wrap up his existing business and make the trip to Dodge—and by that time, it could be all over.

"What you plan to do, Matthew?" Festus asked. He stepped over to the coffeepot and hefted it, and his face fell at its lightness.

Matt shook his head. "Right now, I have no idea. Stucker's men are camped outside of Dodge. Unless they ride into town, I have no authority over them."

"Maybe you could ask the army," Festus suggested.

The big marshal shook his head. "The army has

enough problems of its own and it's stretched pretty thin trying to herd the Cheyenne onto reservations. All I'd get is a polite listen and an equally polite no."

Matt rose from his desk. "Still, I think I'll ride out to the creek and look over the camp, see what Stucker is up to."

"I'll ride with you, Matthew," Festus said. "Like I tole you, those boys are likkered up most of the day an' they could get into all kinds of deviltry."

Stepping to his desk, Matt showed Festus the field glasses. "I'm going to take a look from a safe distance, Festus. Best you stay here in town and keep an eye on things."

Festus nodded. "Whatever you say, Matthew. But you step right careful out there. Them boys could devil you, sure enough."

"I'll be real careful, Festus." He stepped to the gun rack, strapped on his Colt, then settled his hat on his head. "Why don't you bile us up some coffee? I'll need some when I get back."

Matt rode out of Dodge, then swung east toward Stucker's camp. The sun was dropping lower in the sky, but the day was still bright and hot.

He rode to the creek and left his horse on a patch of good grass in the shade of a large cottonwood. Matt slid his Winchester from the boot, hung the field glasses around his neck, then walked along the bank, his eyes searching the way ahead for the Stucker camp.

After a few minutes he found it, at a sharp bend of the creek, where the Cheyenne had camped a time or two years before. Matt stepped into a clump of high grass and got down on one knee, pushing the stems aside to clear his view. The camp was sprawled along the opposite bank of the creek, about two hundred yards away, a scattered collection of tents and lean-tos. Men constantly moved between them. A dozen horses were tethered at the western end of the camp, along with several buckboards. Few of Stucker's rabble owned a horse, and it seemed that the rancher planned to mount them in wagons when he moved against Tyree.

Matt put the glasses to his eyes and scanned the camp more closely. Festus had been right. Stucker had a lot of men, maybe fifty or more. From what Matt could see, they looked like a shabby, dirty, down-at-heel lot—a bunch of worthless scum gathered from the dingiest corners of Dodge, not one real fighting man among them.

Despite the heat of the day, the men were grouped around fires, passing jugs among them. A fiddler was playing somewhere, and now and again Matt heard one of the men at the fires let out with a drunken laugh.

Matt adjusted the focus on the glasses, bringing Stucker's men into sharper view. All wore belt guns and by most of them rifles lay on the grass ready to hand.

On an individual basis, such men would not stand a chance against Tyree, Jenness, Price, the Wyandotte Kid or any one of the other gunfighters. But together, by force of sheer numbers, they could overwhelm them—especially if they caught Tyree's men strung out on the open plains.

Matt had learned all he could and was about to back out of his hiding place when he saw Stucker and Johnny Lomax ride in from the west, a heavily loaded spring wagon following them.

As Stucker and Lomax sat their horses, a few of their men rose up from the fires and began to unload the wagon, cheering as they found sides of bacon, canned goods and jugs of whiskey.

Matt put the glasses to his eyes again. When the wagon was unloaded, Stucker waved his arms, gathering his men around him. Stucker spoke in a normal tone and he was too far away for Matt to hear what he was saying, but the rancher's actions spoke louder than words.

He took a small canvas bag out of his pocket, opened it and poured coins into his hands: five double eagles, as far as Matt could make out. Another cheer went up from the crowd and Stucker accepted a jug from one of the men. He put the jug to his mouth and swallowed, his Adam's apple bobbing. Then he held the whiskey aloft in triumph. There was another burst of cheering and Stucker said something to Lomax. The gunman nodded and grinned beside him.

Stucker had shown his border trash their blood money and now every one of them was hungry for his gold. For such men, back shooting a man and cutting off his head was a much easier way to make a hundred dollars than working for it.

A slow anger building in him, Matt looked down at the star pinned to his vest. Out here, beyond the city limits of Dodge, he was not a lawman, just a private citizen.

The big marshal nodded, smiling grimly to himself. Then so be it. He unpinned the star from his vest and carefully placed it in his pocket.

Across the creek, Stucker's mob was again squatting around the fires, and whiskey jugs were passing from hand to hand. Men laughed and yelled to one another, loudly boasting how they'd be the ones to bring in Sean Tyree's head on a stick.

Matt raised the Winchester to his shoulder, his smile widening into a grin. It was high time the smug trash over there learned what it was like to be in a real shooting war.

The marshal sighted on the nearest fire, then moved his aim to the coffeepot smoking on the coals. He squeezed off a shot and the pot spiraled high in the air, scattering boiling coffee and red-hot ashes in every direction.

The men around the fire yelled and jumped to their feet, frantically brushing burning coals off their clothes. Matt sighted on another fire and shot again. He cranked off round after round, throwing up glowing coals and cartwheeling coffee- and stew pots, scalding hot liquid splashing on unprotected faces and hands. Men were running aimlessly in all directions, bumping into one another, tripping over their own feet. It looked to Matt like he'd just kicked over an ants' nest. A few were firing their guns, shooting into the air mostly, their faces scared and confused.

Johnny Lomax rode among them, swinging his

coiled rope at heads and shoulders, yelling in fury, his face dark purple.

Matt's grin widened. He aimed between the front legs of Lomax's horse and fired. A brief plume of dirt kicked up between the horse's hooves and the animal reared, tossing Lomax over its rump. The gunman hit the ground hard in a cloud of dust, then rose, his face even darker. He roared at his panicked men and lashed out with the rope again. Stucker, yelling something, rode among the panicked mob, trying to restore some order, but without success.

Matt lowered his rifle, threw back his head and laughed. Now Clint Stucker knew exactly what kind of army he'd hired, and by this time the man must be sick to his stomach wondering how this disorganized mob would stack up against Tyree and his professional gunfighters.

Figuring he'd had enough fun for one day, the marshal silently backed out of the long grass and quickly made his way to his horse. He stepped into the saddle, pinned his star on his vest and headed back to Dodge, his thoughts on Sean Tyree.

Matt considered it his bounden duty to arrest Tyree and have him stand trial for the killing of Cage Stucker and three others. There was no right or wrong to the thing. Tyree's guilt or innocence was for a judge and jury to decide.

As he rode, the afternoon shading around him into evening, Matt told himself this was the only reason he was determined to stop Clint Stucker.

Yet, even as he gave thought to that statement, he knew it was not completely true.

The truth was that he liked Tyree. He'd seen him savagely bullwhipped in the street, his face horribly scarred, and then further humiliated by Clint Stucker, who had put the value of his life at twenty dollars.

But Tyree had overcome it all and made his mark. He'd returned to Dodge rich—a young man who had traveled far and successfully moved among men and manners that he might have once considered well above his station.

Tyree displayed almost reckless courage and a fine loyalty to the memory of the friend who had taught him how to make his way in the world. He had kidnapped Festus—that was true—but he'd not mistreated the deputy and, in fact, had showed him a deal of consideration and kindness. To let such a man be slaughtered by Stucker's rabble was unthinkable, and Matt knew he could not stand idly by and let it happen.

Clint Stucker had to be stopped. But the question was how.

chapter 20

Matt Evens a Score

The hands on the clock on Matt's office wall were joined at midnight. Matt rose from his desk, yawned and stretched, then found his hat. It was time to take a stroll along roaring Front Street and check on the saloons and see that the boisterous Masterson brothers were behaving themselves over at the Comique, where Eddie Foy and the beautiful Fannie Garretson were performing.

On Mayor Kelley's orders, Festus had left for the more sedate Front Street across the tracks, Dodge being the only town in the West that had two streets by the same name, one wild, the other not.

Strangely, the deputy had made no complaint. Matt suspected that Festus spent more time in lace-curtained parlors, entertaining the ladies with his tales of derring-do while enjoying their excellent bourbon, than he did alertly patrolling for malefactors.

Matt adjusted his gun belt around his hips and stepped outside. He glanced over at the Long Branch. He'd strolled through the saloon a couple of times recently, but Kitty had studiously ignored him, refusing to look up when he passed, her long eyelashes lying stubbornly on her cheekbones. Not caring to face that humiliation again, Matt turned briskly toward the Alhambra, his spurs ringing on the boardwalk with every step.

A few minutes later, the marshal stepped out of the Alhambra and turned back toward the Alamo, under a sky ablaze with stars. He was passing the Wright, Beverley and Company general store when the huge window suddenly exploded into a million shards of shattered glass.

Matt crouched and swung toward the sound of the shotgun blast, his Colt coming up fast, the falling glass still tinkling around him. The scattergun flared orange again from the dark depths of an alley opposite and the boardwalk at the marshal's feet splintered, buckshot whining past his ankles.

Matt fired at the gun flash, heard a surprised yelp of pain and fired again. Feet pounded in the alley between the Cattleman's Bank and a rod and gun store and the marshal sprinted across the street.

Only a fool would run into a dark alley where a man with a shotgun was lurking. Matt reached the alley and jumped to one side onto the boardwalk behind the sheltering corner of the bank building, just as another round of buckshot whistled in his direction.

The big marshal waited until he heard the metallic click of a shotgun opening. He jumped off the boardwalk, thumbed off a couple of quick rounds, heard a gasp from deep in the alley, then hopped back to shelter again.

Quickly, Matt shucked the empty shells from the Colt and reloaded from his cartridge belt. His gun held high, hammer back and ready, he looked around the corner of the building. Nothing stirred in the darkness.

Behind him, Matt heard running footsteps as men spilled out of nearby saloons to find out what was happening, a few soused roosters loudly demanding to be allowed to join in the fun. The marshal waved the men back, then jumped silently off the boardwalk and stepped slowly into the alley, crouched and wary, his gun out in front of him.

After a half dozen steps, he almost stumbled over a sprawled body. Matt turned and yelled: "One of you men, bring a lamp."

After a few moments a man returned with a glowing oil lamp and Matt held it high. A pool of yellow light splashed over the body of a youngster in a plaid shirt and denim overalls, down-at-heel work boots on his splayed feet.

The dead man's eyes were wide-open, staring into the darkness. He looked to be in his early twenties: a freckled carrot head with the smell of the pig farm still on him.

Matt turned to the crowd gathered around him. "Anybody know this man?" he asked.

A bystander with a short gray beard and wearing

the canvas pants and striped shirt of a railroad engineer stepped closer and peered down at the body. He nodded. "I don't know his name, but I've seen him before. He come into town about a week ago and he's been swamping over to Frank O'Hara's saloon. That is, when he wasn't cadging drinks and trying to get free ones from the ladies."

Matt gave the lamp to the railroader and kneeled by the body. The bushwhacker had taken two bullets, one in the shoulder and a second in the center of his chest. Quickly the marshal went through the pockets of the man's overalls. He found ten new silver dollars and something else—a round brass token.

Matt turned to the engineer. "Bring the lamp closer." He held the token up to the light. Crudely engraved on one side was, FRANK O'HARA'S SALOON AND GAMBLING EMPORIUM; on the other was GOOD FOR ONE $2 LAY.

His head bowed in thought, Matt continued to kneel by the dead farmboy. He stretched and picked up the shotgun and turned it over in his hands. As he'd expected, scratched into the walnut stock of the gun were the initials, F. O'H. Suddenly things began to fall in place for Matt Dillon.

First Tam Elliot, one of Stucker's gunmen, had tried to kill him while he was picnicking with Kitty. He'd blamed Stucker, but the rancher's denial was genuine and it was plain that Elliot had been paid by someone else.

And now this.

Ten dollars was a lot of money to a rube just off the farm, and the token for a pretty girl in a silk dress had sweetened the pot. Some men would kill for a lot less.

Matt shook his head, anger growing in him. He'd threatened to shut down O'Hara because the man was running crooked tables, and it looked like since then the saloonkeeper had borne him a grudge.

The marshal remembered O'Hara's eyes, cold, unblinking, without conscience, like those of a lizard. If such a man harbored a grudge, he would pay other men to even the score for him—and to O'Hara, evening the score meant murder.

Tam Elliot had failed and Matt had killed him. Now this farmboy was dead, maybe too nervous, too scared and too green to shoot his gun straight.

Matt rose to his feet, his face a stiff, furious mask. He had business with Frank O'Hara. It was time to even some scores of his own.

The big marshal, his anger a cold, growing thing, walked purposefully up the middle of Front Street, carrying O'Hara's shotgun, an excited, chattering crowd following at his heels.

When he reached O'Hara's, Matt barged inside. He stepped quickly to the roulette table, brushed the patrons aside and tipped over the table. The wheel crashed to the floor and chips and money scattered and rolled across the rough pine floorboards. Matt stepped from table to table, tipping each one on end. Alarmed cowboys and gamblers sprang out of his way.

A pale gambler in a gray frockcoat stepped in front of Matt and reached for a gun. The marshal's fist crashed into the man's chin and the gambler dropped like he'd been pole-axed, his knees suddenly turned to rubber. A girl screamed and frightened patrons began a rush for the door.

"This saloon is now closed," Matt yelled above the din. "And it won't reopen."

Frank O'Hara, in shirtsleeves, his face livid, stomped down the stairs from the whores' cribs on the top floor. The man wore a Colt in a shoulder holster and the word around Dodge was that he'd used the gun to good effect on many occasions in the past.

Matt looked over, saw O'Hara and said: "You're through in Dodge, O'Hara. I want you out of town now."

"The hell you say," the saloonkeeper yelled truculently, his eyes ugly. "I'm staying right where I am."

"The man you sent to bushwhack me is dead," Matt said. He threw the shotgun at O'Hara's feet; the gun bounced loud on the floor. "I think that's yours."

For a few moments, O'Hara looked like a trapped rat. Then a smile split his round, fiery red face and he said: "You can't prove a damn thing, Dillon. The rube stole this gun. I don't know why he tried to kill you. Maybe he didn't like lawmen."

"And what about Tam Elliot?" Matt asked. "I guess he didn't like lawmen either."

That stung, and it showed on O'Hara. The man looked beyond Matt, at the gawking crowd that had piled in the door, and he touched his tongue to suddenly dry lips.

"I don't know what you're talking—" His voice broke off and he drew.

Matt's draw was smoother and a lot faster. His first shot broke O'Hara's right elbow and the man half turned away from him. Matt fired again, notching a half moon out of O'Hara's left ear. He fired again and blood blossomed sudden and scarlet on the saloonkeeper's remaining ear.

O'Hara screamed and dropped his gun like it was suddenly red hot. "I'm done!" he yelled. "I'm out of it."

Matt took a step toward the man, his blue eyes merciless, shading to an icy gray.

Matt motioned with his Colt. "Move," he said.

"Where?" O'Hara asked, blood running from his ears over his shoulders, his broken arm hanging loose at his side.

"To the livery stable," Matt said. "You get on your horse and ride, and if I ever see you in Dodge again, I'll kill you."

O'Hara put his hands to his shot-up ears and winced. "I need to see a doctor and get my stuff," he whined. "You can't send me away with nothing and all shot to pieces."

"Yes, I can," Matt said, no give in him. "You're a yellow-bellied tinhorn, O'Hara, and you paid other men to do your dirty work. You go now, with only the clothes on your back."

"But I'll bleed to death out there. I can't—"

Matt fired, the bullet splintering the pine between O'Hara's feet. The man squealed and jumped back, his face white. "I'll go, I'll go," he said. "Please don't kill me."

"The livery stable," Matt said.

The big marshal led O'Hara out of his place at gunpoint. The huge crowd that had gathered jeered the saloon keeper, glad that he'd gotten his comeuppance because his crooked ways were known to everyone.

Matt waited until O'Hara awkwardly saddled his horse and just as awkwardly swung into the leather.

"Now you git," the marshal said. "And don't even think of coming back to Dodge."

O'Hara threw Matt a single, venomous look, then kicked his mount into a run. He dodged most of the rocks and clods of dirt the jeering crowd threw at him, and was soon swallowed by the night.

Matt stepped beside the crowd and slipped his watch from his vest pocket. He consulted the time, then waved an arm in the direction of O'Hara's saloon. "I'm reopening O'Hara's for the next two hours," he said. "All drinks are on the house."

The crowd cheered, then stampeded toward Front Street and Matt watched them go. He stood alone for a while, slowly shaking his head.

He had eliminated one problem . . . but a bigger problem still faced him. Getting rid of Clint Stucker would not be as easy.

chapter 21

Stucker Plays a Waiting Game

The morning after his run-in with Frank O'Hara, Matt called Festus into his office.

"I want you to ride out to Duck Creek and keep an eye on that rabble Stucker calls a posse," the marshal said. "If they make any kind of move, hightail it back here and let me know."

Festus nodded, scratching his hairy cheek. "I sure will, Matthew. I'll saddle up Ruth and head out right now."

Opening a drawer, Matt found his field glasses and passed them to his deputy. "Take these. I don't want you getting too close to Stucker's men. They're the kind that would cut your throat for five dollars."

"Not all of them, Matthew," Festus said, his eyes suddenly guarded.

"How do you mean?"

"John Mattingly and Yant McCanles have joined up with Stucker. They say he has a legal right to arrest the man who killed his son."

"Arrest? Is that what Stucker told them?"

"That's the word they used to me," Festus said. "Yup, *arrest* is what they said all right, Matthew."

Matt knew Mattingly and McCanles. Both were solid, respectable ranchers, neighbors of Stucker's back in Texas. Stucker had obviously sold them a bill of goods, enlisting their support by telling them he wanted only to arrest Tyree, not kill him. Neither man would have supported Stucker if they knew he had murder on his mind and had offered a hundred dollars for the young man's head.

John Mattingly and Yant McCanles had ridden with Quantrell during the War Between the States and had later fought Apaches down along the Brazos River country. They were no bargain in a fight, and guns to be reckoned with.

"Anyone else?" Matt asked, feeling oddly depressed.

Festus shook his head. "No, just them two."

"They're enough," Matt said. He slapped Festus on the shoulder. "Better get going and check on that rabble out there on the creek."

The deputy turned to leave, then stopped at the door. "Matthew," he said, hopping from one foot to the other, his embarrassment plain, "this is none of my business, you understand, but something happened between you and Kitty, and ever since then, that lady hasn't been the same. She a-snapping at folks an' moping around the Long Branch. An' I reckon she's off her feed on account of how pale she is an' all."

"We had a disagreement, Festus," Matt said, wanting to end it. "I reckon we'll get together again when Kitty cools down."

"Well, I sure wish you two would, Matthew," Festus said, a frown gathering between his eyebrows. "Miss Kitty has such an overdose of woe, she hasn't given me a free drink in days, or one of them Havana ceegars neither."

The deputy left a couple of moments later and Matt made up his mind to reply to the governor's letter.

Matt picked up his pen and found a fresh sheet of paper. He dipped the pen in the inkwell and laboriously wrote: *DEAR GOVERNOR.*

The big marshal nodded. Well, it was a fair start and he'd finish the rest later. He carefully picked up the paper and slid it into a desk drawer.

He didn't feel much like writing anyway, with Kitty very much on his mind. Was Festus right? Did Kitty have an overdose of woe, like he said?

It hadn't seemed that way the last few times he'd walked into the Long Branch and she'd studiously ignored him. Or was that just the way of womenfolk? Matt sighed. He was no expert on females and Kitty stumped him more than most.

There was one way to find out. He rose halfway out of his chair, the thought in his mind to step over to the Long Branch and apologize for whatever Kitty said he'd done. But slowly he sank into his seat again. What if she turned her back with that little flounce thing she did so well and ignored him? That would be a fine howdy-do. He'd be standing there in the middle of the saloon, feeling like a fool, with his face on fire and everybody watching him.

No, there had to be some other way . . . and the solution would come to him by and by.

Or at least he hoped it would.

Festus rode in just after nightfall and reported that Stucker's men were still camped on the creek.

"They didn't make a move the whole day," the deputy said, a puzzled frown on his face. "They just sat around drinking, and then close to dark, Stucker and Lomax brought in a wagon load of girls off the line. After that, I couldn't see no more." The deputy's smile was thin. "After that, I didn't want to see no more."

Matt shook his head, his own puzzlement growing. "What is Stucker waiting for, Festus? He's got all the men he needs. By this time he should be out searching for Tyree and the others."

The deputy shrugged. "Beats me, Matthew, because I never saw nor heard tell of the like. I've been trying, but I can't seem to dab a loop on a notion about what ol' Clint is up to."

Matt thought it through, trying to find an answer. Finally he gave up and said: "Looking on the positive side, so long as Stucker's men stay camped by the creek they aren't shooting at anybody—and Tyree and his compadres aren't shooting back."

Festus nodded. "That's a natural fact, Matthew. It sure enough is."

"Ride back out there in the morning, Festus," Matt said. "Keep an eye on them."

"I'll keep both eyes on them, if'n it's all the same to you, Matthew. Them boys take a deal of watching."

Matt's face revealed his worry. "Be careful out there. I have a feeling this thing is about to blow."

"Have that feeling my ownself," Festus said.

The deputy's face was stiff and drawn, like that of a man who had forgotten how to smile—and that worried Matt even more.

But the next two days passed quietly. Stucker's men remained by the creek and the rancher himself was back in Dodge at his accustomed chair in the Alhambra.

Then, on the morning of the third day, came the kind of news Matt had been dreading.

Festus rode in before noon on his lathered mule. He burst into Matt's office, his eyes wild, the words on his lips tumbling out in a rush.

"Matthew, you better get out to the creek. There's been a killing."

"Who?" Matt asked, feeling alarm rise in him.

"The Wyandotte Kid."

"Who did he kill?"

Festus shook his head. "He didn't kill nobody, Matthew. He's dead."

"But how? I mean—"

"I dunno," the deputy interrupted. "I was watching the camp like you told me to, an' I seen Johnny Lomax bring in the Kid, facedown over a hoss."

Matt sprang to his feet. "Are you sure it was the Kid?"

Festus nodded, his eyes bleak. "Seen his long black hair a-hanging almost to the ground." The deputy's eyes sought Matt's. "It was the Kid all right."

Matt rose to his feet. "I'm riding out there."

"I'm coming with you, Matthew."

Matt nodded. "And bring the Greener."

The two lawmen rode into Stucker's camp thirty minutes later—and into a wild celebration.

The Wyandotte Kid's back was propped against a tree, his eyes half-open, blue death shadows on his face. Around him Stucker's men were dancing, shooting their guns in the air, most of them already drunk.

Clint Stucker and Johnny Lomax stood to one side, grinning hugely, like they were enjoying a show at the Comique.

As Matt and Festus rode in, Lomax's hostile eyes fixed on the big marshal and he elbowed Stucker and whispered something.

Matt swung out of the saddle and Stucker walked toward him, his hands outspread. "This is none of your concern, Dillon," he said. "The Kid drew down on Johnny and that was the end of it."

"Where?" Matt asked. Festus was beside him, fingering the shotgun, eyeing Lomax.

Lomax spoke up. "Like Mr. Stucker said, this isn't any of your concern, City Marshal."

"Where?" Matt repeated, his eyes blazing.

"North of here," Stucker said quickly. "Beside a lake, kinda big lake at that, east of Elm Creek."

Matt nodded. "I know the place."

The lake was about a half mile long by a quarter mile wide in the rainy season, but in times of drought, it had a tendency to shrink to a small, muddy pond. Matt had caught catfish there, lazily casting his line from the shady cottonwoods that grew along its bank. It was a peaceful spot, not a place where a man should die.

Matt stepped past Lomax and walked to where the Wyandotte Kid's body lay.

The marshal none too gently pushed aside some of Stucker's drunken men and kneeled beside the Kid. The dead man had a wound in front, high on his chest, but it was so torn-up Matt could have shoved his fist into it. This was an exit wound. He turned over the body and saw what he'd been looking for, another bullet wound neatly placed between the Kid's shoulders.

The Wyandotte Kid had been shot in the back and by a large-caliber rifle—like the .44.40 of Johnny Lomax.

Matt stood and found Stucker and Lomax beside him. "This man was shot in the back," he said, his eyes on Lomax hard and accusing.

The gunman shrugged. "Me and maybe a dozen of these men were out hunting when we ran into the Kid. He threw down on us and we shot back. He must have been turning when he caught my bullet."

Stucker nodded. "A dozen men will testify to that, Dillon."

Defeat and frustration gnawing at him, Matt nodded toward the Kid's body. "For God's sake, bury that man decent, Stucker. You got no call to leave him lay like that."

The rancher smiled. "Anything you say, Marshal." He pointed to a couple of his men. "Lawson, Smith . . . bury that."

Stucker turned to Matt again. "Now is there anything else I can do for you?"

Matt nodded. "Yes, you can tell me why you're here"—he waved an arm around the camp—"with this rabble."

Stucker was stung. "Rabble, is it? You know why we're here and you'll see them fight well enough damn soon, depend on it."

"What are you waiting for, Stucker?" Matt demanded.

The rancher's wide, brutal face was guarded and sly. "Big guns. Two of them."

Matt shook his head. "Stucker, you have enough guns already. Why hire more?"

Lomax took a step toward Matt, his eyes ugly. "That's for Mr. Stucker to decide. Now back off."

Stucker's voice was smooth, reasonable, cutting across Lomax's anger. "Johnny is right, you know, Dillon. You're way out of your jurisdiction. We have committed no crime in Dodge, so there's no reason for you to ride out here and bully us."

"A United States marshal might have a different opinion, Stucker," Matt said. He looked around him. A few men had dragged off the Wyandotte Kid's body. The rest were yelling and laughing, staggering drunk, surrounded by more rotgut whiskey than they'd hoped to see in a lifetime.

"Stucker, God help you if you ever meet up with Sean Tyree and Steve Jenness," Matt said. "This drunken trash will cut and run at the sound of the first shot."

The rancher's face revealed only confidence. "The guns I have on the way will make the difference," Stucker said. "Trust me, Dillon. They'll make a big difference." He hesitated, then added, "Send for your United States marshal, but by the time he gets here, this will be all over and I'll be on my way back to Texas with Sean Tyree's head in a sack."

chapter 22

Sean Tyree's Challenge

Matt and Festus rode out of Stucker's camp and headed north, toward the lake where the Wyandotte Kid had been killed. There were a few things Matt wanted to check out for himself.

They rode in silence, each busy with his own thoughts. Even the usually talkative Festus was at a loss for words.

Around them the flat green land stretched, unbroken, for hundreds of miles, the canopy of the sky deep blue with only a couple of puffy white clouds. The air smelled clean, heavy with the warm coming of summer, and the wilting wildflowers drowsily bent their lovely heads to the sod.

The lake was full of water this early in the summer, and it sparkled in the light of the sun, as though someone had cast an armful of diamonds across its wind-ruffled surface.

Matt and Festus splashed through one of the creeks that fed the lake, then swung around the south bank toward a stand of cottonwood and willow. The grass near the bank was flattened, streaked with rusty brown, and Matt stepped out of the saddle to take a look.

He kneeled by the stained grass, and when he touched the brown residue, it left a reddish smear on his fingers. The Wyandotte Kid's body had been dragged along here behind a horse, shortly after he'd been killed.

Matt rose and led his bay toward the cottonwoods, where smoke-colored leaves brushed their glossy palms together in the breeze.

At the base of one of the trees were the cold ashes of a small fire. On the grass a short distance away were piled the innards of a deer and close by a parcel of meat wrapped in the skin. The Kid had shot and gutted the animal and had been in the process of cutting away the meat when he'd been interrupted.

Festus stood beside Matt. "What are you seeing, Matthew?"

The big marshal made no answer. He stepped away from the trees about ten yards, kneeled and studied the ground, and only then called out to his deputy.

"Look at this, Festus. It seems that maybe ten horses stood here in a semicircle, and right in the middle of them, here, are the Kid's heel prints.

"I'd say the riders came up on the Kid and he quit what he was doing to talk to them. While they had his attention, Johnny Lomax circled behind, maybe over there where the cottonwoods are thickest, and shot the Wyandotte Kid in the back."

Matt rose to his feet. "The way the grass is blood-stained, I'd say they put a rope around the Kid's feet and drug him a fair piece before they slung his body over the back of his horse."

Festus scratched his cheek, his eyes clouded. "They sure didn't give him an even break, did they?"

The marshal shook his head. "That kind never does, Festus."

Festus' eyes slid from Matt's face and looked over his shoulder. The deputy's face paled under his beard. "Riders coming fast, Matthew. And the one on the ghost hoss is Sean Tyree."

The deputy split a few yards to Matt's left, the Greener ready across his chest.

Sean Tyree was flanked by Steve Jenness and Nathan Price. The two remaining gunfighters rode behind them.

Tyree swung out of the saddle, looked around him, then stepped quickly toward Matt. "What happened, Marshal?" he asked.

It was in Matt's mind to have hard words with Tyree about the kidnapping of Festus. But for now he decided to let it go. It was a subject he would return to later, after the present crisis was over.

In as few words as possible, Matt related the events of the morning and his theory on how the Wyandotte Kid was killed.

Tyree's face was gray, the scar on his cheek a cruel streak of white. "The Kid was a good man," he said. "He didn't step aside for anybody."

For a few moments Tyree hung his head in silence, a small tribute to a dead warrior. When he looked up, his hazel eyes were ablaze with a green fire. "How many back at Stucker's camp?" he asked.

"Too many," Matt answered. "They're trash, but they're too many."

"How many?" Tyree asked again, his voice hard and flat.

"Fifty at least," Matt replied. "And Stucker says he's waiting on a couple more guns. I reckon they're coming up on the rail cars from Texas."

Steve Jenness had dismounted and stood at Tyree's elbow. "How do we handle that many, Sean?" he asked.

The young man shook his head. "I don't know." He looked at Jenness. "We'll think of something."

The gunfighter's smile was grim under his mustache. "We'd better."

Matt attempted to solve the problem as he'd tried before. "Sean, I have no authority out here, but since you killed three men in Dodge, I can arrest you and take you back to town. I plan to send for the United States marshal and you'd be safe in my jail until then."

Jenness shook his head, answering for Tyree. "I told you before, Marshal, one way or another Sean would hang. We won't let you take him."

Out of the corner of his eye, Matt saw Festus lower the shotgun, the barrels swinging slow and easy on Jenness. "Don't let your finger go looking for a trigger, Steve," the deputy said. "I'm not as fast as you but this here scattergun makes up the difference."

Jenness shook his head. "I don't plan on drawing

on you or the marshal. We got enough enemies as it is and mighty few friends."

"Let it go, Sean," Matt said. "Cage Stucker, the man who gave you that scar and killed your friend, is dead. You can move on now, live your life."

Tyree shook his head. He reached into the pocket of his pants and showed Matt the double eagle. "This is the coin Clint Stucker threw on my bed five years ago," he said. "I've saved it all this time because I want to give it back to him. I plan to tell Stucker what he told me—'Use this to get drunk in some other town or use it to bury yourself if you die. Either way, I don't give a damn.'

"After I tell Stucker that and throw the double eagle in his face, then you can arrest me, Marshal. But until it happens, let me be."

Matt cast around in his mind for something to say, words that would help him get back in control of the situation. He found none but tried with what he had. "Sean, forget the word *arrest*," he said, knowing how lame he was sounding. "Just ride back to Dodge with me and accept the hospitality of my jail."

Tyree managed a smile. "That's way too thin, Marshal." He took a step closer to Matt. "But there is one thing you can do for me. Go talk to Clint Stucker. Tell him that me, Steve Jenness, Nathan Price and the Massey brothers"—here the two other gunfighters grinned and touched their hat brims—"will be waiting for him at Horse Thief Canyon. Tell him he can come looking for us anytime it's convenient."

Matt shook his head. "Sean, this is madness. There's more than fifty of them."

Again a rare smile touched Tyree's lips. "Got our work cut out for us then, don't we, Marshal?"

Matt and Festus stood and watched Tyree and the others ride away, swinging northwest toward the canyon.

Festus laid the shotgun in the crook of his arm and scratched his cheek. "It don't look good, Matthew," he said. "It don't look good a-tall."

The big marshal nodded. "No, it don't, Festus. Sean Tyree and Clint Stucker are two very different men but they share the same mindless obsession: revenge."

"And we're right in the middle of them," Festus said, his long, hairy face gloomy.

"Yes, we are," Matt agreed. "Yes, we are."

chapter 23

Hit and Run

Two days later, Stucker's men had still not moved from their camp on the creek.

But life had suddenly become dangerous for the rancher's drunken rabble. Festus observed most of it through his carefully shielded field glasses and reported back to Matt at night.

"I seen them send out a wood party early this morning," he said, his chair tipped back, his boots on Matt's desk. "Two wagons headed north on the creek. Then I heard firing. Well, a few minutes later those boys came a-foggin' it home, leaving dead men behind."

"How do you know there were dead men?" Matt asked.

"On account of how eight of them boys rode out but only five made it back." Festus removed his battered hat, ran his fingers around the sweatband, then settled the hat on his head. "Next thing I see is Johnny Lomax, looking as mad as a rained-on rooster, taking out of camp with six or seven of them boys.

"After about an hour, I heard more firing, then nothing, then firing again."

Matt leaned forward in his chair. "After that, what happened?"

"Well, lemme see. Oh yeah, after a long spell Johnny rides back in with a face like thunder and he's trailing three men facedown over their saddles."

"Were they Tyree's men? Could you make them out?"

"I could see well enough through them bring-'em-up-close glasses. They were all Johnny's men, every last one of them."

Matt sat back and nodded. "So Tyree is taking the fight to Stucker."

"Looks that way, Matthew. And let me tell you, some of Stucker's boys was looking mighty green about the gills by the time I left. I think a few maybe took off already. Getting too hot for them, I reckon."

Festus rose and refilled his cup from the coffeepot. "Matthew, when do you suppose that U.S. marshal will get here?"

Matt shrugged. "I don't know. Real soon I hope."

The big lawman thought for a while, then said: "Festus, you stay here in Dodge tomorrow. I want to ride out and take a look at the camp myself."

"Suits me, Matthew," Festus nodded. "A man can get mighty lonely for comp'ny jes' a-settin' out there in the long grass by his ownself, to say nothing of thirsty."

Festus turned and glanced at the clock on the wall. "I guess I'd better be headin' across the tracks, no saying what mischief folks could be getting up to over there."

Matt hid his smile, though it still played around his eyes. "Festus, what do you do over to lace-curtain town?"

The deputy stiffened, then drew his dignity around him like a ragged cloak. "Look out for desperadoes mostly, chicken rustlers an' all manner of low persons, like the mayor wants." Festus' left eyebrow crawled up his forehead. "Why you askin', Matthew?"

Matt shook his head. "Just wondered, is all. I don't want you to get too lonely for company over there, to say nothing of thirsty."

Festus' eyes closely searched Matt's face, looking for a barb, but the marshal had hidden even the ghost of a smile.

"Well, that's right considerate of you, Matthew," he said finally. "But I have to do my duty, even when I get all kind of invites to step into the parlor an' set a while." Festus let out a convincing sigh. "Nobody ever said the life of a deputy was easy."

"True," said Matt. "Very true."

"Well, I'll be on my way then." Festus gave Matt another searching look, but the big marshal's face was expressionless.

Only when his deputy was gone and had closed

the door behind him did Matt allow himself a wide grin.

Matt saddled the bay before first light and rode to his hideaway in the long grass opposite Stucker's camp.

As the night faded, shading into a gray dawn, heavy rain clouds rippled across the sky to the horizon and a truculent wind kicked up from the north.

The marshal shrugged into his slicker and studied the camp through his glasses. Nothing stirred across the creek. Stucker's men were still asleep in their tents; the fires scattered around the camp had burned down to ashes.

Easing his cramped position, Matt settled down to wait, though for what he could not guess. Maybe today Stucker's new hired guns would ride in, and they would bear watching.

Rain pattered around the marshal and the air grew cool. Out on the short grass, a quail called and the wind rustled among the thick bluestem surrounding Matt's hiding place.

Across the creek all was quiet.

A slow, wet hour passed as the rain grew heavier and Matt began to feel damp and miserable and more than a little bored. He swept the still camp with his glasses. Obviously Stucker's men would not leave their tents in this rain; most of them were probably sleeping off hangovers. He realized he was wasting his time.

He gathered up his rifle, preparing to back out of

the grass and return to his horse—but then hell came to Stucker's camp.

Sean Tyree and Steve Jenness charged, whooping and yelling, from the sheltering cottonwoods to the north of the creek, with Nathan Price and the Massey brothers close behind. All five had Colts in each hand, letting the reins trail, guiding their mounts with their knees.

Tyree's men were horsemen and revolver fighters, trained in the hard, dangerous school of the feud and the range war to hit and run, trusting in surprise to make up what they lacked in numbers.

The five, their guns blazing, swept through the camp, shooting up tents, stampeding the tethered horses. Bleary-eyed men spilled out of the tents, pulling suspenders over their shoulders, and Matt heard a woman scream.

A tall man, shirtless and with bare feet, swung a rifle to his shoulder. Jenness rode down on him, Colts hammering, and the man fell, his rifle spinning away from him. Another of Stucker's men was hit, and another. An oil lamp fell inside a tent and orange flames flared inside the canvas. A man scrambled out of the blazing tent, his clothing on fire, and ran, screaming, toward the creek. One of the Massey brothers turned in the saddle, raised his gun and cut the man down.

There was no sign of Stucker or Johnny Lomax, and without their leaders, all those left in camp became a disorganized, terrified mob. While they were camped in comfort, drinking Stucker's whiskey, the riffraff hired by the rancher had no problem assuring one another about how brave they were. But now, facing the skilled and relentless guns of Tyree and his men, they showed themselves to be runners, not fighters.

Dozens of frightened men were already streaming away from the battle, splashing across the creek, desperate to get somewhere, anywhere, so long as it was far away from the roar of guns and the screams of the dying.

Jenness in the lead, Tyree and the others rode back into the cottonwoods. They re-formed and charged again, and more of Stucker's men went down. Other tents were on fire and some had collapsed in a tangle of rope and canvas. A naked woman sprinted from a blazing tent and headed for the creek, looking back over her shoulder to hurl curses at Tyree. The young man smiled, waved and let her go.

Matt rose to his feet, shocked by the suddenness of the raid.

He counted six dead men on the ground and there were probably more he couldn't see.

The sudden opening of a tent flap attracted Matt's attention. A red-faced man carrying a shotgun stepped out and looked around. His right arm was in a sling and he held the gun pistol-fashion in his left.

Frank O'Hara had found refuge with his own kind and now he was about to repay their hospitality. Steve Jenness sat his horse, his back turned to O'Hara. The saloonkeeper eyed the gunfighter and raised the shotgun, extending it in front of him as a man would a revolver.

Matt threw his Winchester to his shoulder, sighted quickly on O'Hara and fired. The man took the bullet just under his left armpit and he staggered from the impact, his knees buckling. Matt fired again and O'Hara was hit a second time. The saloonkeeper screamed, sprawled his length on the ground, rolled and lay still.

Jenness turned in the saddle and glanced at O'Hara in surprise. His honed gunfighter's instinct immediately traced the source of the shots and he swung his head and looked directly at Matt, the marshal standing tall and obvious in his bright yellow slicker. Jenness waved, grinning. Matt didn't wave back.

Tyree yelled something to Jenness, swung his horse around and rode out of the camp, the others following after him.

It was over.

Matt looked across the creek at a scene of carnage. Despite the rain, several tents were still smoldering and men lay on the damp ground, some writhing in agony, others sprawled and still in death. A few stunned survivors moved around the camp, rifling the pockets of the dead, and to the south, dozens of Stucker's men were still running as though the devil himself was on their heels.

The attack had been well planned and the surprise had been complete. Tyree had brought the war to Stucker and they had hurt the rancher bad.

Matt turned and walked to his horse. He slid the Winchester into the boot, then stood for a few moments, his head bowed in thought.

By killing O'Hara to save the life of Steve Jenness,

he had chosen sides. Now he had no other choice but to abide by that decision.

Matt nodded to himself. Then so be it. He had rolled the dice and they had come up Sean Tyree—and all that remained now was to finish the game.

The big marshal dug in his pocket, found nothing, then remembered the lawman's star was still pinned to his vest. He opened his slicker and looked at the scrap of metal.

Raindrops ran down the star's polished tin surface, and to Matt Dillon they looked like tears, as though the star itself were crying.

Strangely disturbed, the marshal swung into the saddle. He felt unsure of himself, his motives confused, his future actions clouded by all kinds of nagging doubts.

For the first time in weeks, Matt thought of Doc Adams.

Doc was an old-fashioned, no-nonsense physician with a deal of common sense and the ability to distinguish between what was right and what was wrong. And he held strong opinions on how a lawman should conduct himself.

A loneliness in him, Matt turned his eyes to the gray sky and whispered aloud: "Doc, right about now, I sure wish I could talk to you."

chapter 24

Enter the Big Guns

"Matthew, you better come see this."

Agitated, biting his lip, Festus stood by Matt's desk as the marshal labored over a pile of paperwork.

"You're supposed to be on the other side of the tracks, you know," Matt said. "Keeping the peace, I mean."

The deputy nodded. "I know that. But when I saw what Clint Stucker and Johnny Lomax were unloading off a boxcar, I thought I'd better fog it here to tell you."

"What is it?" Matt asked.

Festus shrugged. "I dunno."

"You don't know?"

"Boxes, Matthew. Two long, wooden boxes."

The marshal rose to his feet. "Sounds like coffins to me."

"Not coffins," Festus said, shaking his head. "They're too big for that." He stepped to the door and opened it. "Better take a look now afore ol' Clint passes by with his wagon."

Matt walked through the open door and onto the edge of the boardwalk. After a few moments, a spring wagon drawn by a pair of Morgans trundled toward him, riders and pedestrians clearing out of its path.

Stucker held the reins, and Johnny Lomax sat beside him. The two ranchers John Mattingly and Yant McCanles acted as outriders, but as they rode past, Matt thought both men looked grim and unhappy.

Lomax and Stucker threw Matt a spiteful glance as they drew opposite him. They'd no doubt heard by now about the raid on the camp and the rout of their men, though Matt doubted they knew anything about his part in it.

As the wagon rolled past, Matt studied the crates loaded in the bed. Both were long, hastily constructed of rough pine and bound with baling wire. There was no lettering on either crate to indicate what they contained.

"Well, what do you think, Matthew?" Festus asked after the wagon swayed and creaked its way out of sight.

Matt shrugged. "I don't know, but whatever those crates hold is big."

Festus was silent for a few moments, deep in thought. Then he said: "Matthew, Clint talked about bringing in a couple of big guns. Maybe he wasn't talking about men, but whatever is in them two crates."

"Festus, I reckon there's nothing in those boxes but supplies of some kind," Matt said. His face changed and a frown wrinkled his forehead. "Wait a minute . . . that is, unless . . ."

"Go ahead, Matthew," Festus prompted. "Study on it some more."

"Big guns—you may be right, Festus. What kind of big guns could be packed into crates like those?"

The deputy scratched his cheek. "Not cannons, that's for sure. Them boxes were too narrow to hold cannons. Besides, I didn't see no wheels. Cannons need wheels."

"No, not cannons, you're right about that. But something else, some other kind of big gun." Matt scowled and stood deep in thought for a few moments, repeating: "Big gun . . . big gun . . ." Suddenly his face cleared. "Gatling guns, Festus! A gun like that would fit into one of those crates just fine. Stucker has bought himself a pair of Gatlings!"

Festus' face was puzzled. "Where would he buy them big guns, Matthew? Off'n the army?"

Matt shook his head. "The army wouldn't sell a civilian a Gatling." He considered the problem for a few moments, then snapped his fingers. "That's it—Mexico! It can only be Mexico."

"Mexico?" Festus asked. "I don't see how—"

"Festus," Matt interrupted, "I read in a newspaper how Porfirio Diaz' government is strapped for ready cash, especially American greenbacks. General Diaz is coming off years of revolution and two bloody civil wars and one weapon he always had in plenty was the Gatling gun. If you know the right people in the government or among Diaz' police—he calls them *rurales*—you can buy as many big guns as you want. I'm guessing somebody placed an order for Stucker in Mexico and that's the reason it took so long to get the Gatlings here."

"An' that's why Stucker hasn't moved out of his camp," Festus said. "He was waiting on his repeating guns."

Matt racked his brain, trying to remember what he knew about the Gatling. As far as he could recall, the gun had ten barrels that revolved around a fixed central frame and it could fire more than three hundred rounds a minute.

The Gatling was a devastating weapon and now Matt understood why Stucker had been so confident. Mounted on the backs of wagons he could move against Sean Tyree with his big guns and shoot Horse Thief Canyon to pieces—along with whoever was inside.

This was a serious development—one that could spell the end for Tyree. He and his four men were all skilled gunfighters, but they stood little chance against a pair of fast-firing Gatling guns. It would not be a fight—it would be a massacre.

Matt thought it through for a while then made up his mind. "Festus, you'll patrol this side of the tracks tonight. I'm riding out to Stucker's camp. I plan to be around when his war wagons are ready to roll and I want to know how many of his rabble are still standing with him."

Festus was silent for a few moments, thinking. Then he asked: "You've chosen a side, haven't you, Matthew?"

"I guess I have," Matt answered, his eyes guarded. "Festus, I don't know if I'm right or wrong, but I do know I can't stand idly by and let Sean Tyree and the others be penned up in Horse Thief Canyon and shot all to pieces."

The deputy's eyes searched Matt's face, then dropped to the tin star pinned to his own stained, wrinkled shirt. "Matthew, I've worn a star like this 'un afore, years back, when I was with the Rangers. I was proud of the star I wore then, but I'm prouder still of this one." He paused, his eyes locking on Matt's. "One other thing, I've always been proud to be your deputy. You've always treated me real good an' I got no complaints on that score."

"Festus," Matt began, "you don't—"

"Let me finish," Festus interrupted. "All I have to say is this—If'n I thought you'd chosen the wrong side, I'd take off this star an' never pick it up again because after that nothin' would ever be the same. You understand what I'm sayin' to you, Matthew?"

Matt tried to answer, but many conflicting emotions choked off his words. Not by nature a demonstrative man, he nevertheless placed a big hand on Festus' shoulder, squeezed hard and managed to say, "Thank you. Thank you for your loyalty. Festus, I . . . I many times think I don't deserve it."

Unlike Matt, Festus had no problem wearing his feelings on his sleeve. His eyes teared up and, his voice ragged with emotion, he said: "You be careful out there, Matthew." He opened his mouth to say more, thought better of it and said instead: "You jes' step real careful."

Matt rode out of Dodge under a broken sky. The moon painted the edges of the clouds with silver and the north wind sighed cool, carrying with it the remembered smell of the rain.

The big marshal swung wide to the west, crossed the lower reaches of Duck Creek, then headed north into the mixed grass country. The shadowless land around him lay in darkness, only the blossoms of the yucca here and there showing white against the gloom.

Matt held the bay to a walk and the horse picked his way confidently, ears pricked forward, alert for the slightest sound. A distance to the east, the coyotes were yipping and a barred owl, a long ways from his usual territory, flew over Matt's head on silent wings, a fleeting gray ghost soon lost in the blackness of the crowding night.

Matt rode past Stucker's camp from the east, then swung the bay a half mile north of the cottonwoods from where Tyree had launched his attack earlier in the day. He stepped out of the saddle, then loosed the horse's girth. Matt ground-tied the bay on a patch of grama grass on the slope of a shallow rise, trusting him to graze and not wander far.

The marshal slid the Winchester from the boot;

then, stepping carefully in a half crouch, he made his way into the cottonwoods.

From there, hidden by underbrush, he had a full view of the camp. The cooking fires were again lit, though not near as many as before.

Hammers sounded from near the horse lines and Matt guessed this was where Stucker was having the Gatling guns mounted on the back of his wagons.

The pounding lasted for the better part of an hour; then the camp fell silent and the fires began to die down. Shadowy figures moved around the tents and Matt estimated that at least eighteen to two dozen men were still there. Stucker's remaining men would be the best of them, and with the Gatling guns, that was enough.

Matt waited another hour, then stepped out of the trees on cat feet and skirted the edge of the camp, heading for the wagons.

Men snored in the tents and grumbled in their sleep, and a horse blew through its nose and stamped a foot. The moon hid its face behind a cloud and Matt took advantage of the brief darkness to walk silently into the camp and make his way to where the wagons were parked. In all, about seven buckboards and spring wagons were scattered around, their tongues raised.

But the two that interested Matt were set a few yards apart from the rest. He made his way to the closer one of these and looked inside the bed.

The Gatling gun was mounted in the wagon, covered by a sheet of canvas. Matt looked around him, then lifted the canvas. A steel tripod had been bolted to the wagon's pine floor to serve as a support for the gun. There was still enough room for six or seven riflemen, in addition to a two-man crew for the Gatling.

It was, Matt decided, a prefect setup. With these war wagons Stucker could attack the canyon at daybreak and be finished with the whole affair in time for lunch.

Unless . . .

The marshal glanced around at the fires glowing outside the tents. He needed only one good flaming branch and he could burn both wagons to the ground and set Stucker's plan back for a day at least, long enough for him to warn Tyree away from the canyon.

Matt's eyes scanned the camp. Nothing moved. He stepped lightly toward the nearest fire, but it had burned down to a few small sticks and gray ash. He would have to try another.

A fire, burning more strongly than the rest, glowed outside a larger tent, shared, Matt supposed, by Stucker and Johnny Lomax.

It was a dangerous move, but Matt saw no other choice.

He walked up to the fire, constantly turning this way and that, checking the darkened tents around him.

So far, so good.

Matt kneeled by the fire and found a thick, well-burning branch, the kind he'd been looking for. All his attention now on the flaming brand, he leaned over to grab it.

But the big marshal never completed the move—because suddenly the sky fell on him and he knew no more.

chapter 25

At the Mercy of the Enemy

Matt Dillon woke to pain.

He opened his eyes and around him the camp was still in darkness, but here and there men grumbled and coughed, stepping, heads bent, through the gloom.

Matt tried to move, but couldn't budge his arms an inch. His head throbbing, he tried desperately to return to awareness. His wrists were tied to a wagon wheel, the rope biting deep, and his long legs were splayed out in front of him.

What had happened?

Slowly, event by event, like a man trying to piece together a drunk the morning after, he remembered.

Judging from the pain in his head, he'd been slugged, probably by a rifle butt, as he bent over the campfire. Then somebody, none too gently, had tied him to a wagon wheel.

Matt turned his head, the movement causing him considerable pain, and glanced over at the two war wagons. Men were milling around, a couple of them inside the wagons checking on the Gatling guns. Two more were leading four-horse teams from a brush corral, the big animals already in their traces.

Footsteps sounded close and Matt turned. Looming over him were Clint Stucker and Johnny Lomax, the rat-faced gunman holding a coiled bullwhip in his right hand.

"The sleeper awakes," Lomax said, his voice thin and mean. Hefting the whip, he turned to Stucker. "Boss, should I have at him?"

The rancher shook his head. "Later, Johnny, when our business is done." He aimed a hard kick at Matt's ankle. "The marshal ain't going anywhere."

Matt's mouth felt like it was lined with cotton. He tried to form words but they dried up in his throat. He swallowed, then tried again. "Give it up, Stucker," he said, the words sounding thick. "Sell your herd and go back to Texas before it's too late."

Stucker laughed, firelight reflecting on his brutal, wide-mouthed face, touching his eyes with flame. "That's big talk coming from a dead man, Dillon," he said. "When this is over, and Tyree is gone, you'll belong to Johnny—and his bullwhip."

Lomax held up the whip. "Do you remember this, Marshal? This was Cage's whip, and when we get back, I plan to cut you to ribbons with it. I guess you recollect what a bullwhip can do to a man."

If Lomax expected Matt to show fear, he was disappointed. "Lomax," the marshal said, "I always took you for a cheap, yellow-bellied, back-shooting tinhorn. Now I know you are."

The gunman nodded, grinning. "Talk big while you can, Dillon. After I deal with Tyree and the rest of that scum, you'll sing a different tune. You'll beg me for mercy—only I won't have none. Then you'll scream because you won't be able to talk no more." Lomax's grin fled his lips, leaving only a mean, twisted sneer. "That's how it's going to be."

Anger flaring in him, Matt tried to kick out at Lomax, but the gunman quickly stepped aside, then slammed the heavy, coiled whip across Matt's face, first left, then right.

Stunned, the smoky taste of blood in his mouth, the marshal watched Lomax walk away with Stucker, both men laughing as they looked back at him.

An hour later, the war wagons rolled out of camp, riflemen clustered around the Gatling guns, about a dozen others, including Stucker and Lomax, riding, the ranchers Mattingly and McCanles bringing up the rear.

Matt watched them go, seeing the funeral procession of Sean Tyree. The young man didn't stand a chance against the firepower Stucker could now muster. By noon, if not long before, it would be all over.

Matt struggled against his bonds, catching the eye of the lone guard Stucker had left behind. The man laid down his coffee cup, got lazily to his feet and tested the ropes around the marshal's wrists.

"Cut me loose," Matt said, desperation driving him. "You want no part of this."

The guard, a middle-aged man with a long, melancholy face and yellow teeth glistening under a drooping mustache, kicked Matt hard in the ribs. "You shut your trap or I'll shut it for you," he said. "I got no liking for city marshals."

Matt winced against the sudden pain that spiked in his side and watched the guard return to the fire. A stick fell and sparks showered up. The man got to his feet and gathered a few more branches and threw them onto the fire. He sat again, yawned, stretched and looked around at the surrounding darkness. Seeing nothing, the guard built a smoke, then poured coffee into his cup.

The only sound in the camp was the sharp crackle of the guard's fire as it guttered in the wind, but out on the plains the coyotes were still talking and the night birds had not yet ceased their calling.

Cramped and uncomfortable, Matt tried to ease his position, drawing another hard look from the guard. The marshal stopped squirming and lay still, and after a few moments the man by the fire spat into the flames and looked away.

Thirty minutes passed and the night showed no inclination to give way to morning.

Matt theorized that the wagons were at least a third of the way to the canyon by now, though the darkness and the steep-banked creek crossings would slow them down.

He tugged on his bonds again, testing the alertness of the guard. The man rose to his feet, fists clenched, and stepped quickly toward the marshal, his mouth under his mustache a thin, angry line.

"Whoo . . . whoo . . . whoo . . ."

The guard stopped, his head swiveling toward the sound, his hand dropping fast to his holstered gun.

"Whoo . . . whoo . . . whoo . . ."

Matt had no idea who was making the noise, but it was about the worst owl call he'd ever heard.

"Whoooooo . . ."

Purposefully now, the guard walked toward the patch of darkness where the sound was coming from. He stopped, peered into the gloom, a Colt in his fist, and yelled: "You out there, raise your arms and come out with your hands empty or I'll cut 'er loose."

A moment later Matt heard a soft *whum . . . whum . . . whum . . .* and caught the steely glitter of a knife blade as it spun through the air.

The knife thudded into the guard's chest, burying itself to the hilt, and the man staggered back, looking down in shocked disbelief at the bowie that had just killed him.

Without a sound, the guard dropped to his knees, both hands tugging at the knife; then he fell flat on his back. His left leg kicked convulsively a time or two and he finally lay still.

Matt heard the swish of footsteps though the grass, and the shabby, stoop-shouldered form of Festus Haggen emerged from the darkness. The deputy strode rapidly to Matt's side, his bearded face revealing his concern. "Are you all right, Matthew?"

The big marshal nodded. "Cut me loose, Festus."

Festus turned and took a step toward the dead guard. "No, not that one," Matt said quickly. "Use the knife in my pocket."

The deputy found Matt's knife and a second or

two later the marshal was free, rubbing his rope-scarred wrists.

"Festus, I'm sure glad to see you," Matt said. "How did you know I was in trouble?"

"I didn't, Matthew, at least not directly. See, I got to worryin' that you was out here all by your ownself and then I got the danged itch at the back of my neck that always warns me all ain't well in the chicken coop. So I saddled Ruth, rode out here and scouted the camp. I Injuned close enough to see you tied up to a wagon an' all, and well, here I am and there you are."

Festus studied Matt's face. "You've been beat up some, Matthew. Your right eye is so bruised and swollen she's almost closed."

Matt nodded, his fingers straying to the back of his head. "And I've got a bump back here as big as an egg."

"Lomax?" Festus asked.

The marshal pointed to his eye. "This was Lomax. He used a bullwhip on me. I don't know who hit me with a rifle butt. Maybe him, maybe somebody else."

"Want to tell me what happened, Matthew?"

Quickly, using as few words as possible, Matt related the events of the night.

"And now Stucker and his war wagons are on their way to the canyon," Matt finished. "And we've got to try and get there before them."

"They got maybe an hour start on us, Matthew."

The marshal nodded. "I know, but the wagons will slow them. Stucker won't hurry the pace. He doesn't want anything to happen to those Gatling guns."

Matt got to his feet, swaying a little as his head pounded. "We'd better make tracks."

Festus disappeared into the darkness and returned leading his mule. He stopped at the guard's body and pulled out his knife, wiping it off on the dead man's shirt before dropping it back into the sheath.

As they walked through the cottonwoods to recover Matt's horse, the big marshal asked: "Festus, who taught you to throw a knife like that?"

"Comanche," the deputy replied. "Ain't nobody can th'ow a knife like the ol' Comanch."

"And the owl hoot?"

"Oh, I was teached that by a white feller."

Matt nodded, a slight smile touching his lips. "Figures."

The bay had stayed close to where Matt had left him. The big marshal tightened the girth and swung into the saddle.

To the east, a smear of pale lemon showed above the horizon and the coyotes were no longer talking.

Holding the bay to a steady, distance-eating lope, Ruth keeping pace, Matt and Festus headed into the flat, long-riding grass country.

Only a couple of hours remained until dawn, maybe less. Time was fast running out on them.

If they didn't reach Horse Thief Canyon before Clint Stucker and his Gatling guns, Sean Tyree and all with him were dead men.

chapter 26

Battle of Horse Thief Canyon

Matt and Festus crossed Duck Creek, then swung east, looping away from the route of Stucker's wagons. After four miles they headed north, splashed through Saw Log Creek and rode toward the lower, shallow tributaries of Spring Creek.

The going was easy, the slowly lightening country around them green with a mix of western wheat grass and bluestem, and vast carpets of pink-blossomed crazy weed grew on the crests of the low rises.

Matt led the way, topped a shallow hill, then dropped down through a narrow draw and up another one. After this, the land fell away gradually and smoothed out again, many narrow streams cutting through the grassy flat, and the marshal swung due north, directly toward the canyon.

As the night quickly faded around him, Matt set

spurs to the bay, and surprised, the big horse stretched his neck and struck out at a fast gallop.

Ahead of him the canyon loomed into sight, still slanted with dark blue night shadows, the dawn light only now painting pale gold the very tops of its craggy sandstone walls.

Matt reined in at the canyon mouth. Festus caught up a couple of moments later, Ruth breathing hard, looking hot, irritable and curly wolf mean.

Festus glanced around at the canyon. "See anyone?" he asked, his mule angrily tossing her head against the bit. "We're not too late, are we?"

Matt shook his head. "I don't see any shell casings. If Stucker's Gatling guns had been cranking, there would be hundreds of them scattered around here."

The marshal stood in the stirrups, cupped a hand to his mouth and yelled: "Tyree! Sean Tyree!"

A few moments passed. Then a man appeared at the entrance to the canyon, a rifle across his arms. It was Tyree and presently Steve Jenness and a small, balding man Matt hadn't seen before stepped beside them.

"Ride in, Marshal," Tyree hollered. "But take it slow and real friendly, like you're visiting kinfolk."

Matt and Festus rode up to Tyree and the others, and both lawmen swung out of the saddle.

"What are you doing here?" Tyree asked, his eyes searching Matt's battered face. "You're a right sorry sight—and a long ways from Dodge, Marshal."

"I know," Matt answered. He touched his swollen eye. "Johnny Lomax gave me this and I've come to warn you that him and Clint Stucker and his men are on the way—and they've got wagon-mounted Gatling guns."

Tyree smiled. "I know."

Matt was baffled. "Didn't you hear what I said? They've got Gatlings, two of them."

Tyree nodded. "Bought them in Mexico and the ammunition to feed them from the *rurales*. I know all that already."

"But how—" Matt began.

Tyree cut him off, still smiling. "Allow me to introduce my lawyer. Marshal Dillon, meet August Jenkins. He brought me the news."

The lawyer, a tiny, spare man with gray eyes that showed all the warmth of frozen bullets, stuck out his hand. "How do, and be careful how you go," Jenkins said. "Consider what you say, Marshal. And remember, I will not be called Gus. Never."

Matt took the man's hand, and it lay cold and clammy in his own huge paw like a dying fish. He dropped Jenkins' hand quickly, introduced Festus, then turned to the lawyer again. "How did you know about the big guns?"

"There is much I know," the lawyer said. He didn't talk in the accepted sense, but rather took bites out of the English language, chewed on what he had to say for a spell, then spat out the words like watermelon seeds. "I do business for the Diaz government and the *rurales* and my spies are everywhere. I knew about the sale of the big guns even before money changed hands."

Jenkins took a step closer to Matt, his voice dropping to a barely audible whisper. "I also handle certain delicate transactions for the Santa Fe railroad. When my client Mr. Tyree wired me a couple of weeks ago and asked me to meet him here, certain, ah, shall we say acquaintances lay on a private train for me, and I got to Dodge very fast."

Matt opened his mouth to speak, but Jenkins stopped him. "Be circumspect now. Consider what you say. Ask for no names. None will be forthcoming."

The big marshal smiled and shook his head. "Well, Mr. Jenkins, for somebody who knew about the big guns, you've landed yourself in a hell of a fix, haven't you? Stucker's war wagons will be here very soon and they'll play hob."

Matt turned to Tyree. "Festus says there's another way out of this canyon. I suggest we all take that route and leave while we still can."

"You can go, Marshal, and so can Festus," Tyree said, apologetically touching his hat brim to the deputy. "But the rest of us are staying."

"You'll be shot to pieces, man," Matt said. "You can't stand against Gatling guns."

Now Jenness spoke up. "We can, Marshal, and we will. We have a surprise lined up for Stucker."

Matt looked around him, into the canyon, his eyes sweeping up to the shadowed cliffs. He saw nothing: neither men nor material that could swing the battle in Tyree's favor.

The marshal felt defeat weighing heavy on him, and his shoulders slumped. "Well, maybe I'll try one last time to talk to Stucker. But since he planned to kill me back at his camp, I doubt that he'll listen."

"You'll do nothing of the kind," Jenkins snapped. "Marshal, one doesn't treat with wild animals. One kills them."

Matt nodded. "That's going to be a tall order."

"And one more thing," Jenkins said. "Now watch what you say. Be circumspect. I will brook no argument." The little lawyer waved a hand at Tyree. "I plan to defend my client against any and all murder charges you intend to bring against him. I will call for an inquest into the killings of Cage Stucker and the others, and I will produce witnesses who will testify that Stucker and his men got the chance to draw their weapons."

"Maybe so, but I guess—"

"Be circumspect, Marshal. I caution you to think before you speak. Perhaps it's best you keep your words for the local justice of the peace at the inquest. Think now. Think very carefully."

Festus' voice cut through the silence that followed Jenkins' warning. "I'm not thinkin', Mr. Jenkins. I'm a-tellin'." The deputy's thumb jerked over his shoulder. "Stucker and his wagons are comin' and them boys are riding so fast, they're cuttin' holes in the wind."

Matt and Festus led their mounts into the canyon as Stucker's wagons thundered into sight, their spinning wheels churning up clouds of gray and yellow dust.

Matt slid his Winchester from the boot, slapped the bay on the rump and watched until Buck trotted deeper into the canyon. He hunkered down behind a rock just inside the mouth of the canyon and yelled over to Tyree, who was also in a firing position alongside Festus.

"Where are Price and the Massey boys?"

Tyree smiled. "They're around. They know what to do."

Matt's face was a study in gloom. "I hope they do for all our sakes, because I sure don't."

Jenness had also dropped out of sight, and the big marshal felt a twinge of worry. Whatever plan Tyree had concocted, it had better be a good one.

Stucker's wagons drew up about a hundred yards away and his riflemen clambered out and flattened themselves on the grass. Stucker and the rest of the mounted men were lined up behind the wagons and Matt guessed at the rancher's strategy.

He would pin down the defenders in the canyon with fire from the Gatling guns, allowing his riflemen to get closer. After the Gatlings and the riflemen had whittled down Tyree's numbers, Stucker would lead a mounted charge into the canyon and deal with any who were left alive.

As a plan it was sound, and Matt figured it would work. Unless Tyree had something up his sleeve that Matt couldn't even guess at.

The Gatlings clattered and Matt ducked as scores of .45 caliber rounds thudded into the rocks around him, throwing chunks of sandstone high into the air. Bullets buzzed angrily over his head and ricocheted off the canyon walls, kicking up plumes of dust and sand around the canyon floor.

There was a break in the firing as Stucker's gunners changed magazines and Matt raised his head. A dozen riflemen were running toward the canyon mouth. Matt sighted on a tall man in a brown coat and plug hat and fired. The man went down, and he heard Tyree yell as the young gambler dropped another.

Seeing two of their number fall, the running men slowed and dived for the grass. The Gatlings hammered again, angrily spraying hundreds of rounds into the canyon, hot lead chewing up the soft sandstone.

Matt turned and yelled to Tyree. "We can't hold them here! We have to get deeper into the canyon!"

Across from him, Tyree shook his head. He cupped a hand to his mouth and shouted: "We need those wagons closer, a lot closer. Concentrate on the riflemen."

Up on the cliffs, Jenness, his gunfighter's instinct honed sharp by the battle, seemed to instantly understand Tyree's problem. Matt heard him yell something and he began firing at the men lying prone on the grass.

The marshal glanced up at the canyon walls.

The Massey brothers were with Jenness, and on the opposite cliff Nathan Price, in a long canvas duster and wide-brimmed black hat, was cranking and firing his Winchester as fast as he could work the lever.

After a few seconds' lull in the firing, the Gatlings opened up again, bullets whining through the canyon, crashing into its steep sides. A man yelped in pain and the younger of the Massey brothers tumbled from his perch on the canyon wall and thudded to the ground just beyond the entrance.

Defying the yammering Gatlings, Matt glanced quickly at the fallen gunfighter. The front of the young man's shirt was bright scarlet with blood where four or five bullets had stitched a straight line across his chest.

But the accurate return fire of the canyon defenders was beginning to tell.

One of Stucker's riflemen got to his feet and backpedaled quickly toward the wagons. Somebody, Matt guessed the surviving Massey brother, cut him down. More riflemen rose and drifted back, only a few of them firing as they retreated.

The Gatlings stopped and Matt heard Johnny Lomax yell angrily as he rode among the fleeing men, beating at their heads and shoulders with his coiled rope.

But the riflemen kept on backing away. They had just experienced the most deadly fire they'd ever faced, and at least for now, they wanted no part of the gunfighters in the canyon.

Seven of Stucker's men ran back to the safety of the wagons, leaving five of their number dead on the ground.

Matt got to his feet, keeping as much sheltering rock between himself and Stucker's guns as he could. He watched as Clint Stucker, his face black with rage, rode up to his wagons and waved them forward.

The man's voice was a furious bellow, clearly

heard in the sudden, sullen silence that shrouded the smoke-streaked battlefield. "Move closer! Clean out that nest of vermin."

Drivers yelled and snapped their reins and the horse teams bent into their loads. Slowly the wagons rolled forward, then gained speed, Stucker and Lomax leading them.

Stucker's horsemen seemed no more inclined to shorten the distance between themselves and the canyon defenders than did the riflemen.

The wagons moved to within fifty feet of the canyon entrance, but the horsemen held back out of rifle range, the ranchers Mattingly and McCanles among them.

Hurried footsteps sounded along the canyon floor and Matt turned to see Jenkins, running bent over, a small wooden box in his hands. The lawyer slid to the ground beside Tyree and dabbed sweat from his forehead with a huge handkerchief. The young man grinned.

"Hey, Marshal," Tyree yelled, "you ever play baseball?"

Puzzled, Matt shook his head. "Saw the soldiers at Fort Dodge play it once," he hollered. "I never took to it my ownself."

Across from him Tyree nodded. "I've played baseball a time or three," he called back. "It's a big thing back east. They say it could become our national sport one day."

Matt shook his head. "I doubt that," he shouted. "Too much standing around if you ask me."

Tyree nodded. "Well, if that's how you feel, I guess I'm the one on the pitcher's mound."

Matt shouted a question, but his voice was lost in the sudden hammer of the Gatlings as the guns opened up again.

Hot lead swept the canyon and all Matt could do was keep his head down. Across from him, Festus, Tyree and Jenkins cowered behind the cover of a boulder, bullets chipping and chewing away fragments of rock above them, the throaty thunder of the big guns echoing and reechoing, bounding off the canyon walls.

High up on the cliff, Matt heard Jenness yell: "Price is hit hard! He's out of it!"

The guns hammered on—a relentless, crashing barrage, clanging like the hammer and anvil of a demented blacksmith.

Matt laid his Winchester beside him and drew his Colt. Two men down, five to go, he thought, his face grim. Six, if you counted Jenkins, who was brave enough but a man who reserved his fighting for the courtroom.

Above him a man screamed and the surviving Massey brother plunged from the canyon wall. Matt couldn't see where he fell.

Five of us left, the marshal thought. At this rate it would be all over soon. Anger prodding him, he raised his head and brought up the Colt, presenting a smaller target than if he'd tried to shoulder his rifle. He ducked as bullets thudded into the wall near him; then he rose again. He slammed a couple of fast shots at the nearest wagon and saw the gunner go down. The man fell across his suddenly silent Gatling and the barrel tilted skyward.

Stucker cursed, rode up to the wagon at a gallop and jumped from the saddle into the bed. He leveled the Gatling and furiously cranked the firing handle. Matt crouched low as bullets again buzzed through the canyon like angry hornets.

"Wagons are charging us!"

It was Jenness' bull's bellow from the top of the canyon wall.

Matt raised his head again. Stucker's wagons were rolling fast toward the entrance. The big guns were firing, the drivers in the wagon bed, crouched behind the seats, reins threaded through the back support.

"Here they come!" Matt yelled. He holstered the Colt and picked up his rifle, determined to sell his life dearly.

The big marshal glanced over at Tyree. The young gambler, the scar on his cheek standing out stark white, opened the box that Jenkins had brought, plunged his hand inside—and came up with a slender stick of dynamite.

The fuse was very short. Tyree thumbed a match, lit the fuse and let it sputter and smoke for a while. He stood, threw the dynamite and ducked down again.

Matt watched the stick tumble end over end through the air and land six feet short of Stucker's wagon. He ducked as bullets scudded around him, then lifted his head again.

Nothing. The fuse smoked for a couple of seconds and died. The dynamite stick was a dud.

The wagons rolled closer. Bullets filled the canyon, whining and bounding off the stone walls. Jenkins cried out and fell to the ground, a streak of blood showing red on the arm of his blue suit coat. Beside him, Festus' face was ashen gray, his Colt clutched in a white-knuckled fist.

There was no backup in Festus Haggen and Matt knew that, like himself, his deputy was preparing for the end.

His mouth a tight white line, Tyree lit another stick of dynamite. He let the fuse burn longer, then jumped to his feet. He again threw the stick at the wagon where Stucker crouched, cranking the Gatling.

"Dynamite!" the wagon driver yelled. The man jumped from behind the seat and landed on all fours on the grass. Lomax rode up to him, his face twisted in fury, and his gun flared. The driver's head shattered into a bloody shower of bone and brain and the man tumbled onto his back and lay still.

The dynamite exploded.

A tremendous, roaring crash was followed by a huge fountain of dirt and sand that mushroomed high into the air. Lomax's horse reared and the gunman cursed wildly and fought to stay in the saddle. The terrified wagon team turned very fast to their left, bolting away from the terrific blast. The left-side wagon wheels sought traction, the steel rims spinning, then bit deep into the grass as the panicked team turned even tighter.

The wagon tilted and teetered on two wheels for what seemed to Matt an eternity; then it fell over on its side, Stucker sprawling clear.

Another deafening detonation erupted near the rancher, showering Stucker with dirt and clods of turf. The man lay flat on his belly and didn't move. A third tremendous blast and this time Tyree's aim was truer. The dynamite landed right in the bed of the second wagon. Three men inside jumped clear just as the wagon exploded into a thousand pieces, a couple of wheels bounding away, bouncing high across the grass. The Gatling inside the wagon tore loose from its tripod and spun twenty feet into the air before crashing close to the entrance of the canyon. Two of the horses in the team were down, badly injured and screaming, and the other pair broke free of the traces and bolted back in the direction of Stucker's riders.

Tyree ran out of the canyon, Festus beside him. The two men stopped just beyond the entrance and their rifles poured fire at Stucker's horsemen, Jenness' Winchester hammering from the cliff.

Matt raised his own rifle and fired at Lomax. A miss.

A couple of Stucker's riders went down, the rest, horrified at what had just happened to the wagons and was now happening to them, broke and fled, streaming away across the flat, working their spurs. Only Mattingly and McCanles, men of a different stamp, still stood their ground. But neither had a gun in his hand and they took no fire from the defenders.

Lomax fired at Matt, cranked his rifle and fired again, his bullets chipping rock close to the big marshal's head.

But now the gunman was everybody's target. Bullets split the air around Lomax and he savagely yanked his horse's head around and fled in the same direction as the others.

A sudden silence fell over the battlefield and the thick, greasy gunsmoke drifting gray in the warm air had laid down the breeze. Matt wearily stepped out of the canyon, his left eye now so swollen it had closed to an inflamed, angry slit.

They had won, but now it was time to count the cost and pay the butcher's bill.

chapter 27

Five-Card Stud

Matt watched miserably as Festus shot the two suffering horses still hitched to the smoking hulk of the exploded wagon. Tyree pulled Clint Stucker to his feet and the big rancher staggered, looking dazed and confused, out of it for now.

John Mattingly and Yant McCanles rode in and reined up near Tyree. Mattingly spoke for both of them. "Tyree, we rode with Stucker, but he told us he only wanted to arrest you." The grizzled rancher waved his arm around the battlefield. "We wanted no part of this."

Tyree opened his mouth to reply, but Jenkins, nursing his injured arm, answered for him. "You two, be circumspect now," he snapped. His face was pale but his voice was acidic as ever. "No statements. Keep your own counsel. You both may have to answer many charges for this in a court of law."

Mattingly nodded. "So be it. But as I said, none of this was our doing."

Stucker was looking around him, his eyes glazed. "Wha—what happened? Where's Johnny?"

"You lost, Stucker," Matt said, not a trace of sympathy in him. "And Lomax flapped his chaps out of here."

The big rancher shook his head, as though he couldn't believe what had happened. "Johnny . . . is gone?"

"Him," Tyree said, "and the rest." His hazel eyes swept the grass around him. "That is, except for the dead."

"And they're the lucky ones, Stucker," Jenness said, his face hard and merciless.

Mattingly and McCanles swung out of the saddle. They helped Stucker stagger to a flat rock by the front of the canyon and made him sit. The rancher buried his face in his hands, whispered, "I lost," and said no more.

Matt and Festus roamed the battlefield while Jenness and Tyree stood guard beside Stucker.

Both the Massey brothers were dead. The younger of the two—Tyree said his name was Luke—had still been alive after he was shot. But the fall from the canyon wall had broken his neck.

Nathan Price climbed down from the canyon wall, his shoulder broken by a bullet. The man was hurt bad, Festus told Matt after he examined his wound, but he would live.

Seven of Stucker's men lay dead on the grass and

another four were badly wounded. "And two of them won't make it until nightfall," Festus said.

Matt, a dreary sickness in him, looked at the blood-stained land around him. He shook his head and stepped next to Tyree. "Seven men dead, Sean, soon to be nine," he said. "Was it worth it?"

The young man's eyes were burned-out, shrouded and unreadable in a face of stone. "Marshal, I told you at Logan's graveside that I'd been handed a bitter cup and I must drain it to the dregs. The cup is not yet empty."

Matt was startled. "But it is over, Sean. You've exacted your revenge on the Stuckers. What more is left?"

"Only the dregs, Marshal. Only that and then it's over."

Tyree turned in the direction of Stucker. "You, Clint Stucker, can you hear and understand me?"

The rancher took his hands away from his face and his eyes were aware and ugly. "What do you want from me, Tyree? Or do you just want to gloat?"

Yant McCanles' anger flared. "Tyree, let the man alone. For God's sake, he's had enough."

Tyree shook his head, the scar on his tanned cheek standing out like a white streak of lightning. "No, he's not had enough, not by a long shot. The reckoning is still to come."

"There will be no more killing," Matt said, his voice quiet, but hard as steel. "There's been too much of that already."

"No killing as you know it, Marshal. I don't want

to kill Clint Stucker the human being. I want to kill his soul."

The young gambler stepped closer to Stucker. "I hear you're a gambling man," he said. "What's to your liking? Five-card stud maybe?"

Stucker looked up at the younger man, anger reddening his eyes. "What the hell are you taking about?"

"Maybe there's somebody you should meet, Stucker," Tyree said. "This is my lawyer, August Jenkins. He works out of El Paso."

"And other places," Jenkins said. He turned his cold gaze on the big rancher. "I advise you to be circumspect. Watch what you say. Be very careful."

Stucker shook his head. "Tyree, your lawyer makes even less sense than you do."

"Maybe so, Stucker, but I asked him to investigate you and he did. In Texas, Mr. Jenkins is much respected by the banking business and he discovered a great deal that was interesting."

Wary now, Stucker said: "What's that to me?"

"Mr. Jenkins was told you are up to your eyes in debt and that the banks are threatening to foreclose on your ranch." Tyree's smile was bitter, without humor. "All that stands between you and ruin are the six thousand head of cattle you have in the pens at Dodge. That's why you've been holding out for a better price and have even tried to gamble your way to money. But now you're flat broke. The cost of hiring guns like Johnny Lomax and paying for Gatlings comes high, doesn't it, Stucker?"

The rancher's anger flared. "I don't know what the hell you're talking about."

"I think you do. Your son, Cage, bragged that you want to expand your range, maybe double or triple its size. You see that as a way to run more cattle and solve all your money problems. You didn't pay off those ten gunmen who helped drive the Rafter S herd to Dodge. You sent them back to Texas and ordered them to wait. Right now they're back at your ranch, lazing around and eating your beans and bacon."

"Now I know you're talking nonsense, Tyree," McCanles snapped. "Mattingly's ranch and mine both border the Rafter S. There's no more range to be had"—the rancher's face froze into a look of stunned disbelief—"I mean . . . that is, unless . . ."

Tyree nodded. "Exactly. Clint Stucker's plan is to start a range war and grab what he needs." The young gambler smiled. "And what he needs is your range and Mattingly's."

Stucker's head swung quickly to McCanles. "Don't listen to him, Yant. Can't you tell he's lying in his teeth?"

McCanles was looking at Stucker in horror, like the man was something slimy and foul that had just crawled out from under a rock. Mattingly's face was stiff with shock, his eyes constantly shifting from Stucker to Tyree and back again.

"Where are those men you sent back to Texas, Stucker?" Mattingly asked finally. "Are they at the Rafter S like Tyree says?"

Suddenly Stucker looked like a trapped animal. But it wasn't his way to just sit and take it. He jumped to his feet, his voice loud and furious. "Damn you! Yes, they are!" He turned on McCanles. "And you, you sanctimonious, whining Bible-banger—yes, Tyree is right. I need your range and your water, and by God, when I get back to Texas, I'll take it."

"Over my dead body," McCanles said, his own anger rising.

"Yant, I wouldn't have it any other way," Stucker said.

Tyree stepped between the two men. "Fortunately," he said, his voice quiet and very calm, "there may be another solution to Stucker's problem—well, at least as far as his mountain of debt is concerned."

Stucker swung on him. "What the hell do you mean?"

The young gambler turned to his lawyer. "Mr. Jenkins, the paper if you please."

Slowly, favoring his injured arm, Jenkins reached inside his coat pocket, produced a folded sheet of paper and passed it to Tyree.

"This," the young man said, "is a certificate of deposit, stating that I have one hundred fifty thousand dollars in my account at the Cattleman's Bank of Dodge."

"What's that to me?" Stucker asked, a suspicious frown gathering on his face.

Matt too was puzzled, trying to figure out what Tyree was driving at.

"I wish to make you a proposition, Stucker," the young gambler said. "My hundred fifty thousand against your herd and the Rafter S. If you accept and win, that's more than enough money to pay off your debts. And remember, you'll still have your six thousand head waiting to be sold."

"Win? Win what?" Stucker asked, his eyes wary.

"One hand of five-card stud or any other game you care to mention. Winner takes all."

Stucker's tongue touched suddenly dry lips. Matt studied the man closely, aware that Stucker's greed and need were battling to overcome his fear of losing everything.

Tyree was right. His hundred fifty thousand dollars could pay off a lot of debt and help fill Stucker's war chest. The man's ambitions were big, very big, and Tyree had shown him the way. Matt watched the rancher, the man's inward struggle betrayed by the white showing around his tightly compressed lips. Stucker had recently been battling a losing streak at the poker table, and the disaster that had overtaken him today suggested it was not over.

Would he take the chance? Could he afford not to?

Stucker looked at Matt and spoke, surprising him. "When this is done and I ride out of here, I want the protection of the law."

Matt shook his head. "I'm not the law here. My jurisdiction ends where the city of Dodge ends."

Stucker thought that through. "No charges back in Dodge then. Nothing at all, Dillon. I walk away a free man."

"Stucker," Matt said, "if it was up to me, I'd hang you right now from the nearest cottonwood. But you've committed no crime in Dodge that I can prove. I have no reason to hold you."

Stucker turned to Tyree. "You," he said, "after it's over, I ride out."

Tyree nodded. "Agreed."

The rancher stood deep in thought for a few moments. His greed finally overcame his misgivings and he said: "Let's play cards, Tyree, and be damned to ye."

Tyree waved his arm, taking in the men clustered around him. "Let all present hear it from you, Stucker. I'm staking my hundred fifty thousand dollars against all you own—your herd and your ranch." The young man looked hard at Stucker, no give in him. "I want your given word that you will abide by that agreement."

Stucker knew well the implications of Tyree's challenge.

At that time in the West, a man's word was his bond. Cattle and land deals worth hundreds of thousands of dollars were often concluded with no more than a handshake and a man's word to follow through with the deal. As long as he kept his word, an honorable man could do business anywhere. But to go back on his pledge, to break his word, meant ruin and disgrace.

Once discredited, a man's word was held as nothing and he himself was considered worthless, a pariah, and he could do no business anywhere.

Stucker understood what he was up against and his trapped gaze swept around the hostile faces of the men around him.

The ranchers Mattingly and McCanles looked at him with eyes tinged by contempt, expecting him to back away. These were men who had accepted Stucker's word in the past, and if he gave it now and then broke it, they would consider him a no-account, a man not to be trusted, and spread the news far and wide.

Nathan Price, ashy white and in pain, Steve Jenness, Sean Tyree, Matt Dillon, Festus Haggen, Austin Jenkins—all men of honor who held a man's word as his sacred bond never, not even one time, to be broken.

Such was the way of the West—an unforgiving way some might say. But all the men around Stucker were raised hard, bred for a hard land, and in the end, the value of a man's given word was what held them together—and made civilized life on a raw, freewheeling frontier possible.

The wind was still, as though holding its breath, waiting for Stucker's answer. The sun had climbed to its highest point in the sky and the day was hot, the only sound the distant hum of bees among the crazy weed and the chuckle of a brawling stream that ran close to the canyon.

Stucker raised himself up to his full height, his mind made up and his tough, brutal face determined. "You have my word, Tyree," he said.

The die was cast and Stucker and all who were there knew it.

Now all Stucker had to do to make his grand, ambitious dreams come true was win a single poker hand. Lose and ruin and destitution lay ahead of him.

"Five-card stud?" Tyree asked, his voice flat and cold. "One hole card."

"Suits me," the rancher replied; then he added a barb, "But I don't want you to cut and deal."

"I'll deal," Festus said quickly as Tyree stiffened, his scarred face showing sudden anger, "if'n that's agreeable to both you gents."

Stucker nodded. "That sets all right with me."

Tyree let out a long breath. "And me," he said finally.

At Festus' urging, Tyree and the rancher sat at opposite ends of the flat rock that had earlier served as a seat for Stucker.

"Cards?" Festus asked.

Jenkins produced a pack from his pocket. He showed the pack around and made everyone confirm, including Stucker, that the seal was unbroken. The lawyer handed the pack to Festus, who removed the jokers, then shuffled the deck.

"Ready, gents?" he asked, holding the deck poised in both hands.

Stucker and Tyree nodded, silent with their own thoughts, and Festus dealt each a facedown hole card.

Stucker was then dealt an ace of diamonds, face up. Tyree drew the seven of hearts.

Festus snapped a second card to the big rancher. Another ace, this time of clubs.

Tyree drew the queen of spades.

Stucker's third card was the jack of spades.

Tyree drew his second queen, diamonds.

Matt and the others moved closer, crowding around the players. Tyree's face was set and expressionless, but Stucker looked tense and ill at ease; his hands trembled slightly.

Festus dealt Stucker his fourth card: the jack of hearts, his second jack. The rancher smiled. He was sitting on two pair, aces high, while Tyree only had a couple of queens showing.

Tyree's last card was the trey of hearts.

"Your hole cards now, if you please gents," Festus said.

"I'm showing the highest hand," Stucker said. "I'll turn first."

Tyree shrugged. "Go ahead."

Stucker was trembling again as he turned over his hole card: the deuce of spades. "Two pairs to beat, aces and jacks," the rancher said, his voice unsteady, knowing what was at stake and what Tyree's hole card represented—that slender piece of pasteboard that could make him rich or destroy him.

The wind had picked up again, scattering the lingering gunsmoke, and out on the short grass a wounded man moaned for a few moments, then was quiet.

Sweat beaded Stucker's forehead as Tyree picked up his hole card and glanced at it. The unreadable expression on the young gambler's face did not change.

Tyree dropped the card onto his two queens. It was the queen of clubs.

"Three queens take it," Tyree said, his eyes on Stucker.

The rancher's face was white, a stricken, tragic mask. He looked around wildly at the men surrounding him as though he expected somebody to say that it had all been a mistake and he could forget it ever happened.

But nobody uttered a word and there was no pity in the cold stares that looked down on him.

Stucker rose to his feet and swayed a little. He looked at McCanles. "Yant, I'm ruined."

The rancher nodded, his face set in hard lines. "I guess you are, Clint."

Stucker's pleading eyes sought those of Mattingly. "John . . . tell me what to do."

"Ride," Mattingly said. "That's all you can do. There's nothing left for you in Texas."

Stucker shook his head in disbelief. He glanced over at Matt, his mouth moving, trying to find words that never came.

Finally the rancher turned away and stumbled toward his horse, a big roan gelding cropping grass just a few feet from a dead man.

Stucker put his boot in the stirrup, but Tyree's harsh shout stopped him cold. "Wait, Stucker! Read the brand on that horse."

Confused, Stucker turned crazed eyes to the young gambler. "I know the brand. It's the Rafter S."

"Then that horse belongs to me," Tyree said. "Leave it the hell alone."

Stucker shook his head. "But . . . but what will I do?"

Tyree dug into his pocket, found a double eagle, a

hole in its center where it had been nailed to the tree. He thumbed it to Stucker. The coin spun through the air and landed at the man's feet.

"Like you told me five years ago, use that to get drunk in some other town or use it to bury yourself if you die. Either way, I don't give a damn."

Stucker stood rooted to the spot for several stunned moments. He looked around at the men facing him and then rubbed the back of his hand across his mouth.

"You're right. God, I need a drink," he said.

Stucker bent, shoved the coin in his pocket and turned on his heel, walking south across the flat grassland toward Dodge, the glowing day bright around him.

chapter 28

The Return of Johnny Lomax

After Matt and Festus returned to Dodge, events moved very swiftly. August Jenkins demanded an inquest into the shooting death of Cage Stucker and three others, threatening the direst consequences if his demand was refused.

Matt was among those who testified that Sean Tyree had called Stucker and given the man a chance to draw.

The local justice of the peace, perhaps intimidated by the forceful presence of a big-city lawyer like Jenkins, quickly declared that Tyree had acted in self-defense and that there were no grounds for a murder trial.

The U.S. marshal—a tall, lean, grim-faced man named McGuire—asked some searching questions about the battle of Horse Thief Canyon. But since all testified that the perpetrator, a former rancher named

Clint Stucker, had now hightailed it for parts unknown, the marshal, having more pressing business elsewhere, gave up and left on the next stage for Wichita.

Three weeks after the inquest, Sean Tyree stopped by Matt's office. The young man was once again dressed in the height of fashion and a pretty girl hung on his arm.

"I just thought I'd say good-bye, Marshal," Tyree said, extending his hand, "and thank you for all you've done for me." The young man smiled. "It was real good of you and Festus not to mention a certain kidnapping. That could have gotten me in a heap of trouble."

The girl giggled as Matt took Tyree's hand. "Festus and me talked about that, but we decided you'd been through enough. Besides, Festus seemed to enjoy lying up in that cave, just sleeping and eating. And he said you made good coffee and had whiskey that was even better."

Matt dropped Tyree's hand and asked: "Where are you headed?"

"Texas. On the ten thirty train. I want to visit the ranch I won. I may decide to stay there since Yant McCanles and John Mattingly have tried their best to convince me that it would be a good idea." Tyree turned to the girl beside him. "This is Angela. I met her a few days ago and she's decided to come with me."

Matt touched his hat to the girl, then smiled. "Sean, you work fast."

The young gambler nodded as the girl blushed and

fluttered her long eyelashes. "Life is short, so a man has to grab on to it with both hands. It's just a bridge you cross over but don't build a house on. Logan St. Clair told me that."

"Wise man," Matt said.

Tyree nodded. "Yes, he was."

What needed to be said had now been said and both men knew it.

"Well, good luck, Marshal," Tyree said finally. "Take care of yourself."

"And you too, Sean. Maybe you'll come back to Dodge someday. Maybe you'll drive a herd up from Texas or just stop by for a visit. Maybe so."

"Maybe so," Tyree said. He touched the brim of his hat. "So long, Marshal Dillon."

After Tyree left, Matt sat at his desk and considered the vexing question of his reply to the governor.

He'd received a second, stinging letter demanding an immediate answer to the state of accommodations in Dodge City for the crown prince of Russia and his large and faithful entourage.

Matt slid a piece of paper next to him and chewed on the end of his pen. He was only a city marshal and he didn't want to chap the hide of a crown prince—or the governor, for that matter.

Matt's eyes slanted to the clock on the wall. It was almost ten. He rose, crossed the floor and buckled on his gun belt.

The door opened and Festus stepped inside. "I'm heading across the tracks, Matthew," he said. "Just so you know."

Matt nodded. "Young Tyree was just here, and he had a girl with him."

"I saw them," the deputy said. "Sean stopped and had a word with me. Said he was headin' for Texas. Right nice feller, and that little gal of his is as purdy as a field of bluebonnets."

Festus' eyes took in Matt's gun belt. "Makin' your rounds? The town is mighty quiet now so many of the cowboys have gone."

"I thought maybe I'd walk down to the station and see Tyree leave," Matt answered. He thought for a few moments and added: "When I watch him step on that train, it will be like an ending. What began five years ago with blood and buckskin will finally be over."

Festus nodded. "I sure hope so, for Sean's sake. You can't plan yourself a future by living in the past, an' that's a natural fact."

The deputy turned to leave, but stopped in midstride. "Oh, it plumb slipped my mind, Matthew, but Doc Adams is back in town. Came in on the railcars an hour ago."

"How is his sister?" Matt asked.

"Doc says she's right poorly an' still riding the bed wagon. But he says she'll be up on her feet in a week or two, the good Lord willin'."

"Glad to hear it," Matt said. "It will be good to have Doc back."

After Festus left, Matt stepped out onto the boardwalk, then turned in the direction of the train station.

Most of the cowboys, ranchers and buyers were

gone, and the residents of Dodge were getting back to their accustomed routine of early to bed and early to rise. Pianos tinkled in only a few of the saloons and the Alhambra and the Alamo had already packed away their bunting until next year.

There were only a few riders on Front Street and Matt counted maybe a dozen cow ponies tied outside the saloons.

A long wind was blowing strong off the plains, banging doors and kicking up the dust along the street, and a full moon rode high, only a few scudding clouds now and then dimming its light.

Matt reached the station, then stepped into the shadow of an awning, where he would not be seen.

After a few minutes Sean Tyree and his girl arrived. A porter took their suitcases and Tyree helped the girl board the train ahead of him.

Matt waited, a strange sense of loss in him. Up ahead, the engine whistled and steam jetted from between its wheels. The carriages jolted once, then rolled along the track, gradually gathering speed.

Soon the train was lost from sight, its rear lanterns glowing like red eyes for a while, until they too were swallowed up by the crowding darkness.

Matt left the shade of the awning and stepped toward the cattle pens. Tyree had sold his herd, and the steer were loaded and gone. All the pens were now empty except for a few that held a late-arriving herd of shorthorns up from a British ranch in the Neuces Plains country.

The big marshal had seldom seen shorthorns, smaller, heavier and less rawboned than Texas longhorns, and he stopped at a pen and looked them over. A cow stepped toward him and he leaned over and scratched the tight, curly white hair on her forehead. The little animal lowed softly, then tossed her head and walked away.

Matt smiled as he watched the cow leave. He turned and walked past several empty pens, then headed back toward Front Street.

But when Johnny Lomax stepped out of the shadows, Matt froze in his tracks.

"Well, well, well, if it ain't Marshal Dillon," the gunman said, a thin, malicious smile on his face. "I guess I don't have to remind you that we have a score to settle."

Lomax's rat eyes were cold. "You didn't think you were gonna hide away from me, did you?" the gunman asked. "That never works with Johnny Lomax."

"Lomax, it will be a cold day in hell when I hide from a sorry piece of back-shooting trash like you," Matt said, his voice steady.

The gunman was stung and it showed in the way his face thinned to an ugly, stiff mask. His hands were very close to the guns strapped low on his thighs. "I was planning to kill you quick," Lomax said, relaxed, eager and confident. "But now I'm gonna give it to you in the belly so you'll die slow and hard. Screaming, maybe."

Matt smiled. "Lomax, are you all through talking?"

"Yeah," the gunman answered, "my talking is done."

"I thought so," Matt said. And he drew.

Lomax was fast, lightning fast. Matt's Colt had

cleared leather but was still not level when the gunman's first bullet hit him.

Matt took the hit high on his left shoulder. He triggered his Colt and saw Lomax jerk as his bullet struck a couple of inches above the gunman's belt buckle.

Lomax staggered to his right and slammed into the iron gate of a cattle pen. The gate clanged loud and, cursing, the man fired again. A miss.

Taking his time, Matt triggered another shot. Lomax was hit a second time and the man's legs buckled. He slid down the gate, setting it to clanging once more, and fired again.

Lomax's bullet burned along Matt's ribs as he thumbed off another shot. Blood blossomed on the front of Lomax's shirt. He tried to bring up his Colt, but the gun turned in his hand, the barrel pointing downward, then slipped from his fingers.

Matt stepped toward the fallen gunman, his Colt ready.

Lomax's eyes were wide, unbelieving, as he tried to comprehend the manner and reason of his death. "You—you've killed me," he whispered, his voice choking as blood bubbled to his lips.

"Looks that way," Matt said, no pity in him.

"But . . . but . . . how?" Lomax asked, his face gray in the brightening moonlight.

Matt's smile was thin. "You were an arrogant man, Lomax, and you never did learn your lesson. You ought to have learned never to underestimate a cowtown marshal."

The gunman tried to say something, his lips peeled

back from his teeth, but then his eyes turned up in his head, showing white and ugly, and life left him.

Without a glance at Lomax, Matt stepped over the dead man and walked onto Front Street. An excited crowd of people quickly gathered around him; then Festus elbowed his way through, yelling for them to make way.

"Matt," he asked, his face a pale, shocked study in worry, "are you hurt bad?"

"Go get Doc Adams, Festus," Matt answered. "Tell him I need him in my office." The marshal hesitated a few heartbeats, then added, "Tell him I need him real fast."

"How many bullets have I taken out of you, Matt?" Doc Galen Adams asked. "I've lost count."

"Three, and one arrowhead," Matt answered, "near as I can remember."

Doc, a stocky, handsome man with a lot of gray showing in his black hair, shook his head, looking down at his seated patient. "Matt, have you ever considered a different line of work, one where people don't shoot at you all the time?"

Matt smiled. "Maybe I'll study on it, Doc," he said.

"You should," the physician said. "I guarantee you'll live longer."

Doc bent over the washbasin and dipped his hands into the water as Matt eased his position in his chair, trying vainly to get comfortable.

The marshal was naked to the waist, a thick white bandage around one wide shoulder, and the burn across his ribs still smarted where Doc had painted some brown stuff that stung like the dickens.

Doc dried his hands on a piece of towel and said: "Take it easy for a few days, Matt, and if that shoulder punishes you too bad, I'll give you something for the pain."

The big marshal nodded. "Doc, you'll be the first to know if it does," he said. "I'll be—"

The door slammed open and Kitty Russell rushed inside. She had been crying and mascara ran black under her eyes. "Oh, Matt!" she said. "I just heard."

The woman ran to Matt, sat on his knee and threw her arms around his neck. "I was so worried. They told me you were hit real bad." Kitty looked at Doc. "Is he going to be all right?"

Doc nodded. "He's as tough as a trail drive steak. I reckon he'll pull through."

Kitty said: "I was so worried. I almost died from worrying about you. I ran across the street as fast as I could but it seemed that I'd never get here."

Matt looked into her beautiful eyes, comforted by the unspoken love he saw there.

Doc snapped his bag shut. "Well, I don't need to be hit over the head with a club to know when three's a crowd, so I'm leaving." He smiled at Kitty. "Don't you go tiring Matt out now, woman. He's got a lot of healing to do."

Matt laughed. "Doc, about right now, I'd say all my healing is done."

Kitty, crying again, laid her head on Matt's unwounded shoulder. "I'm never going to leave you again," she whispered, sounding young and breathless, like a love-struck girl, "not for a day or an hour or a single minute."

"Kitty, that sets just fine with me," Matt said.

Read on for a preview
of the next exciting
Gunsmoke novel
THE LAST
DOG SOLDIER
Coming from Signet
in May 2005

Streaks of winter snow still clung to the Kansas plains and a long wind sighed cold off the distant Rockies as a solitary horseman rode north toward the big bend country of the Pawnee River.

Around the rider, the land lay flat, the grass browned by cold, and when he crossed Sand Creek, his mount's hooves crunched through a thin sheet of ice. So far, the tall lawman had ridden through and around hundreds of McKenna cattle and had identified a half dozen different Texas brands.

Matt Dillon had no idea how Abbey McKenna and her brother, Abe, had acquired their herd, but judging by what he was seeing, he doubted they had come by them honestly.

From what he knew of the McKenna punchers, they were a shabby, work-shy bunch, shifty-eyed border trash recruited from saloons and brothels, not the kind to build a herd by the strength of their backs and the sweat of their brows.

The creaking chuck wagon that had come up the trail with the cattle was held together with biscuit-tin patches and bailing wire. And when Abbey visited Dodge the plain cotton dress she wore was darned and threadbare, her shoes down at heel, a sharp contrast to the fashionable belles from across the tracks in their buttoned boots and rustling silks and satins.

Frowning in thought, Matt reined in his bay.

From where had the ragtag McKennas gotten the two thousand longhorns they'd driven through Dodge and then up to the Pawnee three weeks before? And how had they managed to buy old, cantankerous Andy Reid's thousand-acre spread?

Abe McKenna had put out the word around town that Andy had sold out cheap because he wanted to go east and live with his ailing sister in Boston.

But Matt had never heard Andy mention that he had a sister and the reclusive old retired miner, wary of strangers, was not the kind to welcome the tattered McKennas and their two-by-twice outfit with open arms.

Matt shook his head. He had plenty of questions and no answers.

The big lawman pulled the fleece collar of his sheepskin coat up around his ears, his breath smoking in the cold air. The plains rolled away on all sides, not perfectly flat but undulating slightly, like swells on a green ocean, here and there bands of snow hugging the sheltered slopes of the rises like the white crests of waves.

In the distance Matt watched a small herd of antelope trot toward the Pawnee, seeking water. This early in March, the river was no longer frozen, though ice laced both banks, slow to melt in a truculent wind still cruel with the lingering memory of an unusually hard winter.

Dodge City had been under siege since the late fall, snow crowding in from the plains surrounding the town on all sides. The Arkansas had frozen solid and some of the cottonwoods lining the riverbanks had split in two from the severe frosts with a sound like the crack of a rifle shot.

In late December, it seemed to Matt like the town was shrinking in on itself, as though the saloons, dance halls, stores and houses were huddling closer to one another for warmth. The wind, whispering thin and sharp edged as a newly honed razor, sought out every chink and break in the warped pine boards and probed everywhere with icy fingers, defying the efforts of the cherry red stoves to keep even the smallest room warm.

Bundled up to the eyes, the citizens of Dodge had stepped warily along slippery boardwalks, now and then casting their gaze skyward, hoping to see an end to the gray clouds of winter and a release from the iron grip of the cold.

Now Matt rode under the vast dome of a pale blue sky that stretched from horizon to horizon, the air around him sharp, each breath he took filling his lungs like shattered shards of frosted glass.

Andy Reid's cabin lay a couple of miles to the northwest. Although Matt had a city marshal's star pinned to his shirt under his coat, he had no authority here on the plains. But he swung the bay in the direction of the cabin.

Whether he was out of his jurisdiction or no, it was time to pay the McKennas a visit. The big lawman followed the bank of a narrow stream running due south off the Pawnee, here and there riding wide of lone cottonwoods and the even more rare willows. This was wide-open, level country, where a far-seeing man could scan the land around him in all directions to the horizon.

Yet Matt didn't notice Andy Reid's burro until he topped a shallow rise crowned with buffalo grass, and almost rode right into the little animal.

The burro stood, stiff-legged, at the base of the rise, its head hanging, the morning's hoar frost a silver sheen on its back and flanks, a frayed rope still tied around its neck, the broken end trailing on the ground. Like Andy himself, the burro was impossibly ancient. For nigh on twenty years it had carried the old man's pans, picks and shovels from the desert country of New Mexico and Arizona to the Black Hills of the Dakota Territory with a hundred stops in between.

After he'd moved to Kansas three years before, Andy had done nothing with his land. He used his thousand acres as a barrier between himself and neighbors he didn't like and strangers he liked even less. On his infrequent visits to Dodge for supplies and a jug, he'd paid in gold from his poke, a cantankerous and touchy old-timer who talked to no one and studiously minded his own business.

Matt reined up the bay and the burro lifted its head, looking at him with interest and no sign of fear.

Despite its age and the stiffness of its joints, the old animal made the usual display of good breeding and fine manners common to all burros as Matt swung out of the saddle.

The big lawman took off a glove and scratched the burro's head. "What are you doing so far from home, boy?" he said. He loosed the rope from the little animal's neck. "I'd say you're a ways from the barn."

By way of reply, the burro rubbed its forehead against Matt's leg, blowing softly through its nose. The marshal smiled and patted the donkey's shoulder—and his hand came away stained with blood.

Matt kneeled beside the burro and checked the wound. It looked like the tiny animal had been burned by a bullet some time before. But the wound had reopened recently, maybe when the burro rolled or pushed its way through thick brush.

"Who did this to you, boy, huh?" Matt asked. "Who shot at you?"

The big lawman rose to his feet and looked around. At first he saw nothing out of the ordinary, just the open prairie and, to the north, the bare branches of scattered cottonwoods and willows growing along the Pawnee.

But then, as his eyes scanned the land more closely, he noticed a patch of recently disturbed ground farther along the base of the rise, almost hidden by a struggling yucca.

Matt stepped to the yucca and kneeled beside it,

studying the torn-up earth. Deprived of its deep roots, the grass here had withered and died on the clods of turf, turning a dry, rusty brown. The disturbed area was roughly rectangular in shape and it looked like something had been buried here, laid away shallow and quick in the iron-hard winter ground.

The big marshal carefully lifted away clods of turf. After a few minutes of digging, about three inches under the surface, he uncovered a bearded white face.

It was Andy Reid's face.

Matt dug deeper, clawing at the frozen earth with his bare hands. Clod by clod, he slowly exposed the rest of Andy's body, perfectly preserved in the frost of the topmost layer of prairie. Matt brushed away dirt from the old man's chest and found two bullet holes, no more than an inch apart, on either side of the prospector's middle shirt button.

The marshal continued to kneel for long moments, his head bent, thinking this thing through.

Andy Reid had been murdered by someone who knew how to handle a gun and was lightning fast. When a man is shot, the impact and shock of the bullet will make him jerk away or stumble and a second wound is often inches apart from the first. But somebody had put two bullets into the old man very quickly, so quickly they'd hit close together—and that took a trained, accurate gun hand.

Matt covered up the body and rose to his feet, still trying to piece the situation together.

For certain, Andy had been killed by a gunman

who knew his business. Of the rest, Matt was less sure. Out here on the prairie, Andy would have ridden a horse and left his burro behind. Later, the burro could have broken loose from where it was tied at the old man's cabin and run away. Somebody had taken a shot at it and the bullet had burned along the burro's shoulder. But that hadn't slowed the little animal, and it had instinctively found Andy's grave.

Matt had no way of knowing when the old prospector had been killed or how long the burro had been here. But the animal looked gaunt and wasted, with its ribs showing, so it had been feeding for a long time on the thin graze of the winter grass.

Matt hunched his wide shoulders, deep in thought, his eyes on the ground at his feet.

This had not been a random act of robbery. A thief would have shot the old man and left him lie where he fell. He would have ransacked the cabin, found Andy's poke and hightailed it. A robber certainly wouldn't have taken the time to bury the old prospector.

It was no robbery then. That left Abbey and Abe McKenna as the only people who stood to profit from Andy Reid's death.

It could be that the McKennas had offered the old man a ridiculously low price for his cabin and land, and when he refused, probably angrily ordering them off his property, they had killed him.

It was a wild guess, but Matt was sure he was on the right track.

He had seen Abe McKenna in town, a handsome

young man made less so by a weak chin and small, petulant mouth. Like most men at that time and place, Abe carried a Colt, but Matt's honed instinct had quickly pegged him a sure-thing artist, a back-shooter and not any kind of straight-up gunfighter.

Andy had been shot, but not by Abe McKenna. He had been murdered by a man who used a gun so well and fast he had no doubt killed many times before.

Even at that wild, lawless time in the West, highly skilled gun hands like John Wesley Hardin, Ben Thompson and the man who had killed Andy Reid were a rare breed and, when encountered, best left alone.

But Matt Dillon was not one to take a step back for anyone and he'd do what had to be done to find the killer of a testy but harmless old man.

The cold wind rustled among the winter-dry blue-stem grass and high above the prairie the brightening sky was the color of pond ice. The sun was shining, but gave no warmth, and Matt felt a sudden chill.

The arrival of the McKennas with their mixed herd and the death of Andy Reid nagged at him as if he had a bad toothache.

He sensed a warning carried on the wind that big trouble was coming. He was unsure of its direction or what face it would wear or what words it would use, but he was certain of one thing—however it came, from wherever it came, trouble knew his name.

And it would soon come calling . . . on Marshal Matt Dillon.